BULLETPROOF

Praise for Maggie Cummings

Brooklyn Summer

"I was glued to the page from the first chapter and couldn't put this book down."—*Les Rêveur*

"I enjoyed exploring New York City through the eyes of the main characters. Kellan and Ashleigh had amazing chemistry, their conversations flowed naturally, their relationship was very well paced and the sex scenes very well written. I related to and genuinely liked both leads. The supporting characters were also very well developed."—*Melina Bickard, Librarian, Waterloo Library (UK)*

"*Brooklyn Summer* definitely made me feel a lot, in a good way. It's heartwarming and immensely romantic and it makes me happy... The author does a wonderful job of conveying the sensation of falling in love, the way colours are brighter, sounds are clearer, food and drinks taste better."—*Jude in the Stars*

"[A] pretty straightforward romance that will please fans across the board. Of course, my romantic heart was happy with Kellan and Ash...NYC served as a nice backdrop to the budding romance as well, but without taking over the story like some settings do."
—*LezReviewBooks*

Against All Odds

"*Against All Odds* by Kris Bryant, Maggie Cummings, and M. Ullrich is an emotional and captivating story about being able to face a tragedy head-on and move on with your life, learning to appreciate the simple things we take for granted and finding love where you least expect it."—*Lesbian Review*

"I started reading the book trying to dissect the writing and ended up forgetting all about the fact that three people were involved in writing it because the story just grabbed me by the ears and dragged me along for the ride...[A] really great romantic suspense that manages both parts of the equation perfectly. This is a book you won't be able to put down."—*C-Spot Reviews*

Perfect Partners

"If you like friends-to-lovers romances, you will enjoy this book. If you are a fan of books about dogs, you will love this book. I enjoyed it, and I fit into both categories."—*Rainbow Reflections*

"[A] cozy romance with a touch of spice."—*Broome's Books*

"Maggie Cummings has an amazing talent for writing characters I easily fall for, and she brings them to life with such panache... This is a feel-good tale that left me with a smile on my face. Highly recommended."—*Kitty Kat's Book Review Blog*

Definite Possibility

"I enjoyed this book, well written with well-developed characters, including some familiar faces from the previous book in the series. The leads had good chemistry and the angst level was just right. It was an enjoyable read for a quiet afternoon."—*Melina Bickard, Librarian, Waterloo Library (UK)*

"[T]wo parallel romances give a quick pace to the book with more drama and romance...But what I really liked is that the story goes beyond both romances and is a tale of friendship, family, and love. Overall, a heartwarming and feel-good story with a bit of drama on the side."—*Lez Review Books*

Totally Worth It

"This book was absolutely delightful...A sweet story about love and friendship."—*My Fiction Nook*

"[I]t was...really nice reading about people going through the same transitory period in their lives that I, and many other twenty-somethings, also are...By the end of the book, I was a little jealous that I didn't live in Bay West like the characters. Needless to say, I was pretty pleased when I found out that this was going to be a series because Bay West has so much potential...I can't wait to see where Cummings takes us next."—*Read All About Queer Lit*

By the Author

Totally Worth It

Serious Potential

√Definite Possibility

Perfect Partners

Against All Odds (with Kris Bryant and M. Ullrich)

Brooklyn Summer

√Bulletproof

Visit us at www.boldstrokesbooks.com

BULLETPROOF

by

Maggie Cummings

2020

ISBN 13: 978-1-63555-771-8

This Trade Paperback Original Is Published By
Bold Strokes Books, Inc.
P.O. Box 249
Valley Falls, NY 12185

First Edition: November 2020

Credits
Editor: Ruth Sternglantz
Production Design: Stacia Seaman
Cover Design by Jeanine Henning

Acknowledgments

Once again, I want to express my sincerest gratitude to Rad and Sandy for giving me the opportunity to share my stories. A heartfelt thanks also to the entire BSB team who works tirelessly behind the scenes. Most especially, thank you to my editor, Ruth Sternglantz, for keeping me honest and on point, for both pushing me and coddling me, and for ultimately transforming my words and ideas into a presentable final product.

Real life seems to have a way of always working itself into the narrative somehow. Even when I make a plan, I still find myself drawing from the world I know, the family I love, the friends I cherish. This project was no exception. Special thanks this time around to Bobby for the best contribution to my tiny universe. As always, thanks to KC, Cabe, and Ab for the continual love and support. Shout out to Jane Cramer for keeping me young. Finally, and perhaps most importantly, thank you to every single reader for the valuable time and money spent on my books. I simply cannot properly express how much it means to me.

For my brothers, JPH and Tony D

CHAPTER ONE

I'm in."

Detective Dylan Prescott registered a distant "10-4" from her sergeant as she ended the call and slid the phone into the back pocket of her jeans. She had to actively dial back her excitement. The buzz of a crowded bar on a Friday night, wall-to-wall coeds, the mask of a fictitious identity to hide behind. She absolutely loved being in the center of the action.

She made slight eye contact with two NYPD colleagues inside the Lower East Side bar as she bladed her body, manipulating her way through the college crowd.

Her role in tonight's operation was minimal—the third ghost. Along with the two other undercover police officers, she was in the bar to keep an eye on the New York City Police Department's underage intern who would invariably get served alcohol without providing proof of age. Dylan and the other covert officers were on the scene to witness the transaction, protect the intern, and provide testimony of the crime.

Textbook vice work.

The bartender is a hottie. Dylan shook her head the minute her colleague's text came through.

Bro, you're on point tonight. Pay attention. She hit send but decided to fuck with her partner anyway. *Leave the ladies to me* ;) She was kidding but only because she never blurred the lines while working.

Across the room her colleague rolled his eyes, and it made her smile. She sidled up to the bar, pleased when the bartender stopped what she was doing to wait on her. It was hardly the first time she got immediate attention. Genes played a large part. Dylan had been blessed with a killer combo of ice-blue eyes and dark hair, which she wore super short and styled perfectly. The fact that she was six two literally made her stand out in almost any crowd. Still, she loved that her buddy was witnessing the whole thing. She couldn't wait to rub it in later.

"What can I get you?" The bartender hit her with some major bedroom eyes, and she felt her ego soar in response.

"I'll have a pint of Sweet Action," she said, leaning her forearms on the lip of the bar.

"Sixpoint Sweet Action." The bartender nodded approval, her eyes staying locked with Dylan's. "Excellent choice." Her smile was suggestive. "Can I interest you in anything else, or will that be all for now?"

Game on. The opportunity was there if she wanted it. Her partner wasn't wrong—the bartender was gorgeous, and under different circumstances Dylan would have taken the bait.

"I think that'll be it," she said, offering her best smile as a consolation prize.

"I'll be right back with your beer." The bartender blushed as she flashed Dylan one last invitation. She resisted the desire but let herself indulge a gratuitous look at her body as the bartender poured the draft.

Dylan left a generous tip and stepped away as she tried to blend in. She scanned the crowd until she located the intern battling against the masses to earn a spot at the bar.

"How the fuck are we supposed to talk business here?" A deep voice behind her grabbed her attention with its forceful demanding tone. "I can barely hear myself think."

"You said it didn't matter where we met."

"Well, I thought you'd use your brain. This place is jam-packed."

Dylan turned her head just enough to clock three guys in conversation behind her.

"That's the point. We have our little meeting, then we find some action." She heard obnoxious laughter and saw two of them high-five. Gross.

"Enough." Ooh. Someone was pissed. "Next time, I pick the spot. I'll make this quick. No more excuses. It's time."

"You don't think it's too soon?"

"Stop being a pussy, Goldenballs."

"Yeah, *Goldenballs*." This from a third distinct male voice who punctuated his sentence with a high-pitched juvenile cackle.

Dylan peeked over her shoulder just in time to see one guy jab another in the biceps. "Shut up, dick. Don't call me that." Good for you, Goldenballs.

She turned her attention back to the intern, who was still waiting to order. Dylan shifted her focus to visually check in with her colleagues, but her head was a hundred percent tuned into the conversation behind her.

"All right. Benji," the first guy barked again. He was obviously in charge. From her one-second assessment, it made sense. He was older than the other two with a more refined look and a haughty air about him. "I'm serious," he continued. "You want to make money or not?"

Her interest was piqued. She leaned back just slightly so she could hear the response.

"I do, but..."

"Get your shit together, then. Start moving product. Your little hiatus is over." Her ears perked up. "Otherwise I'm putting George here in charge."

"It's cool. I got it. I'm just worried about the attention. That kid dying fucked me up. I mean...it messed up sales, big-time."

Now this was interesting.

"Christ, Benji, man up already. It's been weeks. The heat's off—everyone's moved on to the next big story. The only one even still thinking about that kid is you. Get over it. We have a lot of shit to sell. Look at these spoiled kids spending Mommy and Daddy's money like it's nothing. Fuck, if they don't get their fix from us, they're going to get it somewhere else."

They were clearly talking drugs, and maybe the NYU senior who had overdosed recently? She tried to remember details of the story that monopolized headlines for the last month. A clean-cut jock, bright future, family heartbreak, the whole nine. Another typical tragedy at the hands of opioids and heroin. She supposed the conversation she was hearing could be a coincidence. For all she knew, every local pusher had their hackles up.

Benji and George. She filed away their names just in case.

"I said I got it." Benji's voice was sharper than before, like he had something to prove. "Just chill out, Paul."

Paul. The ringleader.

"Don't fucking tell me to chill. Do your motherfucking job. Or someone else will."

It was an order and a threat rolled into one, and she felt Paul's body brush her back as he pushed through the crowd to the door.

Over at the bar the underage intern was about to be served. Behind her, the two lackeys were talking.

"Come on, Benji. Let's bail. My buddy just texted me the address of a party on the Upper West Side, loaded with girls. Three-to-one ratio, he says. Can't beat those odds."

Dylan made a split-second decision. The vice team had the operation under control. She let Benji and George get a few steps ahead before she followed them onto the street outside.

Summer still hung in the air, and the sidewalk buzzed with millennials ushering in the weekend. It was the perfect cover. She reached for her phone and speed-dialed the sergeant.

"Sarge, I'm on to something," she said when he picked up on the first ring.

"Everything okay, Prescott?" Sgt. Schmidt's voice held distracted concern.

"Yeah, but I'm off the set. I'm following—" She paused, in the moment trying to articulate what exactly she was doing. "The guys have things under control inside. These two kids were talking about some wacky stuff," she said, knowing it sounded weak. "I just want to see where they go."

"Do you need backup?" he asked.

"Nah, I'm just walking. These guys are about a block ahead of me."

"I see you," he said. "You just passed by on Thompson Street."

Sometimes the intricacy of how the police embedded themselves within the community still impressed her. She knew the sergeant was with a team of detectives waiting to raid the bar, and she still didn't spot him.

"Okay," Sgt. Schmidt said. "Prescott. Don't do anything lone wolf-ish. This isn't TV."

He knew her better than that, but she also knew he needed her to say it. "Of course not, Boss."

"We just got the signal to move in." Sgt. Schmidt sounded a touch harried. "Stay in communication with me, Dylan."

"10-4, Sarge."

Ahead of her, Benji and George turned off Thompson Street onto Bleecker. She hung up and squared the corner just in time to see Benji slide into the passenger side of a jet-black Nissan Maxima. The car pulled away from the curb but not before she was able to capture the plate. Huzzah.

❖

The 15th Precinct detective squad was a ghost town, with multiple teams out on assignment. Dylan expected some of her crew would start trickling in any minute now. Once she was out of the mix, Schmidt had instructed her to head back to the precinct, which was perfect because it gave her time to do some digging.

The wheels of her ancient chair screeched as she slid close to the desk to access the motor vehicle database. She typed in the seven-digit alphanumeric and held her breath. In an instant her screen showed the info she needed. A black Nissan Maxima registered to George Rivas. She cross-referenced his pedigree and uncovered a lengthy rap sheet, including narcotics offenses, assault, and a burglary that had been downgraded to criminal mischief. Nice. Now for the real question. Was Rivas a target in any active NYPD investigations? She keyed his name into the department's case management system and waited.

"Prescott, there's fresh coffee." Captain Calhoun's shoes squeaked as she walked over and leaned against the corner of her desk.

It was almost ten p.m. on a Friday night, and coffee was the last thing she wanted. Captain Calhoun was the tour commander, and she drank coffee around the clock. Dylan wondered if the constant yen for caffeine came with rank or age. "How did it go at the Thompson Street operation?" the captain asked, interrupting her idle thought.

"Good. Pretty straightforward." Except for the fact she left midway through. Calhoun probably knew that detail by now. "Actually, when I was inside the bar ghosting, I got an interesting overhear." Her shrug underplayed how significant she thought it might be.

"What did you hear?" Calhoun's coffee actually smelled delicious.

Maybe she'd get a cup after all once she filled in the details. The caffeine would fuel her stamina in case she found some company later.

"There were these three guys talking about dealing. One guy was pressuring the others."

"Okay." The captain seemed only marginally interested.

"I know. Routine," Dylan said. "But then they started talking about the kid that died. The NYU senior who was all over the news. I think there might be a direct connection." It was a reach, and hearing it out loud, it sounded downright far-fetched. "I mean, it might be nothing. But, Cap, the way they were talking, one guy sounded nervous. Hinky. Like he might have some personal culpability."

"You think he's the supplier?" It was more than a question, like she was already halfway on board with the theory.

"Maybe." Dylan backpedaled, but only because she had nothing concrete to offer in support.

Captain Calhoun nodded at her computer. "Come up with anything good?"

"The license plate of the car they were driving comes back to a guy named George Rivas. Twenty-four years old. His rap sheet is mostly drug related."

"That's a start."

"I know I probably sound crazy because it's not much to go on, but it just felt...I don't know, I can't describe it. It felt like there was something there."

"You have to trust that Spidey sense."

Dylan forced a smile. The captain could be hard to read, and she wasn't sure if she was teasing or not.

"I'm serious," Calhoun said, as though she read the concern. "Half this job is following your gut." Her accompanying nod seemed to be laced with something else. Pride, perhaps. "You run him through our system yet to see if he pops in any cases?"

She touched the computer screen, which had gone into sleep mode since they started talking. Next to Rivas's name was a case number. Her heart started to beat quicker, but the celebration was short lived. Right next to the response was one word standing in her way: RESTRICTED.

"Damn." She didn't even try to hide her disappointment. Without clearance, she didn't have access to get any information on the investigation or what role George Rivas might play in it. Dylan tilted the screen so the captain could see.

Instead of saying anything, Calhoun wrote the case number on a scrap of paper. "Give me a minute," she said, disappearing into her office.

To temper her frustration while she waited, Dylan opened a series of texts that promised to be interesting.

Feel like playing?

I'm wearing your favorite.

Nothing.

She full on grinned at the blatant invitation from Talia, a gorgeous yoga instructor who lived four doors down from her in Brooklyn. Together they had taken friendly neighbor to new heights. There was no denying the rush she felt at the thought of heading right to Talia's apartment after her tour ended. They'd be horizontal in no time. The texts said it all. Talia wanted one thing. It was sexy and uncomplicated. Before she could respond with something equally direct, a new message appeared.

Violet, this time.

Hey Dylan. Haven't seen you around in a while. Me and my friends are at that new bar near your place. Boca. If you're out and about, stop by. Would love to see your face.

It would certainly be a treat to see Violet's face. Not to mention the rest of her body. But that situation was delicate. Violet was sweet with an alluring innocence. Dylan craved more every time they flirted. From their first hookup, Dylan had been up-front that she wasn't looking for anything serious. At the time, Violet echoed the sentiment. But lately, Dylan could sense she wanted more.

That knowledge did nothing to diminish her desire. She just wished their connection had the simplicity of what she had with Talia. Ugh.

Instead of responding to either woman, she tossed her phone on the desk and shifted her attention back to George Rivas's rap sheet.

"Major Case Division has the investigation." Captain Calhoun spoke across the squad from the doorway of her office. "Good news, the sergeant running the case is a personal friend of mine. I took the liberty of making a call." She smiled big, folding her arms and resting her weight against the wall. "They're working on a narcotics ring. Opioids, heroin, fentanyl, coke. The whole nine. Rivas's name has surfaced a few times." Dylan's heart raced even though she was only hearing a summary of the conversation secondhand. "They've been hoping their groundwork would lead to the NYU overdose," she continued. "Turns out it's been one brick wall after the next," she said. "Until right now."

Dylan's mind was fourteen steps ahead, wondering what impact her intel might have on their investigation down the line.

"There's a case meeting on Monday. They're expecting you. I'll send you the particulars."

"Wait, what?" Her head was spinning. Dylan had been fully prepared to document her observations in a report. Perhaps even talk on the phone with the case detective. Presenting it in person, at a meeting, seemed…unusual.

"Pack your bags, kid." Captain Calhoun beamed like a proud parent. "You just made it into Major Case."

It was a massive score to be transferred to such a prestigious division, and with a mere seven months under her belt as a detective, Dylan knew she was especially fortunate for the opportunity.

"No way."

"For now it's a temporary transfer," Calhoun said. But the captain's expression intrigued her. It was like she thought this might lead to something more substantial. "Prescott, this could be a really good thing for you. Go show them what you're made of."

"Cap." Dylan was slightly overwhelmed and almost choked up. "I don't know what to say. I mean thank you, obviously." It wasn't like she could go over and hug out her appreciation, but a big part of her wanted to. She knew it was because of Calhoun's connections she was being given this chance. "I won't let you down."

"Get out of here." The captain waved off her gratitude. "I'm serious," she said. "Go celebrate. This is a big deal."

"Yes, ma'am." Dylan grabbed her things, pumped for the early dismissal. There was plenty of time to reach out to Talia or Violet. But in the back of her mind she already knew it was unlikely she'd contact either. At this hour, she'd hit her Brooklyn neighborhood right when the bars were at peak capacity.

She was feeling lucky.

CHAPTER TWO

I can't believe I let you talk me into this." Briana Logan rested her elbows on her bare knees, enjoying the feel of the August heat on her arms.

"Beats sitting in our apartment by, like, a million degrees." Stef, her roommate, snickered. "Am I right?"

"Meh. If you say so."

"Please. You love it."

"I don't know about love," Briana countered. It was kind of hot outside. At home she could be preparing for her morning meeting.

"If this is about tomorrow, stop stressing. You know you'll get every last detail on the case breakthrough once you get in the office. That's how it works."

Sometimes Briana felt like she'd survived law school solely on her BFF's conventional wisdom. Even though they practiced very different types of law now, Stef's sensibility and rational approach helped channel her own zen.

"It's a gorgeous day," Stef continued. "We're steps from our place, enjoying the tail end of summer in our awesome Brooklyn hood. And there's a basketball court full of women in their prime sweating it out for our viewing pleasure. All we have to do is ogle and clap."

"Cheerleading." Briana widened her eyes to accentuate her jab. "Not really my jam, to be honest."

"How about the ten hot women in peak physical condition? I'm not hearing complaints about that."

"True, but I'm mostly in it for the happy hour afterward." Briana patted Stef's forearm and leaned close. "Tell me again which one you're crushing on?"

"Number five on the orange team. But I wouldn't kick number three out of bed for eating crackers. Or number seven for that matter."

"Always so girl crazy," Briana teased. "Go number five!" she yelled as loud as she could, cupping her mouth and adding a double *woot* for good measure.

Stef yanked her hands down. "I hate you," she said with a laugh.

"You love me." Briana smiled at her own shenanigans. "Ooh and look, one of them just turned around to check you out."

Sure enough, her over-the-top cheer had garnered some attention, and the tallest person on the team had turned around to look.

And whoa, she was hot.

Tall and wiry with piercing blue eyes that were striking even from a distance. Briana felt the tiny hairs on her forearms bristle when their gazes locked across the court for a full five seconds. An unexpected surge of heat followed when the player flashed her an impish grin.

"Bri, much as I hate to admit this"—Stef's whisper was tempered with intrigue—"I'm pretty sure she's looking at you. Like, still."

A whistle blew, snapping the players back into action. Thank freaking God, because that stare was…something.

"Tell me again why you've sworn off women?" Stef read her like a book.

Briana shook out her shoulders, resurrecting her resolve from where it had momentarily melted into the pavement. "Stop. I love women. You know that. I'm not done with them forever."

"Yes." Stef gave a mini fist pump, like she'd won a tiny battle.

"I just need a break."

"So you're riding the dude highway again? I don't get how that's ever appealing." Stef fake gagged, and even though she was clearly going for a cheap laugh, her punch line oddly resonated. Briana based dating decisions on individual personality and mutual click regardless of gender, but if she was being honest, it was hard to compare the emotional intensity that formed seamlessly between women. But, ugh, they were complicated. The last few she'd casually gone out with seemed to be headed for the proverbial U-Haul almost immediately.

"I am decidedly not on the prowl for anyone." Briana added a chin nod, as though the strength of her conviction might dull the desire she felt for temporary companionship. "I'm here to support you. And to treat myself to a frozen margarita. Or two."

"Oh, I know. I was only joking anyway. I support your pansexual lifestyle, even if I can't always wrap my head around it."

"Is it too much to just want to spend time with a good person who's interested in having fun but isn't looking for a relationship?" She asked the question rhetorically, but experience had already given her the answer. "Honestly, Stef. Categorically speaking, women seem to have a harder time with the fact that I don't want a traditional relationship at this point in my life." She hated that it was the truth. "When I go out with a guy and explain I'm not looking for anything serious, most of them seem to respect that. They listen and don't expect more."

"Because they just want to sleep with you."

"That's where you're wrong, young Stefania." Briana was being playful, but it was important her best friend understand the nuance. "The men I go out with are interested in sex. As am I. No one is even invited to sleep over. That's an earned privilege."

"You're so dramatic." Stef clapped when her favorite player scored. "I find it hard to believe there aren't any women who are willing to adhere to these rules."

"From your lips to God's ears." Briana steepled her hands to the sky in fake prayer. The truth was she shared Stef's ideology. "You would think, in this neighborhood, I'd be able to find at least one. I mean, for crying out loud, it's not even one o'clock on a Sunday afternoon, and we're at a women's rec league basketball game. Check out the size of this crowd." She eyed the packed bleachers, the swarm of people lining the perimeter of the court. "But goddamn if they don't all want to settle down and have babies."

"Don't hate."

She touched Stef's shoulder, not wanting to offend her. "I'm not judging. I want those things too. Eventually. Just might be nice to make partner first."

"Or Chief of the Criminal Bureau at the US Attorney's Office. I get it."

"That's a pipe dream, but thanks for the vote of confidence."

Briana loved that even though Stef didn't share her vision or timeline, she still respected it. And she appreciated that Stef believed in her enough to voice her support out loud. "So give me the deets on number five," she said, trying to return the favor.

"Oh my God, Bri, she's so funny. We've been texting all week."

"You met here? At a game?"

"At the bar after last week's matchups. There's an informal meetup at The HB on Smith Street. The cocktails flow. The clientele is—to put it in professional terms—fucking gorgeous."

"Let me guess..." Briana fanned her hand at the court. "Stacked with these lovely ladies?" She was going for coy, poking fun at Stef's weakness for sporty women, but as soon as she said it, she felt an unmistakable rush of hope that the player who'd checked her out might be there.

"You know it," Stef said. "This game is going to end in five. Let's head over now, snag a spot at one of the picnic tables in the back."

"You don't want to wait and congratulate your prospective girlfriend on the court?"

"Ha-ha. No. I want to look like I'm not totally invested. Play a little hard to get."

"Ah, feigned disinterest and trickery," she said, grabbing her purse as she stood. "The way to a woman's heart."

Forty minutes later, Briana stood in the open-air courtyard of The HB, one of her favorite local places to chill, as she indulged the last sip of a frozen pomegranate margarita in the bright afternoon sunlight. The crowd was buzzing and loaded with eye candy, but the sexy player she'd shared a look with earlier was nowhere in sight. She was sure because, despite her words to the contrary, she was looking.

The player's absence was for the best. Briana was in the middle of a big case. One that could bring her career to the next level. She needed to stay focused.

"You having an okay time?" Stef asked.

"Definitely." Briana checked a look at Stef's crush a few feet away. "How's things going with number five?" she whispered.

"Mackenzie." Stef filled in the blanks as she bit her lower lip and pouted. "Good, I think." She crossed her fingers. "Oh, before I forget. Dylan Prescott."

Briana answered her with an eyebrow raise.

"That's her name. The one from the game. You two had a staring contest. Is this ringing any bells for you?"

"We didn't have a staring contest."

"You're right. It was more of an eye-fuck moment." Stef sipped her drink. "She went home to shower. Apparently she lives nearby. Anyway, she should be here soon."

"And you are telling me this because...?"

"Several reasons, really. One, in the name of lesbians everywhere, I selfishly want to keep you on this side of the playing field. Two"—Stef held two fingers in the air—"as your roommate, best friend, study buddy, et cetera, I happen to know you function better when you are not all pent up like you are right now. And three"—she lifted a third finger—"Dylan Prescott is a notorious player. So it's honestly perfect. You can thank me later. When you are fully satiated."

Even though she wasn't convinced, Briana was smiling. She adored her friendship with Stef. Of course she was right. Her mental focus was always sharper when she was physically content. It was a kind of natural mind-body symbiosis.

"Out of curiosity, how do you know all of this?"

"I have my ways. Worry about those details later." Stef looked past her. "She's here."

"Huh?" Her brain caught up but not before Dylan had made her way over to their loose group. Briana watched her greet Mackenzie and the rest of the team with fist bumps and half hugs before turning toward her and Stef.

"I'm Dylan."

She was even taller than Briana had realized, and the hand she extended in greeting was strong and smooth.

"Briana." She smiled and licked her lips before she realized what she was doing. "Nice to meet you," she added.

She tried to look away but couldn't help being drawn to Dylan's delicately handsome look. Her clear eyes were accentuated by a dark blue rim and framed by long lashes. She had high cheekbones and an angular jawline that was somehow masculine but soft at the same time. There was a slight cleft in her chin, and for the briefest moment Briana imagined running the tip of her finger over the smooth skin there.

"I'm going to the bar," Briana said, just to give herself an escape. "Anyone need a drink?" she added to be polite.

"I'm headed that way, too," Dylan answered. "I'll come with, if that's okay."

Briana was full of nervous anticipation as they walked to the bar, but it was for naught. Once they were served she was ambushed by Roger, her needy downstairs neighbor. As he unloaded his latest tale of heartbreak, she watched Dylan chat up two pretty blondes and a curvy brunette. She sighed. Damn if Roger hadn't cockblocked her.

After a solid thirty minutes reassuring him he'd find the right one soon enough, she finessed her way out of the conversation. She was bummed when she didn't see Dylan anywhere but went in search of Stef instead. She held back when she spotted her bestie in the back corner deep in a one-on-one with Mackenzie.

"Think that has potential?" Dylan's voice was low, her breath warm against her neck as she bent in close to speak.

"I don't know. I hope so. I think."

"You think?" Dylan held out a frozen drink toward her. "Pomegranate, right?" She didn't wait for an answer. "You looked like you needed a refill."

"Thank you." Their fingers touched briefly as she reached for the cocktail, and Briana tried not to overthink the fact that Dylan had been keeping tabs on her. "You didn't have to do that."

"No worries."

Dylan toasted her and took a sip of her beer. Briana enjoyed the precise way she used the tips of two fingers to wipe the foam from the edges of her mouth. Ugh, her mouth. She had full lips and a crooked smile, perfect teeth. Briana imagined the graze of their touch along her body, being kissed by her everywhere. Had she really sworn off women?

Dylan pointed at Stef and Mackenzie with her drink. "How come you seem unsure whether or not you're rooting for them?"

"No, I am. I just don't know Mackenzie at all." She was always cautiously concerned about Stef's choices. "Stef has notoriously bad taste in women," she said, giving Dylan a window into the history.

"Ah, gotcha." Dylan nodded. "What about you?" she asked. "How's your taste in women?"

Briana chewed her cheek to keep from grinning. Dylan was sexy and bold, and she loved where this was going.

"Who said I date women?" She teased the straw of her drink with her tongue. Dylan wasn't the only one with game.

"Please don't destroy my wishful thinking by telling me that guy you were talking to has a better shot than me." Dylan looked positively irresistible when she pouted. "I waited a whole half hour just to talk to you."

"You could have interrupted."

"Nah." Even her frown was loaded with confidence. "Not my style."

"Too bad. I could have used a lifeline."

"Yeah?"

"Yes." She lifted the fruit garnish from the rim of her glass and took a small bite, her part in the subtle seduction.

Dylan's eyes were focused right on her mouth. "I didn't know if you were into him."

"Did I *look* into him?"

Dylan leaned into her space, and for the briefest second Briana thought she was going in for a kiss. She wasn't entirely sure she was going to stop her.

"I completely would have helped you." Dylan's voice was husky and full of dangerous promise. "But you didn't give me any signals. Not a wave. No secret call for help. Not a single text."

"I don't even have your number." Briana gently poked Dylan's toned arm, knowing full well initiating physical contact raised the stakes.

"We should fix that right now. Here." Dylan pulled out her phone and handed it over. "This way we avoid this problem in the future."

Dylan's smooth approach should have scared her away, but it was too late. She was absolutely hooked.

"Don't you think your string of girlfriends is going to be upset you're spending so much time over here?" Briana typed in her number and gave the cell back. She was teasing, but she could feel some looks being tossed in her direction.

"Is that..." Dylan scratched her chin like she was searching for the right word. "Jealousy?"

"You wish."

"Kinda do."

Damn, she was good. "Sorry to disappoint." Briana scrunched up her nose, the playful action contrasting with the sincerity of her words. "I don't do jealousy as a rule."

Dylan took a long sip of her beer, and Briana wondered if she was put off. "Why's that?" she asked.

If this had any chance of working, now was the time to lay her cards on the table.

"My life right now is full. I have a great apartment, a job I love. Don't misunderstand me. I like going out, meeting people, seeing where it goes." She wiped the moisture off her glass. Even though Stef had said Dylan was a player, being transparent still made her nervous. "I'm just not looking for a relationship right now. So jealousy doesn't really factor in."

"That's fair." Dylan smiled. "Even though a little jealousy can be hot."

"I didn't say I wasn't enjoying all of your attention right now. Even if those other women are shooting me daggers."

Dylan smirked, her amazing eyes loaded with sin. "There's other women here?"

"Cute," she said with a smile.

She was trying for aloof but Briana already felt herself giving in to the pull of attraction as she indulged in Dylan's sweet woodsy scent. There were notes of cedar and lavender coming through, and for the life of her, Briana could not grasp how those scents melded so well together, or how much it made her want to taste Dylan's bare skin.

"She's married." Stef's voice startled her, and for a split second Briana thought she was warning her with an announcement about Dylan.

"Mackenzie's married?" Dylan caught up before she did, sounding almost as surprised as Stef.

"At least for the moment. Her wife is over there reading her the riot act right now."

Briana turned to see the showdown in the corner of the courtyard. "Yikes."

"I'm sorry to burst into your conversation. I just needed to be away from that drama."

"Of course," Briana said.

"Do you need a drink?" Dylan offered.

Stef rubbed her temples. "No. No. I'm fine. I'm just going to go home."

"I'll come with you."

"You don't have to," Stef said. Briana saw her eyes go to Dylan. "Stay. I'm fine."

"Nope. We came together. We leave together." Briana took a final sip of her drink. "Roommates," she said, explaining to Dylan. "Do you live nearby?"

"A few blocks over. Carroll Street."

"I'm right on President Street. We're neighbors. I'll walk with you both if that's cool." Dylan looked around for a place to put her empty beer, and even though Briana knew she should tell her an escort wasn't necessary, she would be lying if she didn't admit to wanting a few extra minutes together.

"Let's go," she said, leading the way to an exit that placed them right on the street without having to pass through the crowded bar.

As they strolled through the quaint tree-lined streets that made up Brooklyn's Carroll Gardens section, Briana stole glances at Dylan while Stef vented about how things had seemed so promising right up until Mackenzie's secret wife showed up. A few times the back of her hand brushed Dylan's, and as much as she wanted more contact, she knew it was all hormones.

"I'd invite you in," Briana said as they arrived at her apartment. She nodded in Stef's wake when her roommate hurried past them inside. "But I should make sure she's okay."

"No, I totally get it." If Dylan was bothered, it didn't show. "Could we do this again?" she asked. She took one step closer, and Briana's body responded without her permission. Goose bumps lined her forearms, and her nipples hardened under her shirt.

"Maybe not this exactly." Dylan edited her invitation on the spot. "I was thinking just me and you. Something noncommittal, but hella fun. Interested?"

"So interested."

Dylan started to back away slowly. "I'll call you," she said, her grin full of wicked charm.

"I'll answer."

So much for celibacy.

CHAPTER THREE

There's Rivas. Lower right."
       Dylan stood in front of a corkboard in the Major Case Team 2 office, affectionately referred to as The Plant. George Rivas's face jumped out at her from the link chart's bottom row of suspects even before her new colleague pointed him out.

"I see him," she said. Her eyes scanned the board, hoping for a glimpse of Benji or Paul. No dice.

"From what we can tell, Rivas is just a dealer. He's working angles at a bunch of the local colleges. Mostly pills, but he'll sell anything he can get his hands on."

Detective Trevor Gill was the lead investigator on the case. He'd met her in the lobby on the way in and whisked her through the office, rushing to show her the layout: bathroom, break room, lieutenant's office. Now standing in front of the case subject flowchart, he zeroed in on the investigation.

"We've been focusing on this guy here." He pointed to a mug shot of Mike Johnson. "He's got a decent record, but so far we're going in circles with him. Basically he's just a purchaser." He shook his head, seeming pensive. "I'm more interested in identifying some of the players higher up the food chain. I made up folders for you to look through. I'm excited to get your take."

"Definitely." Dylan couldn't keep herself from smiling. Trevor's enthusiasm was contagious. His blind faith in her opinion didn't hurt either. He was about her age, which seemed promising for her future in this division. And his obvious commitment to police work matched her own, even if their energies seemed polar opposite.

For the moment, she was happy he was going Mach 10. It kept her mind in focus. All morning she'd felt herself slipping back into fantasies of Briana. Which was fine. Delicious, even. Their brief flirtation had been the highlight of her weekend, and she couldn't wait to see how things progressed. But today was big, and she needed to keep her head in the game.

"Showtime." Trevor clapped his hands like he was pumping them up.

"What do you mean?" Dylan was lost.

"Big meeting upstairs with our bosses and the lawyers. Let's go."

"Oh, wow, that's happening already?" For some reason she'd expected there would be more time to settle in. She'd envisioned a formal introduction to her new team, the sergeant, the lieutenant. A chance to at least get a sense of how she'd gel in her new assignment.

"I know it's quick." Trevor could already read her. He guided them to the elevator. "I'll give you a proper tour and full introductions after, I promise. It's just that everyone is excited about the big break in the case. The brass wants to hear directly from the rock star who got the intel that's going to get this investigation off the ground." His smile was warm and reassuring. "Don't be nervous. Everyone's cool. Well, except the LT." He lowered his voice as he pressed the button for the tenth floor. "He can be a tool, but you didn't hear it from me."

Not even five minutes later, she was seated at one end of a conference table with the rest of the NYPD crew. Lt. Nieves greeted her with the expected pompousness, and she was grateful to Trevor for the small heads-up in the elevator. Sgt. Hollander was less formal, but perhaps that was because she and Miri recognized each other from the lesbian social scene.

"We're excited to have you on board, Prescott," Miri Hollander said with a welcoming look.

"Yes, we are." Lt. Nieves commandeered the conversation. "Just so we're clear, I'll be presenting the information to Logan. If she has follow-up questions, that's fine. You can answer those."

His tone said this was an order, and Dylan responded in kind. "Yes, sir."

"Logan is the AUSA." Trevor filled her in with a discreet whisper.

Dylan nodded acknowledgment, but there was little time to process the shifting dynamic as the legal team filtered into the room.

They were a mix of men and women, and what she found most notable was that they all seemed young. Why she had expected the United States Attorney's Office to be made up of stodgy old white men, she wasn't sure, but the staff in front of her was refreshingly diverse.

"She'll be here in just a second, Lieutenant," one of the women said, addressing Nieves only. It made sense—he was fidgeting in his chair like an impatient toddler.

As she waited, Dylan assessed their interactions, an occupational hazard. The legal crew seemed to be comparing notes and chatting, and there was even some light laughter. It was in direct opposition to the silence that filtered down from Nieves at the police end of the table.

"Sorry to keep you all waiting." AUSA Logan's voice entered the room a split second before she did.

Was her voice familiar?

As the lead prosecutor took a seat at the head of the table and placed her legal pad in front of her, Dylan let it sink in.

Assistant United States Attorney Logan. *Briana* Logan.

"Nice of you to join us, Miss Logan." Nieves was the only one to laugh at his joke. What a dick.

Briana jotted the date on her pad. "Let's get to work, shall we? I'm excited to hear about this lead."

Dylan marveled at the way she dismissed the lieutenant outright. It was only then that Briana looked up and saw her. The slight stutter in her glance made it obvious Briana shared her surprise, but she moved past it with practiced professionalism.

Nieves sat upright as he started talking. "One of our detectives got a decent overhear while on a different assignment," he started. "So right away we had her transferred to our team."

"This is Dylan Prescott," Sgt. Hollander interjected with a lean forward to introduce Dylan with a wave of her hand. "She comes to us from Vice. She's responsible for the new intel."

"Hello," Briana said with a friendly smile.

With one word, Briana made her feel at ease while revealing nothing to anyone else. Not the fact that they'd met just the day before. And flirted. Hard. Nor had she pretended they were complete strangers, which Dylan oddly appreciated. It was all very…smooth.

Dylan nodded in response and was thankful Lt. Nieves had taken the floor again. She listened to him stumble through his explanation of her overhear, trying not to wince as he butchered the details. The team of interns and attorneys took copious notes, but Briana just listened, taking it all in.

"Did we happen to get names of the two guys Rivas was with?" she asked.

"Benji and Phil, right?" Lt. Nieves looked to Trevor for support.

"It was actually Paul," Dylan piped up. "Benji and Paul." She was a little concerned Nieves would be angry with her for answering, but the specifics mattered.

"Great," Briana said. She lifted her pen and took a note. Dylan felt herself swoon ridiculously at the sight of her delicate hand swirling names across the page with precision. "Trev, if you'd forward me the pedigree for Rivas, I'll start to write for his phone today. Sound good?"

"Sure thing."

Dylan was new to electronic eavesdropping investigations, but she could surmise the bit of information she'd overheard Friday night was probable cause to authorize listening in on Rivas's phone conversations. Being up on a wiretap was a coup in any criminal case. She felt herself beam inside.

"Great job, team." Briana was addressing the entire crew, but Dylan felt her compliment personally.

She wasn't crazy, though—Briana was looking right at her. She could see her gorgeous hazel eyes from behind the tortoiseshell glasses she was wearing. Professional Briana might even be more enticing than flirty Briana from the bar. Her light brown hair was in a messy bun, as though she'd pulled it off her face just moments before the meeting. For the briefest second Dylan imagined releasing it from its rubber band and watching it fall loose across her shoulders. Her head went right to lifting Briana onto the conference table and sliding between her thighs, their kiss full of passion and promise.

"Okay, people. Let's get these guys." Briana collected her pad and stood up. Her staff followed suit.

Nieves rocketed to attention as though he was trying to race her to conclude the meeting. Briana looked as though she might laugh at him. "Go ahead, Lieutenant," she said with a smile offering him the first exit. "I'm in no rush."

Damn, she was good. This was going to be a struggle. Or was it her fantasy come to life? She swallowed her desire, knowing there was hardly a difference.

The remainder of Dylan's first day was characterized by meeting the members of the team. Detectives Ahmed Baisir and Trish Suarez were in the office listening to the phone lines they were already authorized to record. Trevor had explained that there were also guys out in the field doing surveillance. He answered her eight million questions and never broke her chops when every answer prompted a new query.

He showed her the inner workings of the wire room where they monitored and transcribed phone calls. The team took turns doing both plant and field work, so everyone was proficient in all aspects of the case. She read the case jackets of all the identified perps in the network. By the end of her tour she was completely overstimulated.

As a tiny reward for surviving her first shift unscathed, she stopped at Connolly's Public House, a revamped Irish pub with a chill vibe not far from her apartment. She sat at the adorable tiki bar out back watching the sun set as she thought about the day.

Briana was the lead prosecutor. Unbelievable. What were the odds? And what did it mean in light of their promising banter? Just a day ago, Briana had been clear that she wasn't looking for a relationship. But did professional overlap wreck their chances entirely?

There was only one way to find out.

CHAPTER FOUR

*G*ood evening, counselor.

Briana exited the subway. She had yet to process the insane coincidence from today's meeting, but Dylan was already texting. Usually this kind of persistence would irk her, but she felt a smile sneak across her face at seeing Dylan's name on her phone. Even still, she should ignore the message. That was the sensible reaction. At least she shouldn't respond right away.

Detective, she typed back unable to resist.

That was some curveball, huh?

She tried to remain composed. *Unexpected, for sure.*

Most definitely not what I had planned for our second meetup.

Dylan's text came through with additional bubbles indicating another message was on its way. Briana felt her pulse race in spite of logic. She should shut this down immediately. Mixing her professional and social lives was a terrible idea. At the same time, she was grinning like a teenager in anticipation of whatever Dylan might say next.

However...since we've cleared that hurdle... Briana's pulse raced as a final text appeared. *Meet me for a drink at Connolly's?*

Boom. There it was. The invitation she wanted. The one she should most definitely decline. Dylan was typing again.

I don't want to pressure you. But the sky is gorgeous. I'm enjoying the pleasant evening with a beer out back. It might not be a bad idea to clear the air at least...

Briana was only a half a block away from the bar, and even though it went against reason, it was like her legs had their own opinion on the matter. Anyway Connolly's was on her way home, and her hectic day earned her a glass of wine. An opportunity to clear the air, away from their shared workspace, was simply using good judgment. The fact that she got another dose of Dylan's handsome face was collateral she had no control over.

"One drink."

"You came." Dylan's expression revealed a mixture of delight and surprise. She moved to stand in greeting, but Briana stopped her with a hand to the forearm. The touch was unnecessary, and she internally scolded herself for giving in to pure desire.

"I didn't even know this place had a backyard," she said, placing her purse on an adjacent stool.

"They gave it a huge overhaul about a year ago. Now it's one of my favorite neighborhood spots."

"I see why." It was quiet and lovely, just a few patrons scattered about the space. For the first time she looked up at the blue and pink sky. "It's beautiful out."

"Right?" Dylan said with adorable enthusiasm. "Before you know it, winter will be here. We have to capitalize on this beauty while we still can."

"I hate the winter."

"Do you?"

"I don't mind the cold. But the snow. Gross."

"I feel you on that one." Dylan hung her head and let out a husky laugh. It was…divine. "Are you from New York?"

"Yes. Long Island originally. My family is still there. What about you?"

"No way. Mine too. What part?"

"Rockville Center." What was she doing? This was not a date. Why was she acting this way? She'd agreed to a drink to ensure there was no awkwardness going forward. The whole point was to lay the ground rules for a professional relationship. No blurred lines.

"My family is further east," Dylan said. "Suffolk County. But I never lived out there. I grew up here in Brooklyn. My mom moved when she got remarried."

Briana ordered a glass of pinot grigio, and with the first sip she channeled her courage. "Listen, Dylan."

"I'm listening, Briana."

Ugh, even the way Dylan said her name dripped seduction. Dylan looked right at her and her eyes pierced through, like she could see inside. Was it obvious how much she wanted Dylan to kiss her, to take her, to dominate her?

"I think…" Briana said, willing her voice to stay even. She picked up a fray of a napkin that blew off the bar and landed on Dylan's knee. "I think we should keep things on the level. Between us. Professional, I mean." It almost ached to say the words out loud, because her body craved the exact opposite. Like, forthwith. "Would that be okay?" Briana knew why she was asking permission. She wanted Dylan to protest, to convince her to break the only rule that made any sense in this situation.

"You're the boss," Dylan said without missing a beat. Her grin was sly, but her words compliant.

It was the stark truth and the entire reason this couldn't work.

"I'm sorry," she said.

"Don't be."

Dylan's tone told her she wasn't mad, but Briana felt compelled to expound. "I'm obviously attracted to you." She wasn't able to maintain eye contact at her admission. "It's just…in my experience…this doesn't end well."

Dylan smiled. "Do you have a lot of experience with this kind of thing?"

"Oh my God, that is not what I was implying. I just meant with the case, and us…" She waved her hands between them as she stammered out an explanation.

"I'm teasing you." Dylan reached out and stilled her hands. "Relax. We're good."

Briana was pretty sure she registered disappointment in Dylan's unbelievable blue eyes, but it had to be this way. She took a long sip of her wine, letting the alcohol work its magic to calm her nerves.

"How's Stef doing with the whole Mackenzie madness?" Dylan shifted the subject with a swig of her drink.

"She's fine." Even if that wasn't true, Briana would protect Stef to the end of the earth. "Over it."

"That was crazy, though." Dylan shook her head. "I honestly had no idea Mackenzie was married."

"Really? You two aren't buddies?"

"I haven't played with her team for very long. I've hung out with them after games a few times. That's really it." She spun her pint glass on the bar, and Briana couldn't help but notice her long fingers, her perfectly square fingertips. "I'll say this, though—I was shocked. Mackenzie is always looking to score."

"Funny, she said the same about you." Briana sipped her drink, realizing in the moment that she wasn't a hundred percent sure where Stef had gleaned that information.

"Interesting." Dylan shrugged. "She doesn't really know me."

"Perhaps your reputation precedes you."

"Maybe." She seemed unconvinced. "I didn't think I really had a reputation," she offered. "Mostly, because I'm very up front. Like you." Dylan leaned into her space and looked right at her. Briana could smell her cologne. It was intoxicating. "You're direct and honest. It's captivating." Her features softened. "Obviously, you're gorgeous. But I'm sure you know that."

Dylan took another sip of her drink, and Briana was grateful for the reprieve. She wasn't entirely sure how long her resolve would hold. The wine was not helping.

"The way you handled Nieves today. You put him right in his place," Dylan said. "It was…hot."

Dylan thought she was hot. It sent her slightly over the edge. Her chest pounded. The butterflies in her belly were out of control. She needed to rein this in, and quick. It had been too long since she'd had any kind of release, and Dylan's charm was making her weak. If they kept this conversation going, she didn't know how long she'd resist. But she wasn't ready to leave either. So she segued Dylan's compliment into safer territory.

"Nieves is an ass. Men like him make my skin crawl."

"Do you have to deal with that nonsense a lot?"

"Probably the same amount as you." But even as she said it, Briana felt an odd pang of regret at her words, wondering how much flak Dylan caught for her masculine-of-center presentation. There were varied levels of ignorance in the world. Even in progressive New York City.

"Eh, I cope." Dylan finished her beer. "The police department is mostly cool. My old team was awesome. The new team seems fine too."

"How come you didn't tell me you were a detective yesterday?"

"It didn't really come up. I'm sure we would have gotten to it eventually. Honestly, I didn't know you were an attorney either. I wonder if we would've put it all together." Dylan seemed to be pondering those odds when the bartender asked if they wanted another round.

"We shouldn't," she said to Dylan.

"Come on, counselor. One more? We can talk about the case. I'll regale you with the details of my dramatic overhear. We're basically doing work." Dylan coupled the hard sell with a killer smile, but the truth was she would have said yes even if Dylan wanted to talk basketball for the rest of the night.

Staying went against everything Briana believed in. She ordered another pinot on the spot.

True to her word, Dylan gave her the scoop on what was for sure the best case development to date. She also talked a bit about her stint in Vice and her years in patrol. Briana let it slip that she was heavily invested in this particular narcotics case because she believed in getting drugs off the street and holding pushers accountable, but also because a large-scale conviction was important for her career.

"We'll get 'em. Me and you." Dylan held her hand up for a high five in solidarity of their professed teamwork. Briana knew she should pass.

She did the opposite. She touched her palm to Dylan's and didn't protest when Dylan laced their fingers together.

"We can't, Dylan," she said, letting go. But, God, she wanted to. "We shouldn't."

"I know. I know." Dylan seemed apologetic for her small slip across the line. "I know you're right. I just really want to." Her laugh was mischievous and sexy.

"Come on. Let's get out of here."

They settled the bill and continued to chat as they walked along the streets of Brooklyn. Briana liked the natural confidence Dylan embodied when she talked about her job. She could drown in the huskiness of her voice. And the heat she felt emanating from her body as they walked side by side…forget it.

"Is it okay if I walk you home?" Dylan asked politely. "I live right here," she said pointing to a brownstone on the right. Almost on cue, a middle-aged woman passed by and turned up the walkway.

"Dylan, thanks for helping Tom with the air conditioner this weekend. You know him, he'd never ask, and he'd never have been able to fix it on his own," she added with a smile.

"No worries, Marie."

"Are you two coming inside?" the woman asked as she backed toward the stoop. "Should I hold the front door?"

"Nah, I'm good," Dylan answered. "That's my tenant," Dylan whispered in explanation.

"You have a tenant?"

"I do."

"Wait. You own your brownstone?" The shock in her voice was obvious, but real estate in this neighborhood was notoriously pricey. There had to be a story.

"I'll explain on the walk," Dylan said.

"I don't live far—I'll be fine. This neighborhood is completely safe."

"I know, and I'm sure you can handle yourself." Dylan shrugged. "But even as your friend, I'd feel better if I saw you get in the front door."

Briana felt her stomach bottom out. Could she be more chivalrous? "If you insist."

"I do. Come on." Dylan started walking. "I'll tell you how my grandparents used to own this place, and now it's all mine."

"You didn't kill them, did you?"

She felt Dylan's hand on her shoulder. "Is that a deal breaker?"

Briana laughed out loud at the silly exchange. She didn't even allow herself to dwell on the combination of strength and softness in Dylan's touch.

Moments later, when they arrived at her apartment, Dylan said good night like a perfect gentleman, and while her brain said she'd made the right decision, her libido was absolutely devastated.

"Oh my God."

Briana covered her mouth and breathed everything out as she let her body go limp against her apartment door behind her.

"Rough day at the office, honey?" Stef was sitting on the living room couch. She paused *Love Island* to assess her roomie. "Whoa. You look…frazzled. What's going on?"

"Get this." Briana hung her bag off a stool at the kitchen island. She reached in the fridge and poured herself a La Croix. "Dylan Prescott is an NYPD detective who has just been assigned to the narcotics case I'm prosecuting."

"Wait." Stef took a minute to place the name. "The hot butch from yesterday. The basketball player you were talking to?"

"Mm-hmm." She swallowed the crisp beverage, savoring the hint of lime as she continued to wrap her head around the wild turn of events. "The very one."

"Well, that's fucking hot."

"Is it?" she asked with a dramatic head tilt.

"Isn't it?" Stef countered.

"There's not much I can do about it," Briana said. "I have no control over the police staffing."

"Hold on a second." Stef placed her bowl of artisanal mac and cheese on the coffee table, the fork clanking loudly against the dish. "Why are you acting like this is a bad thing?"

"Because it is." Briana pouted. "Is there any more of that?" she asked with a nod at Stef's food.

"Yes. Of course. I'm a team player. I figured you were working late, so I ordered takeout from Wilkie's. There's a turkey burger on the counter for you."

"This is why you're my favorite." She opened the cardboard container.

"It's only one of the reasons," Stef teased. "Now, let's discuss the Dylan development."

Briana took a bite of the burger. "We had drinks just now."

"The whole investigative team?"

"Nope. Just me and her. At Connolly's."

"Shut up!" Stef clapped happily. "It. Is. On."

"It's actually not." Briana picked at the whole wheat bun as she thought about the last hour with Dylan. God, she was sexy. Smart. Dedicated to her job, clearly. It was a damn shame their worlds had collided like this. "We just finished having that conversation."

"That you can't hook up?"

"Basically."

"Why?" She appreciated Stef's support and knew it came from a good place, but still. "Hear me out." Stef took a minute to compose an argument.

Briana grabbed the mac and cheese while she waited. She loved that her bestie was a brilliant corporate attorney. She knew her defense was going to be good.

"On one side we have the lead prosecutor with a fantastic conviction rate. She's beautiful with a slamming body. Amazing hazel eyes. Perfect dot nose and a smile that makes both men and women swoon on the daily," Stef said, going over the top as she listed her physical attributes. "One caveat: she's not ready for a relationship." Stef held up one finger to keep her from interrupting. "On the same side," she said with emphasis, "is the sexy detective. Equally gorgeous. A known player, also not looking for a relationship. Your Honor, the defense rests."

"You're such an idiot." Briana covered her mouth, continuing to chew as she laughed.

"I honestly don't see how it's that big of a deal. I watch *SVU*. I know what happens on those desks after-hours." She laughed at her own joke. "But seriously, I know for a fact you've hooked up with cops before. What's different this time? Dylan's obvious level of hotness notwithstanding?"

"Fuck, Stef." Briana let herself indulge in the memory of Dylan's eyes, her dark hair. A dozen times she'd almost reached forward to feel the sensation of the buzzed fade against her palm as she imagined bringing their faces together. She shook off the thought. "This is different. I have never, ever slept with anyone I was working with. At least not while we were actively working together. That goes for lawyers too." She knew Stef had engaged in a brief affair with one of the partners at her firm last year. She wasn't passing judgment. "I know there's no regulation against it." Briana was careful with her word choice. "I do worry about credibility, though. It's bullshit. But you know as well as I do, as women, we already have to work harder to be taken seriously."

"I can't fight you there." Stef frowned. "Screw the haters," she said, changing her tune. "I think you should be able to have what you want. Dylan seems to tick a lot of the boxes. Let her tick yours." She stuck out her tongue and wiggled her eyebrows.

"Mm." Briana moaned at the thought of Stef's overt suggestion, picturing Dylan for the millionth time. She sighed. "With any luck, this case will break wide open and wrap up while there's still some sparks between us."

"Ah, going for the long game."

"You think it'll fizzle?"

"I think the opposite is true. When you two finally give in..." Stef mimed an explosion with both hands. "Until then, stock up on batteries."

Briana almost choked on her seltzer. Her best friend might be hilarious, but she was also on point.

"Noted."

CHAPTER FIVE

I picked up our sandwiches. Hook us up with a spot to chill."
Two weeks in and Dylan already had a routine established.
Okay, so it was really Trevor's routine, but it suited her just fine. When they were working in the office, they brown-bagged lunch and ate in the wire room as they monitored calls and analyzed intel. On surveillance, they took turns grabbing something on the go and met up at the park under the FDR Drive to stretch their legs. Today was a field day.

"10-4," Dylan said into the portable radio. "I got our location secured."

Her phone buzzed with a text from her mother. She sighed.

She didn't know what was worse, the fact that she had zero desire to message with her mom or that some small part of her had hoped it was Briana. It made no sense.

Since their impromptu drink at Connolly's, they'd had exactly no contact. No run-ins at the office, not a single text. Which was, she supposed, what they'd agreed on. Still, it was a total bummer. Ironing out the boundaries hadn't made the slightest dent in the amount she thought about the gorgeous prosecutor. She could still picture the way Briana dipped her chin slightly when she smiled, the glint in her eye when she put Lt. Nieves in his place. It was confident and authoritative and in such contrast to her sweet laugh that was equal parts rasp and giggle.

"I'm going to miss sitting out here when the weather turns."

Trevor's voice brought her back to reality. Thank God.

"That was fast." She snapped into the present. "Somehow,

I thought you were farther away." She slid her phone back into her pocket and made a mental note to text her mother later.

"I lucked out. Found a parking spot right away." He handed over her lunch. "Here you go. Turkey on rye, extra mayo." He winked. "Just kidding. It's completely dry. I have no fucking idea how a person eats a sandwich like that," he said, biting into his enormous roast beef hero.

Dylan liked that he felt comfortable enough to rip on her.

"I wish Rivas would take us somewhere good," he said, changing the subject as he chewed.

The team had been following George Rivas for days, watching him meet up with lowlife after lowlife. More players in the game, but no one new. They needed another break.

"He's gonna meet up with Benji. We just have to be patient."

Intelligence gleaned from George Rivas's phone records had led right to Goldenballs himself: Benjamin Rafferty. Cross-referencing the phone number led to a DMV search where Dylan was able to place him as Rivas's cohort at the bar with no problem. Rafferty was a recent college grad from a white-collar family. No job, it seemed, but he lived in a nice house in a suburban section of Brooklyn. No criminal record. Thus far, a complete mystery.

"Patience is not my strong suit," Trevor said.

"Yeah, mine either, bro. But you know it's going to fall into place. Trust me."

"I do. Your instincts got us here."

Dylan appreciated the deference Trevor gave her. Even though he teased her for being the rookie on their team, he still listened to all her theories and asked for her take. The other members of the squad were equally welcoming. She liked the camaraderie and the way everyone's opinion was valued. In just a short time she felt connected to the case and to the detectives working it. Like there was a natural cohesion among them. This was where she belonged.

"Before I forget"—Trevor took a swig of Coke—"you up for hanging Friday night?"

"What's Friday?" she asked.

"Nothing special. We try to do drinks every couple of weeks. Usually at Baxter's or someplace local. Trish coordinates it."

"Cool. Yeah, I'm in."

"Good. It's good for us all to blow off steam together. Bond. Laugh. Keeps us nice and tight as a group."

"I hear that." She wanted to tell him that she didn't need convincing. Drinks sounded amazing. Since diving headfirst into the case, she'd barely come up for air. "Is the get-together right after work?"

He nodded. "Basically. I mean, there's no pressure, if you have plans or something." He pulled out his cell. "I should actually make sure I don't have other plans," he said while he texted.

"I'm free." Dylan didn't need to check her social schedule. There was only one person she wanted to see anyway. "Who goes? Just our team?" She knew exactly why she was asking. She hoped her tone was calm enough that Trevor didn't pick up on any ulterior motive.

"Us," he said, making a circle with his hand to reference both the two of them and the rest of their unit. "Sometimes the attorneys show." Bingo. That was the intel she wanted. Dylan could already feel her excitement build. "Trish will send out a message Friday morning with the details. She likes to be in charge."

"That sounds on-brand." No doubt Detective Trish Suarez was the social director. She'd already hit Dylan up for a contribution to the office coffee fund and asked for a commitment to attend the staff holiday party.

"Nieves rarely shows face, but Hollander makes an appearance once in a while." Trevor swirled his soda can like he was gearing up for the last sip.

"Cool. Miri's nice. I used to see her out sometimes."

"Like in…um…" His voice trailed off, and she wondered if he wasn't sure how to articulate referencing the gay scene without offending her.

"In bars near me." On second thought, she wasn't sure if Miri was out at work. Most of the female gay cops she knew were—the NYPD was a notoriously lesbian-friendly place—but she didn't know Miri that well. Better to be vague than blow up her life. "I think she used to date someone from my neighborhood."

"She used to date Trish," Trevor said. He followed his statement with a finger over his lips.

"No way." Even though Dylan had picked up some vibes from Trish, this piece of information was still shocking to her.

"Shhh." Trevor repeated his request for discretion. "You can't say anything. It did not end well."

"I won't say a word—I promise." She wondered if it was an open secret. "Does everybody know, though?"

"I don't think so. I only pieced it together from context clues. Hollander was pretty busted up over it. She can still barely look at Trish. I talk to them both a fair amount. A few months back they were both being super vague about bad breakups. Then I happened to be in the break room with them a few times. The tension"—he opened his eyes wide—"forget it. You could cut that shit with a knife."

"Look at you. Using your detective skills *and* your gaydar."

"I'm all about using all the tools in my arsenal." He held up both hands. "Not that I'm…I just mean…I'm not, but no judgment…" He took a deep breath and covered his chest with one hand. "Love is love," he said.

"Relax, buddy. You're straight. I got it." She laughed at his mini panic. "I just watched you check with your girlfriend to make sure you were allowed out Friday night," she added, teasing him.

"That's basic manners, bro. Plus I used that opportunity to invite Cate to join us. So, there."

"Your girlfriend—Cate—is she a cop too?"

"She is." He swallowed the last of his drink and nodded. "But on the federal side. She's an agent with Homeland Security. You'll like her. Everyone does."

"I'm sure."

"What about you?" He fiddled with the tab on his soda can. "What's your deal? Girlfriend? Wife?" He paused. "Boyfriend?"

Dylan fanned over her body to focus his attention to her attire and also to her overall vibe. "Boyfriend? Really?" She was sure the look in her eyes echoed the challenge in her tone. "You just finished telling me how attuned you are to the modern world. Clue into this, brother."

"No, I get it. I get it." He laughed and held his hands up in surrender. "Still, far be it from me to make any assumptions."

She actually appreciated Trevor's approach, but playing with him was still fun.

"No wife. No girlfriend."

"Playing the field?"

"Something like that."

"Trish will probably invite the crew from Major Case Team 4 on Friday night. We back each other up when extra hands are needed on deck. They're working on a carjacking thing out of their office on the fifth floor. I only mention it because there's some single women there." He shrugged. "If you're looking."

Dylan was always looking. Unfortunately, right now she only had eyes for one specific person. It was foolish. And limiting. And off the table. Did that make it more appealing?

Trevor crumpled his garbage into a ball and angled for a shot at the trash bin. "Think I can sink this?"

"First round on Friday says you don't," she said.

"You're on." He took an extra second to square his shoulders before launching a jump shot.

"And you're off"—she winced in secondhand embarrassment as his shot sailed wide—"by a mile."

"That was ugly." He grabbed his own rebound. "I need a do-over. Double or nothing?"

"Go for it," she conceded with a wave of her arm. "I may not even bring my wallet at this point."

"Heads up, guys." Detective Karrakas's voice crackled through the handheld radio on the bench. "Our boy is headed southbound on the FDR."

Trevor reached for the radio. "Copy that."

"Saved by the perp on the move." Dylan collected her stuff and geared up for action.

"I'll take it," he said with a laugh. "Let's roll."

❖

It was barely five o'clock, and Baxter's was already buzzing with the Friday feels. The start of the weekend always brought a party atmosphere, but the team's energy was boosted today by a trifecta surveillance featuring George Rivas, Benji Goldenballs Rafferty, and their sophisticated looking puppet master that Dylan had recognized as Paul from the night of the overhear.

"Coming through." Trevor's deep voice bellowed above the happy hour crowd as he lowered a tray of shots on the high-top table.

He doled them out and raised his shot glass high in the air. "To this fucking amazing team."

"To us," Karrakas said, ready to pound.

"Hold on, hold on," Trish said. "Let's take a second to officially welcome our newest member. We tease her as the rookie of the crew, but the truth is, Dylan, without you, we'd all still be in the freaking dark on this caper."

"Hear, hear." Trevor seconded the gesture.

"To Dylan," the gang cheered in messy unison as they downed tequila.

Dylan couldn't help but be moved. Even though it was cheesy, their praise felt genuine and honest.

She was so busy drowning in sentimentality that she almost missed the entrance of the legal team. The lawyers and interns were all smiles as they greeted the detectives, scooting past to claim a free table. It might have been her imagination, but Dylan would swear that she felt Briana's hand brush her back when she squeezed by.

"Dom, those girls are checking us out." Karrakas elbowed his partner and nodded toward two women at a table near the front window. "Hurry up and finish your beer so we can go buy them a round. I call dibs on the ginger."

Dylan shook her head. If circumstances were different she would have educated him on the spot that women weren't property to be claimed even, and perhaps especially, as part of flirting. But her whole focus was on the sight of Briana at the bar, and she downed her beer just for an excuse to get another.

"Next one's on me," she said to Trevor and Trish as she headed to the bar.

It was too eager, but she hadn't seen Briana in forever, and she wasn't taking any chance of missing the opportunity to talk to her.

"Hey there," she said sidling alongside Briana.

"Hi, Dylan." Briana smiled but didn't make eye contact. "Are you having fun? I heard you guys caught a good meet today."

"We did." Dylan looked around to assess the makeup of the crowd. Baxter's was a cop bar, and the clientele was mostly made up of their colleagues from the police department and the US Attorney's Office. It was probably safe enough to discuss the details, but she didn't want to talk work. She wanted to ask Briana about her life. Find out what she had been up to in the last two weeks and where she'd been hiding. She wanted to keep it social, in hopes there might be an opening to invite Briana to the rec league championship and afterparty on Sunday. "Do you need a drink?" she asked, but as she said it, the bartender delivered Briana's chardonnay.

"I should get back to my people." Briana nodded toward her staff in the corner and lightly tapped Dylan's forearm. "See you later."

What the fuck just happened? Not blurring the lines was one thing. But this interaction was barely cordial. Even her touch seemed... distant. Unnecessary, but also cold. Her head was spinning. Against her better judgment she watched Briana saunter away and sit down, hoping for a last glance, a final look, something.

Zilch.

Dylan let out a deep breath, trying to release her negative energy. She was a grown-up—she could do this. She collected her ego from the floor and returned to her crowd with a round of drinks.

"You must be Cate," she said to Trevor's girlfriend, who had arrived in her short absence. "I'm Dylan." She extended her hand in greeting. "Your boyfriend neglected to tell me what you drink." She lobbed a playful wink at Trevor. And just like that, she bounced back.

Her team made it easy. She spent most of the night in a pleasant foursome with Trevor and Trish and Cate. It was fun and lighthearted as the conversation bounced between work and life. Cate teased Trevor openly, but he obviously loved it. They were sweet together. After a while a few detectives from one of the other squads joined their crowd, and Dylan recognized one of them from her police academy class. The entire night she resisted the urge to even look in Briana's direction but somehow still felt her presence the whole time. Even now, she struggled to avoid trying to figure out who had her attention.

"Word on the street is that you're single." Trish stood slightly too close, her eyes glassy and her speech slurred.

"Where'd you hear that?"

"I have sources." She ran a manicured fingernail along the rim of her glass. "I am a detective, you know."

"I did hear that," Dylan played back.

"Is it true, or should I be vetting my intel more carefully?"

Dylan laughed. Trish was adorable. Even in her altered state her big brown eyes stood out. Long silky hair and gorgeous curves didn't hurt either.

"You can keep your confidential informant on the payroll," Dylan said, confirming her relationship status.

"Good to know."

"What about you?" she asked even though she had some of the details. "What's your story?"

"Single and available." Trish licked her full lips.

"I'll be sure to file that information away," she said. Her phone vibrated in her pocket, saving her. Dylan knew better than to hook up with a detective on her team. Especially the ex her sergeant was still pining over.

"Uh-oh. Looks like I have competition," Trish teased.

Dylan smiled as she waved her phone. "I should answer this. Excuse me." She stepped outside the bar and took the call.

"Hello, Cynthia."

"I hate when you call me that."

"It is your name."

"Can't you just call me Mom?"

"I guess." She crooned into the phone, "Hi, Mom."

"Kevin told me you got transferred. Is everything okay?"

"Of course it's okay. Why would you assume my transfer is a bad thing?"

"Well, I've been texting you. You don't answer me."

"What are you talking about? I messaged you back the other day."

"Two lines, Dylan. And you didn't say anything about your transfer. I'm your mother. You should be telling me these things."

Her mother was only needy when it suited her. There was something else going on here. She racked her brain to figure it out.

"How did Kevin hear about my transfer?" Her mother's husband was a veteran patrol guy with over twenty years of service. They worked in different boroughs, in different divisions. Their paths never crossed.

"I asked him to check on you. See if you were still alive." Typical Cynthia. So dramatic. "Kevin's birthday is tomorrow," her mom continued. "You don't call me. You don't text. How am I supposed to know if you're even coming?"

There it was. Dylan swallowed a small chuckle. This call was entirely about party planning.

"I'll be there, Mom." She peered into the bar, but the table where the lawyers were seated was obscured by patrons milling about. It was probably a good thing. She had no desire to see Briana giving her attention to anyone who wasn't her. "What time's the party start?"

"We'll eat around five. But come whenever you want. Your brothers miss you."

"Okay, Mom. I'll come out early."

She hung her head and made her decision right on the spot. It was time to head back to Brooklyn. Tomorrow's full day of family would require all her energy. Kevin would no doubt have a zillion questions about work, and her mom would pry into her love life. Zach and Conor, her teenage half-brothers, would demand one-on-one matchups on loop in the driveway basketball court. She'd collapse before letting them win.

Plus, Briana was inside giving her zero attention, while Trish was down to party. Absolutely no good would come from that dynamic.

CHAPTER SIX

I need a caffeine boost for this. You interested?"
Dylan watched Trevor upload Friday's surveillance photos
of Paul Last-Name-Unknown as they prepared to cross-reference the
police department's mug shot database. With any luck Paul would have
a record, and they'd be able to fully identify him.

"I'm good. Better make yours strong, though." Trevor focused on
the computer screen. "We're going to be here scouring pics all freaking
day."

"My point exactly. I'll bring you a cup in case you start to nod
off," she said as she shuffled out of the plant's wire room.

She felt for her wallet, on the fence over whether to make coffee
in the office or run across the street to Gregory's. The decision became
a no-brainer when she spotted Briana fiddling with the Keurig machine
in the break area.

Dylan stopped dead in her tracks.

"Hello." Briana called out the greeting over her shoulder like her
presence in the plant was an everyday occurrence.

It was not.

In fact, Dylan had never seen her in the squad area before today. It
took her a full three seconds to respond. "Hi."

"Morning," Briana said. "How was your weekend?"

"Fine." She shook her head, still trying to process what Briana
was doing on the third floor instead of the law offices on ten. "Sorry. It
was fine. How about yours?"

"You left early Friday night," Briana said over the squeak of a
cabinet door as she closed it and opened another one.

Dylan looked around dramatically to make a point. "You are talking to me, right?" She tilted her head from side to side. "Because Friday you barely spoke to me, and now you're all buddy-buddy, so…" She waved between them letting her sentence trail off.

"You're the one who left early," Briana challenged with a lyrical tone as she searched another cabinet.

"Not like you noticed," she said, meeting Briana's spirited, if confusing energy.

"I think I just pointed out that I *did* notice." Briana opened and closed a drawer, still on the hunt for something. "Was the Downtown vibe too bland for you? You went back to Brooklyn, I assume?"

Dylan was completely into the fact that Briana was curious where she'd gone after she left, but she wasn't done deconstructing the happy hour scene yet.

"I actually tried to talk to you at the bar, if you remember. You blew me off."

"I didn't." Briana shifted her weight to one hip and leaned against the counter. Her expression softened, and she scrunched her nose up in the most adorable way. "I'm sorry if it seemed that way. It's just that my supervisor was there. And my staff." She tapped her finger on the edge of the counter. "I felt like I had to put in legit face time for a good portion of the night. Then when I finally could scoot away, you guys were all in a group, knee deep in war stories."

"Your presence would have been a welcome interruption, I assure you."

"Eh, it felt weird." She shrugged. "I looked for you again later, but you were gone. Off to greener pastures."

"More like my apartment."

"Really? I figured you were out on the town in our hood."

It was the second time Briana made that point, and even though Dylan was dying to know if that thought made her even the slightest bit envious, they were having a nice conversation, and she didn't want to ruin it by pushing too hard. "I just went home. I had a family thing all day Saturday."

"Oh yeah? Out on the Island?"

She nodded. "My mother's husband's birthday."

"Your mother's husband. Does that mean your stepfather?"

"Technically, I suppose." Kevin was a decent enough person, but she never thought of him as a father figure. Bestowing such a significant title on him just felt odd. "Kevin's a good guy. He makes my mom happy, but he was never really a dad to me. I never even lived with them." She didn't know why she felt the need to justify his label, but Briana seemed to accept her explanation. "What about you? What did you do this weekend?"

"I was at my parents' too. It's a shame we didn't talk Friday—we could have coordinated." Briana touched her lightly just above the wrist. "Oh, hey. I heard your team won the championship game yesterday. Congrats."

She had no idea what was happening here. Was Briana setting some kind of ground rules for acceptable office banter, or was she this touchy-feely with everyone? Either way, Briana's hand was still resting on the tattoo on her forearm.

"We did win. Thanks." She resisted looking at Briana's hand because she didn't want her to think the contact was unwelcome. "Stef?" Dylan said, inquiring about the source of her information.

"I think she only caught the end of the game. She didn't want Mackenzie to think she'd gotten the best of her."

"I get it." Dylan had seen Stef at the postgame happy hour. It had given her fleeting hope that Briana might be present also. She didn't want to revisit the funk that eclipsed her entire day at the realization she wasn't there.

Rather than give a platform to any of those thoughts right now, she kept it simple. She ticked her head to the coffee setup. "Are we doing coffee or what?"

A sweet laugh escaped Briana, and she shifted her gorgeous eyes to the floor. "I was searching for those fancy K-Cups Trish gets. I know they're in here somewhere."

Dylan reached up to the highest cabinet with ease. She moved a box of organic sugar and pulled out two boxes. "Crème brûlée," she said, placing one container on the counter as she twisted the second box in her hand to find the flavor. "Spiced chestnut. Which actually sounds disgusting," she said examining the ingredients with a laugh. "Trish hides them up here because Nieves gloms on to them, and he never contributes to the fund."

"Shocker." Briana rolled her eyes and took out a crème brûlée pod. "I'm dying for one of these. Our coffee upstairs is the worst. You want one?"

"Sure," she said, selecting a pod for herself.

"Thanks for your help." Briana placed a paper cup under the spout and pressed the brew button. "I don't think I would have found them. I definitely wouldn't have been able to reach."

Briana made her coffee and splashed the tiniest bit of skim milk in it. Dylan tried not to stare at her like a fucking stalker. She was just so…pretty. And sweet.

"You want the milk?" Briana asked, catching Dylan looking.

"No thanks. I'm a half-and-half person all the way."

Briana walked to the small fridge and replaced the skim, grabbed the half-and-half, and handed it to Dylan. "So tell me about this Paul guy," she said, sipping her coffee.

"Come here, I'll show you."

Dylan led the way to the link chart they'd updated this morning. A close-up of Paul's face zoomed in from a surveillance photo was tacked to the side of the semi-filled pyramid of suspects.

"I think he's going to fall somewhere in this tier." Dylan pointed one level above George and Benji. "Problem is we have no pedigree on him at all. When Trevor and I saw him the other day, it was just the two of us in the field. We lost him in pedestrian traffic, so we didn't even see him get into a car we could trace back or anything."

"That's tough." Briana seemed to be studying the players, and Dylan wondered what she was thinking. Almost on cue Briana added, "Thank God you're here. I honestly don't know where we'd be if you hadn't come to us when you did."

Dylan thought she knew exactly where the two of them might be if not for their worlds intertwining in this semi-unfortunate yet perfect way. Briana must have had the same thought because she blushed and cleared her throat.

"I meant with the case. Sorry about that." She tipped her head to sip her coffee.

"No worries." Dylan took a drink to clear her mind of the perfectly inappropriate image that had materialized. "Anyway, Dom and Karrakas are following Rivas right now. Trish and Ahmed are on Goldenballs. I mean Benji."

"Goldenballs." Briana shook her head but smiled. "Men."

"It's a ridiculous nickname—I'm not arguing that point. Thing is, though, it's telling. There's a closeness there. Maybe even a jealousy. It's the kind of dumb thing my half-brothers would say to tease each other. My guess is Paul and Benji end up being related."

"Makes sense." Briana's hazel eyes held both depth and sincerity. "You're very smart, Dylan." Her compliment made Dylan feel like a superstar, and she shifted her attention to the floor, so Briana wouldn't see the effect it had on her.

"We'll see. Intel is trying to dig as much as possible through Benji Rafferty's records. In the meantime, me and Trevor"—she nodded to the wire room a few feet away—"are going to attempt to find a needle in a haystack."

Briana crinkled her forehead in question.

"We're going to search through old booking photos to see if we can find Paul."

"That's ambitious." Briana's expression showed she was equal parts impressed by the level of commitment and skeptical about the chance of results.

It truly was a ridiculous undertaking, but Dylan loved a challenge. "It's a long shot, for sure." She shrugged. "No harm in trying."

"I have complete faith in you." The smile Briana gave her was worth every second of being ignored on Friday. "In all of you." She did the cute scrunchy thing with her nose again. "But especially you."

Dylan looked right at her. She wanted her expression to show the gratitude she felt over Briana's confidence in her. But when their eyes met, something else took center stage.

Heat.

"Yo. What's up guys?" Trevor popped his head out of the wire room and broke the moment. Which was probably a good thing. It was, Dylan told herself repeatedly. She was not going to make a move. Not today. Not tomorrow. Most definitely not *at* work. But man, that one look sent her heart into A-fib.

"Anything yet?" Dylan had to fight through a thicket of tension to speak.

"Nah. The program is still booting up." He looked at their coffee cups. "You two went for the secret stash, I see. Nice." He stuffed his hands in the pouch pocket of his hoodie.

"Sorry, bro, I completely forget to make you one."

Trevor let her off the hook with a dismissive wave. "I really didn't want one anyway." He nodded at the diagram of the criminal enterprise under investigation. "We're getting there, Briana. I'm telling you. Benji and Paul are going to be key."

"Dylan was just saying the same thing." Briana held her coffee with both hands, sort of cradling the cup. She swayed a little in place. "I should let you guys do your thing," she said as she backed toward the door. "Tell Trish I'll Venmo her my monthly coffee contribution. And if you two need anything at all"—she flashed that million dollar smile—"I'm right upstairs."

"She's the best," Trevor said.

Dylan wondered if he picked up on any of their energy but simply agreed with a nod. She had no confidence her voice wouldn't completely betray her if she spoke.

"Ahmed called in a few minutes ago," he said, still one hundred percent focused on the chart. "Nothing doing in the street. I told him the phones were quiet too. These boneheads are probably still asleep."

Dylan checked her watch: 10:10. "Ah, the glorious life of a middle-class pill pusher." She clapped his shoulder. "Come on, let's see if we can put a full name to his face."

For the rest of the morning and well into the afternoon, they pored through hundreds of pictures but got no closer to identifying the elusive Paul.

It was almost three o'clock when Dylan's phone vibrated with a message from Briana.

Any luck with the photo booking system?

Nothing at all.

Don't give up :)

Dylan tilted her head to the side, fully analyzing Briana's choice of words. On the one hand, the language was completely harmless. The prosecuting attorney communicating a boost in morale to the case detective, possibly even issuing an assurance it would all work out.

But Briana was a smart woman. She had to see the possibility of a double meaning, intended or not.

I won't, she typed back.

Briana's response was immediate: *Good.*

Was this subtext or was she reading in to it? Either way she was thankful Trevor was too engrossed in their project to notice her huge smile. She contemplated continuing the reverie but instead put her phone away, letting the contact end on this ambiguous high note.

It wasn't until much later that evening when she was settled into her cozy apartment with her feet up on the end of her living room couch that Dylan reached out again.

Sorry to bother you at home, Dylan started.

Briana's response was instant: *Who says I'm home?*

It was a gut punch she wasn't expecting. She closed her eyes and swallowed hard at the image of Briana laughing and flirting at dinner or drinks. She took a deep breath, knowing she needed to be cool, but when she opened her eyes again, there was a new message.

Just kidding. What's up?

I wasn't sure if anyone updated you on what we found today...

Haven't talked to anyone but you. OMG. Did you actually find an old mug shot of Paul?

No. That was a complete bust.

Briana hadn't spoken to anyone but her. The tidbit made her disproportionately happy. Even though she knew her information could wait, she'd wanted an excuse for contact. Whether Briana chose to read between those lines remained to be seen. *However, records analysis uncovered someone of interest. J. Paul Rafferty. He's a cousin of our boy Benji.*

See! You knew it. Several clapping emojis followed.

She felt her chest puff out in response to the praise. *We don't know much yet*, she typed back, not wanting to oversell the info. *I could give you the details over crème brûlée tomorrow...*

Sounds delicious.

Dylan felt herself smiling ridiculously and wondered if a mere few blocks away Briana was doing exactly the same.

CHAPTER SEVEN

So he's an attorney?" Briana asked, even though the answer was in front of her in black and white. *J. Paul Rafferty, Esquire.* She sat at the NYPD lunch table in the squad area perusing the LexisNexis printout. Rafferty's law firm and home address were listed on the public records site, as well as his undergrad and law school degrees.

"Apparently." Dylan leaned over her and tapped her finger next to a line at the bottom of the page. "Did you see this yet?"

"Wine Bar," she read aloud. "What is that?"

"Hold up." Dylan returned the carton of half-and-half to the minifridge. "Let me just grab this, and I'll come sit with you." Briana watched her reach beyond a cubicle partition for a folder. She pulled up a chair and sat so close Briana could smell her hair product.

Dylan set her coffee down and pulled three grainy prints out. "This is the Wine Bar. It's going to be the key to everything. I can feel it."

"Okay." Briana took an indulgent sip of her crème brûlée. She wasn't a hundred percent sure where this was going, but she was enjoying the company. It was barely eight a.m., and the plant was empty except for the two of them. Right or wrong, she could get used to these one-on-one sessions. She leaned over and brushed Dylan's shoulder with hers. "So tell me about the Wine Bar."

"The Wine Bar." Dylan held one finger in the air. "Admittedly we don't know much." She hung her head and let out a low sexy laugh. "Trev and I took a ride by last night to see if the place looked legit."

"And?"

"It was quiet. But it was hard to get a good view from the car. That's where we snapped these pics." She lined up her pictures precisely. "It's right next to this restaurant, Victor's"—she pointed to the farthest image—"but we're not sure if the two establishments are connected or not."

"You think they might be?"

"I really don't know. Trevor and I have some theories, though."

"Where is Trevor?" she asked, looking around.

"He had to make a stop on the way in. I told him I was going to update you, though." Dylan put a finger over her lips to indicate a level of secrecy. "We haven't briefed Nieves yet. So this has to stay between us for now."

"Ooh," she crooned. "I feel special."

Dylan gave her the hint of a crooked smile, and Briana sensed something devilish and divine in her pale blue eyes before she shifted her attention to the paperwork on the table.

"I know it shouldn't matter," Dylan said. "You're more invested in the case than he is." She tapped her coffee cup on the table. "But he's a stickler for chain of command. So obviously we'll bring him up to speed when he's here later. Probably around noon." She chewed her lip and looked a touch unsettled. "I'm only mentioning specifics because I'm sure he'll call you right after and expect credit for breaking the news. It would be cool if you could act surprised. I hate asking you to lie..."

"Don't worry, I can fake it."

Dylan hitched one eyebrow up at the expression, and Briana felt her face turn red.

"I didn't mean...I just meant..." She took a small moment to collect herself, owning her embarrassment with a grin. "No need to worry. I'll make sure Nieves thinks he's the hero." She tapped Dylan's knee. "But tell me the plan because I'm curious."

"So I was thinking...and I know it's early still." Briana watched her study the pictures and printouts as she spoke. "I bet this bar is the place where Paul meets up with Benji and George."

"Why do you think so?"

Dylan chewed the inside of her cheek for a few seconds. "I don't know. Gut feeling."

"But the surveillances haven't led there, have they?" She hated poking a hole in Dylan's hypothesis, but it was the truth as far as she knew.

"No." Dylan seemed loaded with confidence as she leaned back in her chair. "We've only been on them for a few weeks. What we've covered so far is mostly drug deals. George selling to his clients. We think Paul is higher up the ladder. He's probably supplying George and Benji with their stash. So they have to meet up somewhere for that to happen. I think it's going to be the Wine Bar. If we catch them in there together, I'm thinking maybe we could put a bug inside."

"Put an eavesdropping device in the location?"

"Yes."

There was absolutely no hesitation in Dylan's answer, and Briana wanted to agree on the spot. The way Dylan talked about the case, her lack of indecision, her total control—it was a complete turn-on. But what she was suggesting was still well beyond their reach.

"I'm not saying no, but we need a lot more probable cause before we could even consider such an aggressive tactic." She saw Dylan's face fall at being shot down, and she longed to fix it.

Briana reached over and touched Dylan's thigh for comfort and reassurance. "It's a good idea, Dylan. It really is. Let's just take it one step at a time."

"Of course." The spirit returned to Dylan's eyes and Briana felt herself smile ridiculously.

"What's the plan?" Briana sipped her coffee indulgently. She could sit and listen to Dylan talk all day and convince herself it was for the furtherance of the investigation. Even though she knew it was complete bullshit.

"We're going to shift the focus to Benji, hoping his relationship to Paul comes through for us. Right now we're spread a little thin. So I'll be in and out of the field. Trevor too."

"Did I hear my name?" Trevor barreled into the office with a ton of gear in tow. "You guys and this terrible coffee." He shook his head in disapproval. "Mind-boggling," he muttered, barely under his breath. "Buddy, did you tell Briana the master plan to get inside the place?"

"I was getting there."

"With a bug, you mean?" Briana asked.

"Actually, a body."

Briana was lost and she looked to Dylan for an explanation.

"We were thinking to gather PC to get authorized to install the bug, maybe I'd go in and see if I could get these guys to talk to me. Or at least in front of me."

"Undercover, you mean?"

"Light undercover, but yeah."

"What's light undercover?"

"I would just go in and chat," Dylan said. "Be a patron. A person going for a drink."

"The two of you?" Briana waved a finger between them. She watched Dylan and Trevor exchange a glance.

"Eh, prob not." Trevor uncovered his gourmet coffee and took the first sip. "We were thinking Dylan and Trish."

"Okay," she said, waiting for more explanation.

"I look like a cop," Trevor said, answering her silent question. "Me and Dylan don't read as a couple anyway. But Dylan and Trish, that could work." He let a moment pass. "Think about it. Two good looking women who are together—that's eye catching for sure." He took another long drink of his coffee before adding, "In my opinion this approach could accomplish several things. First, we'd have eyes inside. Plus Dylan and Trish are less likely to get pegged as law enforcement, and their presence might garner some attention from our targets."

"And that's a good thing?" Briana didn't hide her shock.

"I know what you mean," Trevor said with a slight laugh. "And you're not wrong. Typically, the goal is to blend. But in this scenario…" He flashed a look at Dylan, and Briana could tell this was something they'd thought through. "We think attention could foster interaction."

"Briana, these guys…" Dylan looked right at her. "I know I was only in their presence that one time. But I hear them talk on the phone. They are always looking to hook up." She rolled her eyes. "They think they're, like, studs, players. My guess, they go for the bait in no time."

"Even if they suspect you're a couple?" Briana countered. But even as the words came out, she knew the challenge was part of the game. Dylan dropped a look that was probably meant as playful disbelief, but behind those amazing eyes all Briana registered was smolder. "Point taken," she said, finding her voice. Dylan's confidence was persuasive, but she still didn't love the idea. It was a massive gamble that was risky and dangerous with Dylan in the epicenter of it all. "Have you ever done anything like this before?"

"Not exactly like this, no." Dylan's voice was soft but full of competence as though she was trying to reassure her. "But I've done research, and I know of investigations where this type of setup has worked to infiltrate gangs, organized crime families, terrorist cells..."

"Dylan's right," Trevor piped up. "Sometimes you have to take the risk, even if it's unconventional."

"You can trust me to be smart and not do anything crazy." Dylan's voice was measured and smooth as she made her case. "I just think, I don't know, it's amazing the things people will brag about to get attention."

Briana knew that was true. More than once she'd witnessed defendants take the stand just to have a captive audience. Her mind was going a mile a minute as she envisioned the possibilities rife with danger.

"Briana." Dylan's eyes were almost pleading. "If George and Benji talk to us, maybe we get an introduction to Paul."

Trevor hoisted his coffee cup in the air in a kind of anticipatory celebration. "Imagine if Dylan can identify Paul in the Wine Bar *and* she can put him at the bar the night of the overhear? When they were talking drugs and specifically about the student who overdosed, that's like a legal home run, right?"

It was such a long shot, but Briana had seen unlikely things work in the past. Still, she hated the thought of Dylan putting herself in any kind of vulnerable situation. She also despised the thought of Dylan partnering with Trish and posing as a couple, particularly after she'd seen them flirting at the happy hour a while back. The whole thing irritated her in a way that it most definitely should not.

"A connection of that nature would be very strong for our case," she admitted, channeling professionalism. "But again, we're way ahead of ourselves."

"Absolutely, Briana," Trevor said. "We're going to take it one step at a time. Start with a heavy tail on our main three. With any luck they'll lead us right to the Wine Bar. If that happens—"

"When that happens," Dylan interrupted.

"When that happens." Trevor was calm, clearly trying to appease everyone in the room. "Then we'll make some real decisions."

"We just wanted you to be in the know," Dylan explained.

"I appreciate that." Briana hoped her tone and expression showed her support of the tentative plan. But she also needed both detectives to understand that everything needed to be done by the book. For this tactic to be effective during prosecution, planning and precision were paramount. "I'm on board," she said. "Let's just all be careful. Obviously we want a conviction, but not at the expense of anyone's safety. Okay?"

"I promise."

The sincerity in Dylan's expression was almost too much for Briana to handle. "I should get to work." She smoothed her skirt as she stood. "Great job, you two," she said, making sure Trevor got some attention.

"You should come back for coffee tomorrow," Dylan said with a smile.

She was already planning on it but tossed a playful warning glance at Dylan's overt banter just the same.

"You never know—we might have a new lead by then." Dylan defended her invitation with a grin.

"You miss a day, you miss a lot." Trevor offered his two cents.

She rolled her eyes but couldn't contain her smile as she backed to the elevator bank. "Good-bye, detectives."

CHAPTER EIGHT

I literally cannot stop touching her."

Briana looked over the mountain of case folders on her desk at Stef picking through her Cobb salad.

"Am I supposed to be surprised by this?" Stef speared a piece of chicken.

"You're supposed to yell at me. Tell me to get my shit together and act like a goddamn officer of the court."

"Yeah…you invited the wrong person for lunch here if that's the lecture you were hoping for."

"What am I doing?" Briana flopped her head on her desk with dramatic flair.

"These little encounters happen when? Over coffee every day?"

Briana sat upright and pulled the plastic lid off a bowl of mixed greens. "Not every day." She stared at the ceiling tiles, pretending to calculate. She knew precisely how many times they'd interacted. Where, when, and what she'd been wearing. "A couple of days last week," she said. "And yesterday."

"Like I said, every day basically."

"I can't help it if the cops have good coffee."

"Don't even." Stef dropped a look on her. "I passed three gourmet coffee shops on my walk here. And you're drinking Keurig. By choice. This is about Dylan. Admit it."

Briana answered with a weak shrug. Even though it was the truth, she wasn't ready to say it out loud.

"What does she do?"

"What do you mean?"

"I mean, what does Dylan do when you touch her?"

Briana stopped to think about it. It was entirely possible Dylan didn't even notice. She never reacted.

"She doesn't stop you," Stef said, answering her own question. "My guess, she's into it." She pierced some lettuce on the end of her fork. "So why are you stressed?"

"Because *I* set boundaries. *I* said we needed to stay professional." She heard slight desperation in her tone. "And I'm sending the complete opposite signals." She rubbed her temples.

"May I make a suggestion?"

"As if I could stop you."

Stef placed her salad on the edge of Briana's desk and folded her hands over her crossed legs. "Your body is telling you what it wants. It's trying to give you a message."

Briana dipped her chin. She knew where this was going.

"I'm not being snarky. Or salacious," Stef said, reading her with ease. "I'm stating a fact. You need something. You want it from her."

"It's a bad idea and you know it."

"I am not on that train." Stef shook her head and reached for her lunch. "But have it your way. Find someone else, then. Because you're driving yourself crazy."

"That's the thing, though." She pushed her salad around as she ruminated on her social life. "I've been out a lot lately. I even ran into Max last week. Do you remember him? Finance guy. Very nice, really good in bed."

"No. But go on."

"I could have easily gone home with him," she admitted, hoping she didn't sound vain. "I had no desire. I can't get her out of my head."

It was quiet for a second as they both focused on eating. Crunching a crouton, Briana wondered if her confession would garner a response or if they'd move on to another topic.

"When are you going to quit doing God's work and come make some real money?"

A deep voice broke through the silence, and Briana recognized her former colleague's signature rasp before she even looked up to see Jill Jessup standing in her doorway.

Briana swallowed and smiled, taking her time to put up a little sass of her own. "Are you offering me a partnership?" she asked.

"Well, not right away. But you and me together, I'd say it's definitely not out of the realm of possibility."

"You defense attorneys, always with the big lead. But present one simple challenge and you have nothing to back it. How does one win a case like that?" Briana winked at Stef, who was watching the spirited volley with interest.

"I wouldn't say *nothing*. I've been told my charms are very persuasive. With a jury, obviously."

"Obviously," Briana deadpanned. "Stef, this is Jill Jessup. She used to work here before she went over to the dark side." She made sure to add a smile so JJ would know she was mostly kidding. "JJ," she said, continuing the introductions, "this is Stefania Tariq. Stef's with the legal team at the Wellington Group."

"It's a pleasure to meet you, Ms. Tariq." Briana watched JJ give Stef a full once-over. "The Wellington Group. Impressive." She reached into the inside breast pocket of her designer suit and produced a business card. "Jill Jessup. Managing Partner at Jessup Finch Silo Toussaint, if you ever need anything."

"How are you, JJ?" Briana crossed the small office to greet her old crony with a hug.

"I'm doing well. I just wanted to say hello. One of my clients just had a proffer session with AUSA O'Rourke."

"Does it feel different being here, but on the wrong team?" she teased.

"So young and naive. Still believing the government holds justice as a core value." JJ covered her heart dramatically. "I do love that angelic outlook, though." Her whole demeanor dripped confidence. "Anyway, ladies, I didn't mean to interrupt your lunch. Briana, think about my offer."

"Was there even an offer?" she challenged.

"Think about it." JJ's voice faded as she backed out of the doorway.

Briana let her eyes trail JJ's path until she was gone, idly pondering the vague employment offer. She loved being an Assistant US Attorney. The work was fulfilling personally and on a macro level. The narcotics case downstairs exemplified that. But the truth of the matter was she had big career aspirations, and there were moments she worried if her CV was broad enough to achieve her goals.

"Um, hello?" Stef waved a plastic fork in the air, and the small action brought her back into the moment.

"Hi."

"Who the fuck was that?"

"Jill Jessup. JJ." Briana shook her head, still lost in the memory of working together. "We had a few years of crossover here, before she started her practice. She was basically my mentor."

"Were you two ever…"

"No."

"Really?" Stef's voice was loaded with disbelief, and she understood why. JJ was her type. Tall, dapper, and brilliant. She was older than Briana by about ten years and her short dark hair was beginning to gray at the temples in the best way. Even age somehow improved her classic sexy vibe. It figured. JJ had a way of seeming to always get her way.

"We worked together. I have a code, remember?"

"You don't work together now."

Stef had a point. Still, she had zero desire to pursue that path, and she knew it had everything to do with her off-limits obsession with Dylan.

"I'm just saying, if you're not going to allow yourself to have fun with the sexy detective, a hot butch lawyer could be a formidable substitute. You literally just said you were looking for a distraction."

She waved off Stef's suggestion. "Don't misunderstand me—JJ's great. She's very smart."

"But?"

She's not Dylan. "I don't know, her whole shtick is a little smarmy."

"Smarmy, charming. Potato, potahto."

Briana laughed out loud. "Stef, she just flirted with both of us. Right in front of each other."

"I know. The cockiness." Stef fanned herself. "Whoa."

"Go for it," Briana said excitedly. "But full disclosure, JJ is a total player."

"At least I know it up front."

"That makes it better?"

"After the Mackenzie debacle, I think it does." Stef focused on her phone. "Anyway, I'm going to invite her to the Wellington event tomorrow. You have twenty-four hours to reconsider. After that, she's fair game."

Briana laughed. It was cute to see Stef trying. "I am one hundred percent not interested. I have a one-track mind these days."

"Ridiculous. Even though I'm a little happy it might work to my advantage." Stef winced. "Does that make me a terrible friend?"

"It makes you human. And I'm all for it. But one question."

"Shoot."

"What's tomorrow?"

Stef hung her head. "The Wellington fundraiser. In our neighborhood. You promised you'd come."

"Oh right. At that chichi whiskey place." The details came back to her. "Why do you need me there?"

"I don't. You can bail if you need to. But I convinced my boss that investing in a community outreach program was a good idea. Which it is." Stef covered what remained of her lunch. "Tomorrow is a meet and greet with other stakeholders and community leaders, so my presence is required. Wellington is picking up the tab."

"Okay. I'll be there." Stef always had her back. It was the least she could do to support her friend. "Want me to call JJ and extend the invite?"

"Honey"—Stef shook her head—"my assistant is already handling that."

"Wow, you work fast."

"You have no idea."

Oak and Vine was crawling with corporate ego. It wasn't a total surprise—Briana knew Wellington's clientele was heavily moneyed and mostly male. In the back of her mind she'd held out slight hope she might find someone cool to connect with just enough to help get her past her current fixation. But the wall-to-wall suits weren't doing it for her, and after two glasses of wine, she was ready to happily find comfort in cozy pajamas and guilty pleasure TV.

She did feel slightly bad leaving Stef flat. Company events at this level required game face even in the off hours, and it was fun to witness her friend in action. Stef was clearly the driving force behind the successful event, and she radiated confidence as she worked the room. JJ would eat it up if she showed. Hmm, Stef and JJ. She wondered if that had a shot, as she swung her light jacket across her shoulders.

"Please don't tell me you're leaving." Dylan's voice in her ear caught her completely off guard.

"Oh my God, hi," she said with the unparalleled enthusiasm of a middle school science nerd talking to her quarterback crush.

"Hi," Dylan said smoothly.

"Have you been here the whole time?" Briana asked.

"I just got here a few minutes ago." Dylan looked right at her, and her eyes were pleading before she said, "Please have a drink with me."

"I guess I could stay for one more." Against all sound reasoning, Briana knew she'd stay for last call if Dylan continued to look at her like that.

"Excellent. Wine or bourbon?"

"Dylan, you don't have to get it." Briana touched Dylan's forearm in protest. "I can pay for my own drink. In fact, I feel like I owe you from the last time. Let me get this." She started to reach for a credit card, but Dylan stopped her.

"It's open bar." Dylan's smile was adorable. "Corporate sponsorship and all."

"Of course." She blinked long and slow, mortified over her assumption Dylan was trying to pick up the tab.

"I was headed to the bar, though." Dylan swirled the last of her bourbon before downing the last sip. "What can I get for you?"

"Cabernet, if you don't mind."

Ten minutes later, as they sipped their drinks, Briana asked, "What are you doing here?"

"I could ask you the same question." Dylan's smile was devious and charming as hell.

"Stef works for the Wellington Group." She fanned her hand at the crowd. "The corporate sponsor."

"Well, that makes sense."

"What's your excuse?"

"I'm here as a member of the community board."

She said it with such nonchalance that Briana thought she was kidding at first. "Wait, for real?"

"Yes. Why are you surprised?"

"I don't know. I just…I suppose I didn't think that would be your thing." For some reason she'd assumed the community board was all old money.

"Anyone can be part of the community board," Dylan said, as if reading her thought process. "It just requires devotion to the neighborhood and issues that affect it. There's some volunteerism expected, but it's not a huge commitment." She paused to take a quick sip of her bourbon. "I enjoy giving back. This neighborhood has always been my home. Normally I'm not down for this type of social event, but this program is of particular interest to me. I wanted to show support."

"I came for Stef," she admitted. "I honestly don't even know what's being promoted."

Dylan reached into her back pocket and pulled out the glossy postcard highlighting the program's benefits. She placed it on the bar between them. "They're developing a privately funded sports and arts program that's the exact type of thing I would have loved to be in when I was a kid."

"Really?" She was insanely interested in hearing about Dylan's life. Her third glass of wine was erasing any kind of barrier that might have kept her from asking for details. "Tell me why."

"My mom was only sixteen when I was born."

"Wow," she said, unable to mask her shock. "That's very young," she said, finding her composure. "I just…it must have been hard."

"It was actually okay," she said with an easy laugh.

"Your dad…?"

"Was also a teenager," Dylan said with her signature smile.

It was decades too late, but Briana was sure her concern was obvious.

"It's okay." Dylan's smooth voice forgave whatever pity must have showed on her face. "Honestly. We lived with my grandparents. In the brownstone where I live now. The one you saw. Me and my mom, and my uncle Tim. My grandparents were amazing. They were both nurses."

"Both of them?"

"Yep. My nana worked days and my grandfather worked nights. They did that so someone was always home with me. They gave up so much of their lives for me."

"And look at you now. I'm sure they're so proud of you."

"They would be." Dylan's nostalgic expression was steeped with adoration. "They're both gone now."

"When did they pass away?" Briana lowered her voice and placed a hand on Dylan's midsection, telling herself the contact was for support.

"Nana died when I was eighteen. She had cancer. My grandfather moved in with my uncle in New Jersey after that. He died five years ago."

"After they left, you stayed in the house? With your mom?"

"Actually, my mom moved to Long Island with her second husband when I was in high school."

"Oh, right. You mentioned that."

"My grandfather got sick shortly after he moved in with Uncle Tim. At that point, Uncle Tim and my mom decided to keep the brownstone, instead of selling it. Growing up, we always rented out the apartment on the top floor and lived in the space on the two main floors. When everyone but me was gone, they decided they could flip that situation. Rent out the first two floors as a big apartment and make some decent money. I could live on the top floor, rent free, in exchange for acting as the landlord and property manager."

"That's a sweet deal."

"It's fantastic. I didn't want to leave. They took care of me."

Briana was hanging on every word. She loved Dylan's deep slow cadence and the genuine affection that came out when she talked about her family.

"Do you have to fix stuff? In the apartment?"

"Sometimes. I'm pretty handy. My grandfather taught me everything. I followed him around like a puppy when I was a kid."

"Oh my God, I would love to see pictures of baby Dylan." It was out before she could filter it, courtesy of her third cabernet and general lust.

A wolfish smile spread across Dylan's handsome face. "That can be arranged. My apartment is very nearby." Dylan brushed a hand over her fingers, which were still hovering around her abdomen.

"Dylan, we can't." Briana's words stood in contrast to their fingers gently caressing in the dark bar. "You know we can't."

"You worry too much." Briana knew she should pull away when Dylan laced their fingers together. "We both want this." Dylan leaned in close. "I think about you all the time."

How was she saying no to this? She was digging deep for restraint, but Dylan was still whispering in her ear. "We know the boundaries. We both want the same thing. I can be very discreet."

"We work together. Do you know how people would talk about us?"

"Who's going to tell them?"

"I don't know. I already wonder if Trevor suspects something. I come there for coffee almost every day."

"Where we are completely professional and talk about the case."

"True. But I can barely keep my hands off you."

Dylan squeezed their clasped hands. "That's my favorite part."

Despite every internal lecture she'd given herself over the last few weeks, Briana felt herself caving. "No, no, no," she said, reversing her thought process on the spot. She heard how weak her denial sounded, and her eyes bored into the ground. "I have to go home."

"Okay. I'm not going to pressure you into anything. Ever." With one finger under her chin, Dylan tipped her head up. "But I am going to walk with you."

"Dylan," she started to protest, even though she wanted the company.

"Uh-uh"—Dylan covered her lips with one finger—"that's just common courtesy. Okay?"

Briana could only nod in response. She was using all her energy to resist what she most definitely wanted. Bad idea or not, her body longed for Dylan in her arms, in her bed. Thank God Dylan moved her hand, because in another second she might have caved and given in to her urge to suck on Dylan's finger right there at the bar.

"Let me grab my jacket," Dylan said. "Wait here."

Across the bar, Briana saw Stef flash her a look and a subtle thumbs-up at her read of the situation. It made her laugh, and she shook her head, hoping to convince her roommate—and herself—that a walk was harmless.

The night was brisk with autumn in full swing. Oak and Vine was a good few blocks from her place, and they spent the time in comfortable conversation about the neighborhood, their favorite restaurants, where

Dylan had gone to elementary and high school. Their hands brushed a multitude of times, but when they were at her corner and Dylan's index finger hooked with her pinkie, she didn't even attempt to separate them. In front of her apartment, Dylan faced her. "I'm so glad I ran into you tonight. I know we see each other every day." Her laugh was a deep throaty chuckle. "It was nice to not talk about work, if that makes sense."

"I completely agree." They were still holding hands, and she could feel herself pulsing everywhere. She was one millisecond away from inviting Dylan inside and throwing her self-imposed restrictions out the window.

Dylan pulled her in for a hug, and Briana didn't fight it when she swayed them in place a little. Everything about the way they held on to each other felt both familiar and enticing. With each small degree of movement, Briana felt herself relenting.

"Good night, Briana. See you in the morning." She felt the outline of the words as Dylan's lips brushed against her neck.

"'Night," Briana said to the sidewalk, knowing if she made even the slightest eye contact, she would give in completely.

CHAPTER NINE

Too much wine, a drought of physical activity, and close proximity to Dylan Prescott were a disastrous combination.

In the light of day, this was clear, and as Briana walked from the subway to her office, she weighed her options.

So long as she didn't allow those three elements to align, everything would be fine. The solution was simple, now that she understood the equation. She mostly saw Dylan in the office where there was no alcohol. If they ran into each other in the neighborhood, she'd be sure to go easy on the sauce. Or leave. This was not a problem. She would have to put a moratorium on the innocent touches too. That indulgence was the most difficult to part with, but a necessary sacrifice to ensure success.

Briana pressed the button for the third floor and wondered if Dylan realized how close she'd come last night to breaking her own rules. The thought washed out of her head as quickly as it had come in when she opened the squad door to a flurry of activity.

The entire investigative team was assembled around the table.

"Briana." Sgt. Hollander acknowledged her presence and pulled out a chair at the head of the table. "I'm so glad you're here. Please sit. We can fill you in on the break we caught last night."

"Oh?"

"Ahmed and Karrakas followed Benji Rafferty to the Wine Bar." Miri tacked a picture of the establishment to the corkboard. "Paul Rafferty was there. George Rivas showed up too."

"Wonderful." She looked at Dylan, who gave her a soft smile in return.

"It gets better," Trevor said.

"After about forty-five minutes, the three musketeers left the bar, walked to Paul's Mercedes SUV, and unloaded several boxes into Rivas's Maxima and Benji's Audi."

Sgt. Hollander updated a whiteboard with the make and model of Paul Rafferty's high-end vehicle. "You guys got pictures of this?"

"Pictures and video, Boss," Ahmed said.

Trevor clapped once in excitement and turned to Briana. "Obviously we don't know what's in the boxes."

"Could be anything," Miri echoed. "Including drugs to sell to college kids."

"This is fantastic. Great work."

"Okay, folks. You know the drill." Miri capped her marker and put it back on the ledge of the board. "Find your targets and stick to them like glue. Without getting burned, obviously. We'll reconvene this afternoon. Be safe out there," she said in dismissal.

The crew scattered, and Briana began to collect her belongings while Miri turned to her and began to flesh out the details of the previous evening's surveillance. Briana listened intently even though part of her brain was trying to figure out if Dylan was still in the office. Miri laid out basic next steps, but before she was finished she introduced the possibility of sending Dylan and Trish inside the Wine Bar in an undercover capacity.

"I'm not downplaying the work of these detectives, Miri. You know that. But we need more than one sighting of nondescript boxes being loaded into cars."

"Of course. We'll get you more. You have my word."

"All right," she said, still not sold on the risky method. "Let me go upstairs and brief my supervisor. I'll get started researching the case law. Just so we're up to speed when your team gets the probable cause necessary for moving forward."

"Thank you, Briana."

Briana waved over her shoulder just as a text from Dylan appeared on her phone.

Sorry I didn't have a chance to warn you about the group hug going on in the squad, lol. I only got in a few minutes before you. I'm in the field all day. Hope you got some coffee.

With one simple text it was clear that despite their sidewalk quasi-cuddle the night before, everything with Dylan was just fine. A hundred percent normal. She felt at once relaxed and disheartened at the realization.

I passed on coffee. Truth is, I'm in it for the company as much as the crème brûlée. She dropped in the shrug emoji even as she wondered what the hell she was doing.

Dylan's response was the rosy cheeked smiling emoji. *Same.*

You heard your boss. Go get some bad guys. Dylan, be careful.

Always.

Ugh. How did one word hit her so hard? She shook it off, and for the rest of the day she threw herself into work, trying to focus on the intricacies of legal procedure and not Dylan out in the street following dangerous drug dealers.

At five forty-five, she was thinking about calling it a day when her desk phone rang.

"Are you available to come downstairs for a meeting?" Lt. Nieves barked before even saying hello.

For a fraction of a second she considered telling him to come up to her office, just to pull rank, before realizing she really didn't care. Plus, a meeting in the plant might mean a chance to see Dylan. "Is everything okay?" she asked.

"There's been a few developments in the investigation. I know you spoke with Sgt. Hollander this morning. I'd like to brief you personally if you're available."

"Sure, Dan," she said dropping formality altogether. "Give me fifteen minutes."

"Whatever you need. We'll be here."

A half hour later, she listened to Nieves drone on with details she'd already heard at the morning meeting. Somehow, he had a way of making the surveillance and the likelihood of subsequent leads sound less exciting than it had earlier. Maybe it was because only Nieves and Sgt. Hollander were present at the break room table, and her hopes of seeing Dylan were all but dashed. The sheer disappointment she felt was absurd. Internally calling herself on it, she made sure to stay focused for the next hour as the three of them hashed out police procedure and legal process for moving the investigation forward.

While they were chatting, Nieves checked his phone. "The team is following Paul Rafferty as we speak," he said, giving fresh intelligence.

"Just Ahmed and Trish," Hollander clarified as she looked at her own phone, clearly getting the same set of updates. "Ianelli and Karrakas are on Rivas right now. He's over in Chelsea."

"Old Goldenballs hasn't moved in hours." Nieves giggled like a schoolkid at the moniker. He turned to Hollander. "Pull Gill and Prescott off him for the day."

"Should I cut them loose?" she asked.

"Have them report here. I'd like to talk to them directly about their observations."

"Yes, sir," she said, typing as she spoke.

While Briana believed Nieves was flexing his brass, she was secretly happy because she knew his orders meant she'd get to see Dylan after all. For the next while, she hung around when she could have easily gone home. Instead she stayed at the table rehashing case law and tactics that had held up in court in similar investigations. Her patience paid off just after eight p.m. when Trevor and Dylan arrived.

"Any news?" Nieves asked before they even put their stuff down.

"Trish and Ahmed lost Paul in traffic heading crosstown from the Upper West. Just came over the air." Trevor held up his portable radio for emphasis. "Dylan and I were hoping we might pick him up on our way here."

"And?"

"No luck, Loo. They're going to check up by the Wine Bar again and over at Benji's house too, just in case."

"They can break off after that," Nieves said. "It's going to be another long day tomorrow."

Briana wondered if there was any point to extending this briefing, but then she hardly cared when Dylan gave her a sweet smile as she set her gear on a vacant chair.

"Hey," Dylan whispered as Trevor briefed Hollander and Nieves. "You're here late."

"Nieves asked for a meeting." Briana rolled her eyes. "It was mostly a recap of the morning session."

"He made you stay late for that?"

"It was no big deal. We talked about the progression of the case going forward. It wasn't a total waste of time."

"Still, though." Dylan seemed suspicious, but at least her disbelief was aimed at Nieves's motives and not hers. She watched—okay, stared—as Dylan switched out one radio battery for another. Like the rest of her, Dylan's hands were long and lean, and Briana watched her work swiftly, wondering for the hundredth time what her fingers might feel like inside her. "Long day for you," Dylan said, interrupting her X-rated thoughts.

"But I get to see you." She said it out loud, for the moment letting her guard down and forgetting where she was entirely.

Dylan's look was gratitude, surprise, and desire rolled into one, and even though Briana hated herself for sending mixed messages, the smolder she got made it worthwhile.

"What can I say, I missed my coffee buddy today," Briana said, dialing it back on the spot.

"Coffee buddies. Right." Her laugh was so smooth and sexy. "We could have some right now." Dylan's eyes went to the cabinet where the fancy coffee pods were hidden.

"But then he'll know." Briana looked in the direction of the lieutenant and mouthed, "Nieves."

"Oh, I forgot." Dylan faked a grimace and whispered, "The big secret."

Were they still talking about coffee?

"Prescott." Nieves looked over from his mini confab with Trevor and Hollander. "Good work today."

"Thank you, sir."

"And Ms. Logan, thank you for letting us take up so much of your time. We sort of kidnapped you down here." He laughed heartily. "I'd like to get you a ride home as a show of my gratitude."

She wondered if he was truly grateful for her input or if he was just trying to show off in front of his staff. Either way she appreciated the gesture. "That's not necessary, Lieutenant."

"Nonsense." Nieves leaned back in his chair and folded his hands behind his head. "Prescott. You live in Brooklyn. Drive the good counselor home. Door to door. Understand?"

"Sure thing, Lieutenant." Dylan hopped off the desk she was perched on. "I'm ready when you are."

"I have to run upstairs and get my things," Briana said as her head spun at the turn of events. "Are you sure you don't mind?"

"I've been given an order." Dylan winked. "I'll meet you in the lobby."

❖

Briana hugged herself for warmth against the biting cold. How was it so frigid right now when just twenty-four hours ago she and Dylan had enjoyed a lovely, if brisk, stroll in their shared neighborhood? Furthermore, did Dylan assume she felt entitled to a constant escort? Selfishly she was excited for the time together. She hated that their coffee date was bumped this morning. It was silly, but she'd come to count on the one-on-one time. But being the recipient of forced goodwill made her feel like a nuisance.

"I'm sorry you have to do this. Again," she said with a lilt in her tone, hoping to infuse the situation with some levity.

"You know I don't mind." Dylan pressed the key fob, and the headlights flickered on her sedan a few feet ahead of them. "It's almost ridiculous we don't commute together all the time."

"I think we keep different hours."

"Do we, though?" Dylan's voice was light. "We got here within minutes of each other today, and now we're leaving together."

"Good point." She slid into the passenger seat of Dylan's Chevy Malibu. "How was your day?" she asked as Dylan settled in behind the wheel. She tried to keep her eyes straight ahead when Dylan set up her radio, adjusted the mirrors, buckled her seat belt.

"Busy. We were all over the city. What about you?"

"Same. Busy." Briana was distracted by all the little gadgets she noticed. Near the top of the windshield was a discreet light bar hidden by a swath of subtle window tint. "Hold on a second. Does this car have lights and sirens?"

"Does that do it for you?" Dylan faced her and narrowed her eyes dramatically. "And to think this whole time I've been *walking* you home when I was sitting on this gold mine."

"Shut up." Briana rolled her eyes.

They were still parked, but Dylan pressed a button and the lights flashed red and blue. "Anything?" she asked playfully.

Briana punched Dylan's biceps. "You're a jerk."

Dylan chirped the siren. "How 'bout now?"

"You are insufferable—you know that?"

She reached for the control panel to shut everything off, but Dylan beat her and blocked the switch with both hands. "I'm just making sure," Dylan said, full of frisky spirit.

Briana was laughing in spite of her protest as she tried to permeate Dylan's makeshift shield.

Finally, Dylan gave in. "Okay, okay. You win." With a few quick movements Dylan shut everything down, but her smile stayed as she looked over her shoulder and pulled away from the curb.

"I can't believe you did that." Briana covered her chest, which was beating a mile a minute. "My heart is racing."

"I told you." Dylan wiggled her eyebrows, and even though Briana knew it was all in jest, her pulse was high from the company more than the silly game. If only Dylan knew the effect she had on her all the time. Lights and sirens didn't even hold a candle to simply being in her presence.

"This is probably a stupid question, but how come you have all of these accessories in an undercover vehicle?" she asked just to change the topic.

"It's not a stupid question at all." Dylan looked both ways at a four-way stop. "When we're doing surveillances, following someone and all that, we try to blend in," she explained. "So nondescript cars, common colors, et cetera. But"—she turned into the flow of traffic—"there are times when we need to chase vehicles. Pull them over." Dylan checked her mirrors before switching lanes. "Lights and sirens are necessary in those situations."

"Of course."

"But it doesn't happen that often. Which is why this light package is a bit more low profile than you might expect. On a patrol car or even an unmarked police car participating in traffic regulation and stuff like that, there'd be four times as many lights."

Briana liked the way Dylan explained it without making her feel foolish for asking. She also enjoyed the way Dylan wound through the narrow streets of downtown New York City like it was no big deal. She couldn't tear her eyes from her long, smooth fingers as she gripped the steering wheel and adjusted the temperature. In a moment of silence, the radio crackled with activity, and she heard Trish Suarez report there was no activity at Benji's residence. A second later, Ahmed Baisir called out negative hits for suspect vehicles near the Wine Bar.

"How do you follow someone and not get caught?" Briana surprised herself with the question.

Dylan smiled as she drove. "There is an art to it."

"And you just know how to do it?"

"We help each other out." She shrugged. "By talking on the radio. We take turns being the eye, that's the lead car, and we do that by communicating and switching on and off. This way no one gets made."

"It sounds hard," she said, letting a laugh slip out.

"It's not. Honestly, all it takes is practice." Dylan waited at a stoplight. "I hadn't done it too much before. Not this kind of surveillance. So I'm learning as I go. Trevor gives me pointers. The other guys too."

"Are you good at it?"

They were still at the light, and Dylan turned to make eye contact. "I'm okay, yeah."

"Is that...modesty?"

"Might be." Dylan chewed her lower lip, and Briana stared at her perfect teeth, gleaming white in the darkness. She was pretty sure Dylan was staring at her mouth too, but the light changed, and just as they started to inch forward, a dark blue Mercedes-Benz cut them off.

Dylan hit the brakes. "Holy shit."

"What?"

"That's Paul Rafferty. In front of us. Hang on."

"Are you sure?"

"Yes." She keyed the mic. "Hey, guys. I got eyeballs on Paul Rafferty. Northbound on Water Street. Possibly headed for the FDR. I'm going to stay with him."

"Pres, what's your cross street?"

Dylan glanced up at the street sign. "Fulton Slip. I think he's gonna pick up the Drive at Houston."

"I'm headed your way."

"Who was that?" Briana wasn't sure why she was whispering.

"Dom Ianelli." Dylan accelerated, but only slightly. She let a car get between them and Paul's Benz. "Shit, Briana." Dylan braked. "Are you okay with this?" She touched Briana's shoulder softly. "I don't want to scare you."

Fear was the furthest thing from what she was feeling. Incredibly turned-on watching Dylan in action, check. Completely aroused from one small touch, you bet. Fear, not even on the radar.

"Of course not. Do what you need to do. Pretend I'm not even here."

Dylan agreed but did the exact opposite. For the next fifteen minutes, she fully explained every move she made. She pointed out the ding in Paul's rear bumper that had initially caught her attention and explained how she'd committed all the subjects' license plates to memory. She clued her in when Ahmed joined the surveillance, then Trevor.

Briana took it all in, mesmerized by the wacky shorthand Dylan and the other detectives communicated with over the radio. She was completely grateful when Dylan broke down the coded language, so she could truly follow what was going on. And, ugh, the way Dylan controlled the situation and made it seem perfectly routine was possibly the sexiest thing she'd experienced in her life. When they dropped off and let the rest of the team take over the surveillance, Briana was buzzing with secondhand adrenaline.

"Do you need me to get out so you can stay with the rest of the team?" Briana was a full step behind. "I can take a subway. It's no problem." She touched her temple, more than a little embarrassed at her mental delay. "Dylan, I should have made that offer earlier. I guess I got a bit swept up in the excitement."

"It's fine." Dylan laughed. "The team has it covered."

"Are you sure? I don't want to get you in trouble." She had botched everything. It all came rushing to the surface. "Will you get in trouble for taking me on, like, a ride-along?" She knew there were always liabilities to be considered. She hated the thought of Dylan getting punished for doing exceptional police work in the middle of doing her a favor.

"I won't tell if you don't," Dylan answered with a real laugh.

"But won't Nieves know? From listening to the radio and stuff."

Dylan winced, and Briana wondered if she was considering the consequences of her spur-of-the-moment decision. "Eh, he barely listens to the radio. Miri won't out us. Trevor's a vault. And no one else knows. I think we're good."

They were doubling back on the FDR, finally on the way home.

"You have to promise to tell me if you get reprimanded. This way I can speak on your behalf."

"Absolutely not." Dylan's tone was completely jovial. "Stop worrying. It's fine. I promise." Dylan leaned slightly over the console. "So, what did you think? Was it fun?"

"So much fun."

Briana bit her lip and nodded in support of her short answer, positive her face showed the excitement that was coursing through her veins. At least she had the car chase to blame for the heightened sensation she felt. She couldn't bear the thought of Dylan knowing how turned-on she was. How having a front seat to seeing Dylan in action made her want to chuck all her restraint right off the Brooklyn Bridge.

They were in front of her apartment in no time, and as much as Briana wasn't ready for the night to end, she needed to be out of this car.

Dylan pulled into a parking spot and cut the engine.

"You don't have to get out," she said, unfastening her seat belt and avoiding eye contact altogether. "You've already driven me all the way home."

"With a massive detour."

"An exceptionally cool detour."

"Still."

"Where I got to watch you take charge," she said, processing out loud. "It was—you were…amazing."

"Thank you." Dylan's eyes narrowed as though she wasn't sure where this conversation was headed. Briana wasn't sure either. She was certain of only one thing: Dylan made her want to break all the rules.

Briana peered out the passenger window and let it all pour out.

"It's just…I have a good time with you. You make me laugh. Last night, tonight. You're so easy to talk to. And fun. I haven't connected like this with anyone…" She studied the stars and tried to remember the last time anyone had this effect on her. "I don't even know," she admitted. She let her head fall back against the headrest and closed her eyes. "I cannot stop thinking about you."

"Don't." Dylan's voice was low and sexy. "Look at me."

"I can't."

"Please."

Briana tilted her head to the side and opened her eyes. Dylan was there.

"You're overthinking everything."

"I'm aware."

"So stop." Dylan mimicked her position as she leaned her head back against the headrest. In the seat her body canted just the slightest bit toward her. For a second, Briana thought she might be imagining it. Dylan was only inches from her face, her gorgeous blue eyes loaded with desire. "You know where I stand. I don't see the point in denying ourselves what we want." Dylan seemed to swallow a laugh as her attention shifted from her mouth to her eyes. "But I know you have rules and doubts, and the last thing I want is for you to have any regrets. So come on, counselor." She ticked her head toward the world waiting just outside the car. "As hard as it is to say good-bye to you, I'm still walking you to the front door. I gave my word on that."

Briana didn't stop to think about it, or if she did her body was so far ahead of her brain that she'd already committed to what she wanted. It all seemed suddenly so clear. Without another word, she leaned all the way across the center console and right into Dylan's space.

No regrets.

CHAPTER TEN

Dylan's lips were so much softer than she expected. It was literally the first thing Briana noticed as she sank into her embrace. Briana had started the kiss in a rush, afraid she'd lose her nerve or come to her senses—or both. Instead she dove in with everything she had and kissed Dylan like she'd imagined literally dozens of times. It was hurried, even a little sloppy, if she was being honest, until the second Dylan took over.

How the shift occurred, she wasn't even sure. It all felt so natural and organic. Out of nowhere Dylan was simply in control. Briana felt a hand at the base of her head, and Dylan's thumb caressed her face as she kissed her over and over. Her tongue moved slow and deliberate, the passion between them escalating ever higher as they kissed for what felt like a divine eternity.

For a second Briana thought it might end here. Just one heart-pounding, heat-inducing, sexy kiss in the undercover police car in front of her house. Maybe that was enough to release the pressure between them. But that thought terrified her more than never having kissed Dylan at all, and she heard herself whimper at the idea.

Dylan pulled back and tucked a strand of hair behind her ear. "Are you okay?"

"Not even a little." It was a completely honest response, and she didn't bother to try to qualify it. Logic and passion seemed to be at war inside her. She was pulsing everywhere. She should say good night. Her body felt like it was on fire. No good would come of this. She wasn't even close to ready for it to be over.

Ignoring all reason, Briana leaned in for another searing kiss and didn't stop Dylan when she felt Dylan's hand slide over the front of her body. She needed to be out of this car. She tipped her head back, and Dylan kissed her neck. Her mouth was warm and wet and demanding. She wanted all of it.

"Inside. Right now," she whispered in Dylan's ear.

Briana didn't stop to assess Dylan's reaction if there even was one. She didn't make any eye contact whatsoever as she grabbed her purse and virtually ran up the walkway, into her foyer, and up the stairs to her second-floor apartment.

It wasn't until the door was shut safely behind them that she registered the hunger in Dylan's eyes. It was matched only by her signature devilish smile. The look both enticed and relaxed her, but she hardly had time to process before Dylan leaned in and kissed her.

Where she'd seemed controlled and measured before, Dylan was all desire now, and Briana was here for it.

Her bag dropped to the floor, and Dylan's mouth was all over hers. Her hands were in Dylan's soft sculpted hair, and she moaned into her mouth. Dylan leaned back against the door, and Briana leaned into her, pressing her body up against Dylan. With seemingly no effort, Dylan lifted her, and she instinctively responded, wrapping her legs around Dylan's torso, not caring one bit when her skirt hiked all the way up.

Dylan carried her to the kitchen island, kissing her the whole way. Her lips were all over her face and neck, and her blouse was off before Briana even realized it. Dylan pushed the material of her bra down and kissed her bare breast. She gripped Dylan's hair and pushed herself in deeper, needing to feel Dylan's teeth against her flesh. Dylan's fingers pressed against her center, and she groaned, knowing she was wet, fully aware Dylan knew it too.

In the dark she felt Dylan expertly remove her panties. Briana knew she should stop her. They were in the freaking kitchen. Stef could come home any minute. But she simply could not bring herself to do it. Instead she leaned back and let it all happen.

And oh God, her mouth was nothing short of a goddamn miracle. Dylan found her sensitive spot in seconds, and the first baby orgasm ripped through her in record time. Dylan could obviously tell—Briana could feel her smile against her skin after she let out a series of gasps and stifled moans.

Clearly Dylan was just getting started as Briana felt her add a finger to the action. It already felt amazing but was too much for the kitchen counter.

"My room," she managed.

"Of course. Yeah," Dylan said as she stood and graciously helped her down. Briana was genuinely touched when Dylan bent down and picked up her shirt and underwear off the floor. It was such a simple action, but oddly thoughtful. She reached for Dylan's hand and laced their fingers as she guided them down the hall to her bedroom.

Standing next to her bed, Briana felt shy for a second. Somehow the ambient light from the street drew attention to the state of her semi-undress and made her just the slightest bit self-conscious. It literally made no sense considering what had just occurred—in the kitchen of all places—but facing a fully clothed Dylan while she was half-naked made her feel exposed instead of sexy.

"You're beautiful," Dylan said. Briana wondered if she paid the compliment because she could sense her nervous energy, but then the look in her eyes seemed so sincere, it moved her regardless of the motive. When Dylan leaned forward to kiss her, she let all her defenses drop and stopped analyzing altogether. She got lost in the softness of Dylan's lips, her tender touch, the way she asked permission before progressing onward. It was as though Dylan wanted to make sure even if this was a fluke, it was one Briana felt confident in pursuing.

Briana was beyond speechless over what was most definitely happening. The irresponsibility of this decision did absolutely nothing to tamp down her need, and in the semidarkness she responded the only way she could manage, via tiny moans of approval and decadent kisses of encouragement.

At first Dylan seemed to want to go slow, but Briana needed her too much to have any real patience. It was as though any deceleration might give her pause to consider the repercussions of their actions, and more than anything she wanted to live in this moment.

She slipped her hands under Dylan's shirt and lifted it off, letting it fall to the floor. She followed suit with a sports bra that was barely necessary, before Briana let her hands and her mouth explore with complete abandon. Dylan was wiry and muscular, all sharp angles and taut skin covered with multiple tattoos. She wore a single religious medal that caught her so off guard she almost stopped to ask questions.

But before she could say anything, Dylan's mouth was on hers, hard and demanding and so clearly ready to go to the next level.

Briana scraped her nails along the outline of a six-pack before she made her way to Dylan's belt, not breaking away from the deep kiss as she loosened the buckle. She undid the button of Dylan's jeans and started on the zipper, but Dylan stopped her.

"Just let me take care of this," Dylan whispered as she removed her firearm from where it was secured to her belt. Briana was half mesmerized as she watched Dylan place the holstered weapon a step away on the nightstand. "Is it okay if I leave it there?" she asked.

"Yeah. Yes. Of course." The truth was she'd forgotten all about the fact that Dylan was armed, and while she didn't have a cop fetish, this whole night was making her appreciate the allure. "I'm sorry if I got too close…"

Dylan reentered her personal space. "You're fine." Dylan held her face. The kiss that followed was soft and sweet for one second before it turned right back into full heat.

Briana broke from the kiss more than breathless. She inched back to the bed, never letting go of Dylan's hand. Pulling back the covers, she felt Dylan embrace her from behind. She couldn't contain a whimper when Dylan ran her hands over her breasts and her belly and kissed her neck. Briana turned around and met Dylan's mouth as they fell into the bed together. She pushed Dylan's boxers down, the need to feel her everywhere superseding all else.

She held onto her shoulders as she felt Dylan's fingers slide inside her. It felt amazing. Dylan seemed to know exactly where and how to touch her. How much pressure to use, when she should pull back, and when Briana needed her to go hard and deep and fast. Briana opened her legs wider ready for every last inch Dylan had to offer.

Dylan kissed her neck, her chest, her mouth. Her actions were tender and raw at the same time, and they created an intimacy that somehow underscored the sensation. When Dylan hovered over her, Briana registered her slightly ragged breathing, and she wanted to make her feel even a fraction of what she was feeling with every kiss, with every thrust.

"Can I…" Briana managed. She brushed her hand over Dylan's center, completing her sentence with the promise of her touch.

Dylan's mouth hung slightly open as she nodded assent.

At the contact, Dylan's moan was deep and guttural and sexy as fuck. Briana felt herself gush in response, but she was already so wet she wondered if Dylan even noticed. Dylan moved in sync on top of her and inside her, and Briana moved with her, bucking and gasping and begging for more. She was barely in control of what she was even saying, but it didn't matter. She was almost there and Dylan clearly knew it. Briana felt slight perspiration on Dylan's back as she pumped harder and faster. If she didn't know any better, she'd swear Dylan was about to come with her. The thought evaporated as quickly as it came when all brain function ceased as her nerve endings took center stage.

The orgasm started in her center but swept over her in full ripple effect, reaching all the way to her fingertips and her toes. Even the insides of her eyelids buzzed like a fuse was shorting out. It was only after she came back to reality that she was even aware of Dylan's dead weight sinking into her.

Briana smiled, loving that they'd climaxed together. She opened her eyes and placed a small kiss on Dylan's temple. She loved how intertwined their bodies were and how they jointly seemed too depleted to even begin to unentangle. She didn't have a clue how that would even begin—figuratively or literally. But that was a problem for tomorrow. Right now, in this moment, she was content basking in the post-sex haze, in Dylan, in sleep, in the sheer ecstasy of it all.

CHAPTER ELEVEN

Dylan sat on the edge of the bed and reached for her shoe, tugging it on with as little movement as possible.

"Are you leaving?" Briana's voice was gravelly with sleep, her fingertips delicate as they drifted along her back.

"I was trying not to wake you up."

"What time is it?"

"A little after midnight." She shifted on the bed to face Briana, who was covered under a pile of rumpled sheets. Spent and sated and half-asleep, she was as gorgeous as ever. Dylan leaned forward and caressed her face. In return, Briana kissed her palm. The action was decidedly tame, but it turned her on just the same. "I should go," she said, even though she was dying to take her clothes off and get back in bed. She wanted to do everything over again. Slower, this time. Savor every second.

The night had been a divine rush, and she knew it was what they both needed, but it already seemed a blur. She wanted another chance, and she wasn't sure she was going to get one. Her heart plummeted at the thought. Looking at Briana's sleepy smile affected her in a way that was unfamiliar. She wanted Briana to tell her to stay, to fall asleep in her arms.

"Text me when you get home?" Briana whispered.

"You'll be asleep." She placed a kiss on her cheek. "You're asleep now."

"Do it anyway?" Briana's request was almost a plea, and it touched her.

"Okay," she said, agreeing on the spot.

Briana held her face and kissed her. It was more than a peck but fell short of leading to anything more. At once sweet and passionate, it was the perfect good-bye.

She stood and finished dressing in the dark, at last securing her gun inside the waistband of her jeans.

"It's ridiculous how sexy that is." Briana covered her eyes with her forearm as she shook her head back and forth on the pillow.

Dylan grinned. She'd heard it before. There was a brand of woman who dated cops as a rule. They dug the mystique, the uniform, the badge. She never really understood it, and she never sought them out the way some of her coworkers did. Right now, she was beaming inside because Briana Logan thought she was sexy. If all it took was taking her gun on and off to get those flushed cheeks, she'd do it all day long.

"I hate that you know it," Briana said, misreading her flattered expression for smugness.

Seizing the moment anyway, Dylan leaned in for a final kiss. "Sweet dreams," she said. "I'll see you in the morning."

Dylan let herself out and walked home practically on cloud nine. It hadn't been that long since she'd gotten attention—or action, for that matter—but she simply could not remember the last time she felt like this.

❖

Why she'd assumed they'd do coffee this morning, Dylan wasn't one hundred percent sure. She supposed it was because she expected—or at least hoped—Briana wanted to see her as much as the reverse was true.

In that spirit, Dylan had sent a good-morning message coupled with a coffee emoji when she arrived at the office but never received an answer. By ten thirty with no word whatsoever from Briana, Dylan made another move.

You are alive, right?

It was several minutes before Briana's curt response appeared.

In a meeting. Sorry.

No worries, she typed back.

She waited all morning for a follow-up, a simple explanation. She didn't need much. Common courtesy, good manners, that was all she was looking for. But hours passed with nothing. Not a phone call, not a text, not even a goddamn GIF indicating Briana was swamped with work. In her head she knew Briana was probably redrawing the line. She'd made it clear for weeks that she didn't want to cross a boundary, but then they had. And now she was freezing her out. It was an unnecessary, over-the-top reaction, and even though she was pissed, Dylan wanted to fix it.

At two forty-five, she found the courage to be the bigger person. Plus, she was ready for a break from a full day of monitoring and transcribing phone calls.

Dylan thought carefully about wording, trying to keep her text to Briana breezy. *I'm making three o'clock coffee. You in?* She waited a second and reread it. It seemed to have the right tone, with no room for misinterpretation. She hit send.

Briana's response was immediate. *Busy. I'll text you later.*

Wow. Wow. She didn't think their hookup last night meant they owed each other a commitment, but she also didn't deserve to be treated like crap.

Yeah, okay, she responded, mimicking the icy tone.

There were bubbles for a second, but then they disappeared entirely. What was Briana about to say? Did she even want to know?

Despite her commitment to do the exact opposite, Dylan kept one eye on her phone all day, but it was for naught. It wasn't until she was home from work, unpacking her few groceries from the corner farm stand, that Briana contacted her.

We should talk.

Dylan rolled her eyes at the dramatic one-liner. They should have been talking all day, and part of her wanted to say exactly that. But before she had a chance to respond, a second message came through.

Are you still working?

No. I'm home.

Oh. I thought you might be on overtime.

So you were hoping I might NOT be available…

It was frustrating that text messages had a way of omitting emotion, because right now she wanted Briana to know she was annoyed. Caps were the best she could do.

No. There were bubbles and then none, and then bubbles again.

A small part of her felt guilty for instigating this tiny squabble, but technically Briana had started with the cold shoulder. Finally a message appeared. *I was hoping to catch up with you. I just checked the plant, but you weren't there. I thought you might be in the field.*

At least Briana seemed to be thawing. Thank God.

We could meet somewhere if you want. She knew better than to offer her apartment. Surely Briana would be suspect of her intent, and if she was being honest, she didn't entirely trust her motives either. *Connolly's?* she suggested.

How about the Starbucks on the corner of Court and Kane?

More coffee, the last thing she wanted. *Sure*, she typed.

I'm just getting on the subway now. See you in about a half hour? See you there.

Dylan got there early but waited outside. She was curious about the randomness of picking Starbucks for their first post-sex sit-down, but rather than fixate on it, she scrolled her phone while she waited for Briana to arrive.

She was halfway through an interesting article on DNA testing when a vaguely familiar strawberry blonde approached her.

"Hey, Dylan. Fancy meeting you here."

The woman bounced on her toes to kiss her cheek.

"How have you been?" Dylan asked, completely drawing a blank on her name. She put her phone away and racked her brain, but nothing surfaced.

"Oh, you know. Same old, same old." She scrunched her curls as though she was primping on the spot. "Are you going in?" She nodded at the door.

"I'm meeting a friend," Dylan said. In the distance she saw Briana crossing the street and heading her way.

"You should come to Boca tonight," the woman said. "The vibe is amazing on Fridays."

"Uh, maybe."

The woman placed a hand on Dylan's forearm. "Or we could meet up somewhere else. Shoot me a text. You have my number."

She might. Be helpful if she knew what name it was under. It would also be fabulous if Briana wasn't catching this entire exchange.

"Hey," Briana said, arriving at the tail end of the convo.

The woman looked at Briana and then back at Dylan. "Anyway, it was good to see you, Dylan." She squeezed Dylan's biceps as she opened the door.

"Thanks, sweetheart. You too."

"Sweetheart?" Briana mouthed. "Am I interrupting?" She waved between Dylan and the woman who was already inside at the counter. Her tone was completely tongue-in-cheek, but Dylan rolled her eyes in response.

"I don't remember her name," Dylan admitted in a low whisper as she held the door open.

"What's worse is that you think that makes it better," Briana said, still teasing.

She hung her head like a scolded puppy, but the truth was she really didn't know what to say. The back and forth outside had thrown her off her game, and she wanted to get some mojo back. "Hi," she said, starting over and keeping it simple.

"Hi," Briana said.

It was only one word, but Briana's expression was soft and warm, and even after not talking all day, Dylan felt ridiculously close to her.

"Do you want coffee?" she asked.

"What are you getting?" Briana responded with a question.

"I'm thinking about a vanilla latte." Dylan turned to study the specialty drink menu just to make sure there wasn't something else that piqued her interest, when one of the baristas squinted at her. "Dylan Prescott, is that you? Haven't seen you around in ages."

"Mairead. How are you?" she said with a smile. At least she knew this one's name. The name tag she wore was only a minor assist. But honestly, how the fuck was this happening right now?

"For real?" Briana didn't even try to hide her judgment.

Mairead was still batting her eyelashes. "What can I get you two?" she asked.

"Do you want to go somewhere else?" Dylan said to Briana.

Briana slow-blinked and shook her head. "No." Dylan thought she heard a small laugh sneak out. "It might not be any different."

"Ouch." Dylan covered her heart.

"You love it," Briana teased. "I'll have a caramel macchiato," she said to Mairead. "And a vanilla latte for the neighborhood stud."

"Okeydokey. Are you two staying or going?"

Dylan looked at Briana as she paid for their drinks.

"Staying," Briana answered for both of them.

"Sit anywhere you want. I'll bring your drinks over when they're ready."

"Thank you," Briana said. She turned to Dylan. "And thank you for paying."

"I'm not above buying your goodwill at the moment."

"Not necessary." Briana touched her arm gently as they settled into a corner. "Even though I was not expecting the twofer, I'm just teasing you." She shook her perfect hair off her shoulders. "The reality is that neither of us was a saint before last night."

Last night. Dylan had almost hoped to avoid the topic entirely. She knew why. Her gut told her Briana's standoffishness today was the first baby step to putting the kibosh on any future extracurriculars. Avoiding the topic altogether at least left room for a chance. But it was too late—Briana was already talking.

"The thing is, Dylan, I just don't think we should let that happen again."

Dylan nodded stoically. "I knew you were going to say that."

"Perhaps because you know it's the right decision."

"I wouldn't go that far."

"I am sorry about this morning. All of today, really." Briana leaned forward and touched her knee. In past interactions the gesture had meant desire. Right now, it signaled sincerity, and it was amazing the dismal effect that difference had on her entire being. "I wasn't lying when I said I was busy today," Briana continued. "We got hit with a multitude of ticking time bombs at once." She took a deep breath, appearing to steel herself. "Nonetheless, my behavior was immature, to say the least. I don't really have an excuse for that."

Dylan wanted to suggest that it was possible Briana's conduct was her subconscious's way of telling her she didn't want to be mature. That deep down she didn't want to make the decision that was right *on paper*. Her body and soul wanted to splurge, to indulge. But even in her head, it sounded like an appeal.

Mairead brought their drinks over, and it bought her a little more time to think about what she wanted to say. But nothing came to her.

"You're awfully quiet over there." Briana took the first sip of her drink.

"I don't really know what to say." She shrugged. "I disagree with you. I think you know that."

"What's the alternative?"

Was Briana really asking that? It seemed so straightforward to her. "We take it day by day. See where it goes."

"I know you think it's that simple."

"It's not?"

"I think as women, particularly working in male-dominated fields, it's foolish of us to assume we won't be judged. And treated differently."

"Don't you think people talk about us already?" Dylan tasted the froth on her drink. "I mean because we're strong and independent women, not to mention queer."

"Yes. Of course. I'm sure there are people who talk about you for being an out lesbian and criticize the way you choose to present yourself. Undoubtedly people consider me loose for openly identifying as pansexual, not that the haters even understand that label," she said. "But that's not what I mean." Briana took another sip of her macchiato. "I guess what I'm saying is we can't dictate the things people will judge us for that are beyond our control. I am who I am, you are who you are. But we shouldn't add fuel to the fire by doing something that, while not strictly verboten, is arguably unprofessional. I'm an Assistant US Attorney, you're the co-case detective."

Briana had a valid point and Dylan hated it.

"What about our feelings?" Dylan asked even though it made her vulnerable.

"I think this case could be paramount to both of our careers. Right now, I think that surpasses all else."

"Wow, that's cold." Dylan forced a laugh.

Briana's face fell at the barb. "Dylan, I like you. Obviously, I'm attracted to you." She chewed her bottom lip. "If you had any doubts before, I'm pretty sure last night put those to rest." She blushed a little. "As far as feelings go"—she raised her drink aloft—I think that's where we can take it one day at a time. "If real feelings develop, they'll keep."

"Until after the case is done."

"Ideally, yes."

"The fact that you make so much sense is very annoying. You know that, right?"

Dylan took a hefty sip of her latte, letting Briana's message sink in. She still didn't wholly agree with the approach, but she could at least respect the ideology behind it.

"Hold on a freaking second." Briana stared at Dylan's paper cup and then lifted and inspected her own. She spun it all the way around on their shared table before dropping her jaw in disbelief.

"What's going on?" she asked.

Briana pursed her lips and pointed at Dylan's cup. "She put a heart on your cup. The barista."

"Mairead?"

"Mairead," Briana singsonged in mock frustration.

Dylan waved her off with a laugh. "It's probably her signature thing."

"I don't have one. See for yourself." Briana offered her drink for inspection, but Dylan pushed it away.

"You know, you sound a teensy bit jealous." It was true and Dylan reveled in it. Even though she knew she couldn't expect anything from it, for now, just knowing was enough.

"I mean, it's a little rude. I'm sitting right here with you."

"Do you want me to go yell at her for insulting you? My non-girlfriend. My boss? What is our relationship exactly?"

"We're friends?" Briana suggested. "Friends who had one super-hot, amazing hookup. Now we work together. To put bad guys in jail."

"We sound like a TV show I would actually watch."

"Right?"

Dylan loved Briana's silly laugh and her real smile. It was just a bit giggly and oddly goofy for such an attractive person. It was worth everything just to see it.

"So we're back to normal?" Dylan asked.

"Whatever that is," Briana said with a laugh.

"That's you and me and coffee. We talk, we laugh. We know there's something here"—Dylan waved between them—"but we don't act on it. That's our normal."

"To our normal." Briana toasted with her drink.

Dylan didn't miss a beat, meeting her midair. "I'll drink to that."

CHAPTER TWELVE

That was kind of a wild-goose chase," Dylan said. "I'm sorry I dragged us all the way out here."

"No big." Trevor shrugged. "Would have been a home run if it had panned out."

Dylan had road tripped with Trevor to New Jersey to speak to a female who'd woken up from a months-long coma after a heroin overdose. Since the young woman had done a semester at NYU before transferring to Princeton, they'd hoped she'd be able to point out George or Benji as her supplier. No dice.

"I haven't really done too many interviews since making detective. It was good experience for me."

"How did you like Vice?" Trevor asked as he steered up the turnpike entrance ramp.

"It was fine. A little rote. I felt like we did the same thing over and over."

He dropped a look on her that questioned how that was different from day after day of surveillance and wire monitoring.

"Not the same," she said, answering his unspoken question. "I feel like what we're doing here could really make a difference. There…" She took a second to organize her thoughts. "It was all a stats game. We'd raid a bar for serving minors, and the owner would pay the fine but not get any stricter with their policy." She thought about dozens of busts she'd done in her first months as a detective right up until the golden overhear. "I get that it served a purpose, but sometimes it felt a little useless, if that makes sense."

"I get it." Trevor nodded. "I had some of the same experiences in Narcotics. We'd collar one street corner dealer, and another would pop up in his place within twenty-four hours. It was disheartening."

"George and Benji and Paul have a nice little network going. Nailing them might actually have an impact. At least that's what I believe."

"I'm with you. We need another fucking break, though. We're getting cold."

"I know."

He switched into the left lane to pass a slowpoke doddering along. "See, we have enough good observations to arrest Rivas for sure. Benji too, I think. But Paul is careful on the phone. He doesn't say much. And he's got to be getting his supply from somewhere. Even if we scoop up the two nimrods, unless one of them talks, Paul will just find new henchmen to get his product on the street."

Dylan knew he was just thinking out loud, but she liked to be privy to his process. Hearing his theories helped her build on her own. She was chewing through some ideas when he started talking again.

"Getting you and Trish inside the Wine Bar is key. I'm still pushing that."

"What's Nieves say?" she asked.

"He's not the holdout. It's Briana."

She'd known Briana wasn't a fan of the aggressive plan from the outset. Dylan didn't really understand her strong opposition, but she'd hoped time would soften her a bit. "I thought it would be more up to Nieves than her," she said.

"With a tactical decision like that, technically Nieves could make the call. But it's always a good idea to have the blessing of the AUSA. She'll have to defend it in court at some point. It's ultimately better for the prosecution if everyone's in agreement. And at the moment, she's not."

"She's tough." Dylan said it mostly just to say something, but she felt Trevor's gaze on her.

"How are things with you two?"

"Fine," she responded. It wasn't a lie. In the two weeks since their Starbucks rendezvous, they'd gone back to being pals. They did coffee at the plant, they chatted. Sometimes it bordered on flirty, but they kept their word to each other. No acting on whatever feelings might be simmering beneath the surface. Dylan did feel like her clit might break from the amount of masturbating she was doing to keep the edge off, but Trevor didn't need to know that.

"Just fine?" he asked.

She held her palms up in surrender. "Fine is good, no?"

"It is." He drummed the steering wheel. "I guess I was hoping you might have some sway with her. You two seem chummy."

"Chummy?"

"Close. I think she trusts you."

"She trusts you too."

"It's different. I can tell." She wondered how much he was attuned to. "Maybe it's a chick thing."

She breathed a sigh of relief to know he wasn't picking up on their mutual attraction. "You think because we both have vaginas I can get her to change her mind on the undercover idea."

"Oh my God, do you have to use that word?"

"Vagina?" She laughed.

Trevor covered one ear as he guided the car into the Holland Tunnel. "Yes."

"Vagina. Vagina. Vagina." She was laughing hysterically as she watched his panic on display. "Your girlfriend has a vagina too. You know that, right?"

"Can we not talk about my girlfriend's...vagina?" He stuttered out the word.

"You're such a pussy."

"See, was that so hard?" he countered with a chuckle.

Dylan controlled her laughter. "Seriously, what influence do you really think I'll have on Briana?" she asked, steering the conversation back on track.

He took a minute to answer like he was considering his words with care. "I don't know," he finally said with a shrug. "You think infiltrating the Wine Bar is a good idea?"

"I don't think it could hurt."

"So convince her of that. Get her to see it through your eyes. Maybe work on her tomorrow night."

"What's tomorrow night?"

"Trish is organizing a get-together at some new place. The Pounding Gavel."

"Sounds lawyer-y."

"Exactly." He squeezed into a parking space in front of the office. "Which means the legal beagles will definitely show."

❖

Dylan shouldered her way through a row of suits to deliver a round of drinks to her colleagues. For over an hour she'd kept close watch on Briana across the room to see if there might be an opportunity to bend her ear on the undercover operation, but she'd been tied up with the same dude the whole night.

Finally, she threw in the towel. She told Trevor and her crew she was headed to the bathroom, but she beelined it for the exit and the subway when she thought no one was paying attention. It took forty-five minutes for Trevor to call her out.

You're such an Irish good-byer.

Sorry bro. I need to be around my people.

I thought we were your people.

She laughed because it was kind of true. *You are. I'm headed to Boca in Brooklyn*, she typed, even though she was halfway thinking about going home. *It's down the block from my apartment*, she added.

He answered with the thumbs-up emoji before adding, *I hear you. Have fun. Get lucky.*

She texted him back the smirking emoji, even though she wasn't sure she even wanted any company that wasn't Briana. With the gorgeous counselor on her mind, she sent a final text to Trevor.

I'll try to talk to Briana about the UC thing next week. Promise. I didn't get the chance tonight.

No worries, dude.

Except she was worried. Not about the case, though. All night Briana had been in close conversation with one guy. A handsome guy, even though it annoyed her to admit it. Dylan conducted some mild recon at the bar. His name was Dante Miller, and he was an attorney, but didn't work at the US Attorney's Office. Which meant he had a shot with Briana. Dylan was sure he was interested. Who wouldn't be interested in the prettiest, smartest person in the bar? The one with the best laugh and sweetest smile.

She clenched her teeth in frustration. When she and Briana

made a deal not to act on their shared desire, she wished she'd had the forethought to include a rider clause banning any other hookups as well. Dylan laughed at the ridiculousness of her thought process. She was literally on her way to another bar that would be loaded with prospects. She rolled her shoulders and her neck in an effort to shake off her frustration.

Her neighbor Talia might be at Boca. Violet too. Social media said she frequented the local hot spot every Friday.

Filled with the hope of at least some attention, she mustered the energy to socialize. A stop to freshen up and change at her apartment helped rejuvenate her spirit, and half a drink into Boca she was actively blocking Briana from her brain.

"Hey, sweetheart."

It was the strawberry blonde from Starbucks two weeks ago. Dylan had done her homework since then.

"Skye. Hello again."

Skye dropped her mouth open in a teasing manner. "Somebody studied up." She poked Dylan's shoulder with two fingers. "I knew you didn't remember my name last time."

"I'm sorry." Dylan winced in apology. "I could buy you a drink to make up for it."

"I'm all set." Skye fingered the straw in her cocktail. "It's nice to see you again, though." She ran her eyes the length of Dylan's body. Dylan saw her eyes widen a little as she registered the slight bulge in her pants. "Fuck, I hope that's what I think it is."

Dylan swallowed her smile. She loved this part. Loved it, loved it. The anticipation. The game. Any other day, she'd be rock hard and ready. But looking in Skye's baby blues only made her miss Briana's deep hazel eyes. Skye's curly hair had her reminiscing over Briana's light brown waves. What the fuck was she doing?

"If memory serves, your place is right near here." Skye leaned in close and ran her tongue over her lips seductively. Dylan felt Skye's hand graze the front of her jeans. "I say we finish our drinks and get out of here."

She felt her phone buzz in her back pocket. Briana. She opened the text on the spot.

Not her. Please?

Dylan stood tall and looked around. Near the doorway Briana gave her a small wave coupled with an even tinier pout. Dylan scooched out of Skye's semi-embrace and excused herself. She was standing next to Briana in no time.

"What are you doing here?" she asked, hearing the elation in her tone.

"Trevor told me where to find you."

"Oh," she said, trying to piece together how that information transfer might have come to pass.

"You bailed without even talking to me."

"I'm sorry." She leaned her head all the way back knowing she had to be honest. "I couldn't stay and watch you talk to that guy. It was just…too hard."

Briana pursed her gorgeous lips. "How do you think I feel? I walked in to see that display." She nodded toward the spot where Skye was still standing.

It was probably against the rules, but she reached for Briana's hand. "There's nothing going on there. I swear to you."

"I know I can't expect you not to have a social life." Briana's shrug was positively adorable. "But I kind of wish you didn't have a social life."

"I get that." She squeezed Briana's hand. "Do you want a drink, or do you want to walk?"

"Walk?" she said with a questionable lilt. "I feel bad making you leave, though."

"I want to be with you. Pretty much always. Sort of the problem." She said the last part under her breath as she led them outside, and she wondered if Briana even heard her. It was the truth, and she didn't really care one way or the other if Briana knew how she felt so long as it didn't make her balk.

In the cold, they both put their hands in their respective pockets as they strolled. It was for the best, but it made Dylan sad. At work, she had no problem respecting the boundaries, but on the streets of their shared neighborhood, following the rules was exponentially more difficult.

"Would you have gone home with her? The Starbucks woman?" Briana asked. "One of the Starbucks women, I should say."

"Ba-*zing*." Dylan pretended to wrench an arrow from her chest. "I guess I deserve that," she said with a smile.

"You don't. This whole night. My showing up here. It isn't fair. I know that."

"Would you have gone home with Dante Miller?" Dylan asked.

"I came to Boca looking for you," Briana countered.

"I had to pep talk myself to come out here tonight. To try to get my mind off you for five minutes." Dylan didn't bother to sugarcoat it. "It didn't work." She turned up her block out of habit but paused to lean on a tree near the corner. "I was talking to Skye and thinking, Briana has nicer eyes, a better smile, is a thousand times more interesting. So no. I would not have gone home with her. Or anyone."

"Skye." Briana rolled her eyes. "Fake name."

"But Dante isn't pretentious at all." She frowned just to lay it on nice and thick. "Nope. Completely regular. Run of the mill."

Briana laughed, and it was giggly and silly, just the way Dylan loved. She could listen to it all night.

"Poor Dante didn't have a chance." Briana stepped forward and rested her forehead on Dylan's chest. "I basically don't stop thinking about you."

Dylan circled her arms around Briana's back. "What are we doing to each other?"

"I'm not sure torture is the right word, but I think it's pretty close."

"Why, though? Maybe that's the real question." She smoothed her hand along Briana's hair, just to feel its softness through her fingers.

Briana looked up and all her defenses seemed to drop. "I honestly don't know." She stood on tiptoe to bring her face close to Dylan's. "Right now, I just want you to kiss me."

Without hesitation, Dylan found Briana's lips and kissed her over and over. In contrast to the last time, she was in no rush, and she took the time to appreciate Briana's full lips, her warm mouth. It was soft and slow and sweet as they made out in the dark against a giant oak on her quiet street. Dylan held her face and savored every fucking second of Briana pressed up against her.

Briana made no move to stop it. On the contrary, Dylan heard tiny moans as the kiss intensified. She pulled Briana closer, forgetting for a second that she was packing. Briana realized, though. That much was clear from her sharp gasp and the sexiest whimper she'd ever heard.

"Jesus Christ, Dylan." Briana was more than a little breathless. "It's like you're trying to kill me."

"The way I see it"—she moved Briana's hair to kiss her neck—"people are going to gossip anyway." She nibbled an earlobe. "Why don't we do what feels right?"

Briana bit her lower lip. "I have a pretty good idea what's going to feel right in a few minutes."

CHAPTER THIRTEEN

As titillating as Briana's street corner comment might have been, Dylan was committed to making the night that followed positively romantic.

After walking the very short distance to her brownstone, Dylan didn't rush into anything. Instead, she took her time showing Briana around her third-floor apartment and answering questions about the transition from growing up on the first two floors to becoming the property manager of the whole house. She basked in Briana's praise of her kitchen redesign and bragged just a smidge at having done all the renovations herself.

Dylan hooked them up with glasses of wine and leaned against the kitchen island, listening intently as Briana talked about her own upbringing in central Long Island, her favorite golden retriever who she missed desperately, and her star turn on the high school debate team that made her realize she was going to be a litigator.

Dylan was as turned-on by just talking to Briana as she was from anything else. Briana seemed to be enjoying herself too. Dylan liked the way Briana watched her mouth when she spoke and probed for additional information with each new tidbit. It was as though learning about one another was part of the seduction.

When they finally made it to her bedroom, their small touches and heavy kisses seemed so organic she barely stopped to make sure Briana was truly comfortable moving forward.

It wasn't until they were shirtless on top of her bedspread that she made her final check-in. She kissed Briana's breasts but stopped grinding against her center.

"You sure you're okay with this?" she asked, looking up to assess Briana's facial expression.

"Yes. I promise." Briana brought her face close for a kiss. "I don't know what we're signing up for. Not really." Briana danced her tongue along Dylan's neck and wrapped her legs around her body. "But I am sure I want you." She looked down devilishly at Dylan's pronounced bulge. "All of you."

It was all the encouragement Dylan needed and more. She made quick work of Briana's skirt and panties, and when she stood to take off her jeans, Briana sat on the edge of the bed and pushed her hands aside.

"Uh-uh. I've been waiting hours for this," she said, unbuckling Dylan's belt and leaning forward to kiss along the waistband of her boxer briefs.

If Dylan wasn't ready to burst before, watching Briana kiss her stomach and trace the tattoo on her midsection with her lips about did it for her. After under a minute of delicious torture, Briana leaned forward and found her mouth, kissing her hard and possessively.

Ushering them under the covers, Dylan sank two fingers inside Briana. Oh my God, she fucking loved how wet she was. She loved knowing it was because Briana wanted her. That in spite of conventional wisdom, they were in her bed. About to have sex. Again.

Against logic and reason, it seemed, Briana needed her.

Dylan moved in a steady rhythm before she kissed her way down Briana's beautiful torso. She paused by her hip bone, licking and biting and sucking as Briana writhed beneath her. Finally, when she couldn't hold back any longer, she made it to her center and took her time teasing with baby kisses and touches until she buried her face with purpose. When she focused her attention on Briana's clit, she felt Briana's muscles tighten around her fingers. Dylan smiled at the reaction she generated and groaned when Briana gushed in her mouth.

She was hot and hard and dying to be inside Briana. She withdrew her fingers and removed her boxers, leaning her body weight on one hand as she used the other to guide herself inside.

Briana responded with a moan that sounded both fulfilled and still yearning at the same time. Dylan felt her fingernails scratch her back. Briana's hands gripped her and pulled her impossibly closer. She felt Briana's lips on her neck, her throat, her chest, her shoulders. With every thrust, Dylan moved deeper inside and inched closer to her own climax.

Thankfully she heard the cadence of Briana's breathing change. She saw her mouth drop open.

"Fuck, Dylan," Briana breathed in her ear, "I'm going to come."

The distinct knowledge pushed her over the edge. She watched Briana squeeze her eyes shut and bite her lip just as Dylan's orgasm took over, coursing through her body until she had absolutely nothing left. More than a little short of breath, she collapsed next to Briana and fell sound asleep almost instantaneously.

Dylan finally regained consciousness as she registered the smooth touch of Briana's fingertips caressing her forearm.

"Hey," she whispered into Briana's hair as she opened her eyes. Her room was still pitch black and she rolled onto her back to check the time.

"Fuck. It's one fifteen. I totally passed out."

Briana turned to her and rested her head on her chest. "I fell asleep too."

"That makes me feel less bad." She draped an arm across Briana's back and hugged her close.

"I should go home," Briana said with a sigh.

"It's the middle of the night and it's cold out." Dylan kissed the top of her head. "You should stay. You know I'll walk you, though, if you want," she said, editing on the spot. She didn't want Briana to leave, but she also didn't want her to feel trapped.

"I don't want you to feel suffocated," Briana said. She snuggled the tiniest bit closer. "But your bed is amazing. I really don't feel like moving."

Dylan kissed her forehead and her lips, happy that it was settled. "Maybe you should shoot Stef a text so she knows you haven't been abducted." She laughed at her own dark humor. "Do you two do that? Check in on each other?"

"We do, kind of." Briana traced the outline of her St. Michael pendant as she spoke. "We don't have a set system in place, but we do keep tabs to make sure everything is okay." She reached for her phone on the nightstand and read through a series of texts.

"She's not home."

Dylan nodded. "Is that okay?"

"Yeah, definitely. She's seeing someone new. A friend of mine."

"That's good? We like this person?"

"We do." She sat up and thumbed out a quick message. "Sorry, I'm just letting her know I'm out for the night also. There," she said. "All present and accounted for."

"Out of curiosity, did you tell her where you were?"

Briana smiled. "I didn't. But only because she's either asleep or will have a million questions." She scrunched her nose. "I'd rather handle that interrogation in person, quite frankly."

"Fair enough."

Briana stretched out next to her, and Dylan took the opportunity to appreciate her gorgeous body. She traced her outline from temple to hip. "You're beautiful." She saw her nipples harden. "Are you cold?"

"Not really."

"Do you want a shirt or something?"

"It's embarrassing."

"What is?"

"You look at me and my nipples get hard. It happens all the time. At work. At that fundraiser. Even at the basketball game that first day."

"Really?"

"Yes." Briana looked bashful and adorable when she nodded in confirmation. "That has never happened to me before."

"Well, that's fucking hot."

"I don't know why I'm telling you, because you clearly do not need an ego boost." She shrugged, seeming to give in to the moment. "You do have an effect on me, Dylan Prescott."

Dylan leaned forward and kissed her softly. "Just because there's no physical evidence, don't go thinking you're not making an impact on me."

"Is that so?"

"Yes." She nodded. "I'm pretty sure we're both doomed."

Briana turned on her side and baby spooned into Dylan. "Let's go to sleep. At least we'll be well rested when our lives fall apart."

"I knew you were the smart one," Dylan said, fully nuzzling as she let everything go, ready to drift into dreamland.

CHAPTER FOURTEEN

Is that fresh coffee?"

Briana had put on a T-shirt and old sweats that Dylan left folded on the edge of the bed. They were swimming on her, but she was grateful for both the gesture and having something to substitute for yesterday's skirt and blouse.

"Good morning." Dylan looked up from her iPad. "Did you sleep okay?"

Briana smiled and nodded in response. She had slept like a freaking baby. It was unusual because she usually hated not sleeping in her own apartment. But then, everything about last night was unpredictably divine. The conversation was easy, the bed cozy, the sex phenomenal.

"Thank you for the clothes," she said, pulling on the hem of the navy-blue shirt to look at the white NYPD lettering.

Dylan came around from the counter and kissed her. It was sweet and unexpected and made her melt just the tiniest bit. "My clothes are gigantic on you. But you look cute." She shrugged. "I thought you might not want to put on work clothes again."

"It was sweet. You're sweet," she said, not bothering to filter.

"You sound surprised by that," Dylan said with a laugh. "I think I should be offended."

She rubbed Dylan's abs over her soft sweatshirt. "I guess I am," she said honestly. "You're smart. You're sexy." She placed a kiss on Dylan's chest. "You're the neighborhood stud. I guess I didn't expect sweet too."

It was kind of a backhanded compliment, but it was out before she could massage it. Dylan seemed to take it in stride.

"Thank you?" Dylan said with a slight chuckle as she stepped away and reached for two coffee mugs. "I don't have skim milk. Is two percent okay?"

"Of course." Briana nodded at the news app still open on the tablet. "What's going on in the world? Anything exciting?"

"Nothing good, that's for sure." Dylan poured their coffees. "Are you hungry? I have fruit and yogurt. I could make toast, if you want."

"I can't eat first thing in the morning. Thank you, though." She reached for the sweetener and prepped her coffee. She sat on a stool and watched Dylan move around the kitchen. Dylan fixed her coffee, and Briana shook her head at the ridiculous amount of half-and-half she put in.

"Is there even any coffee in that mug?" she teased.

"Says the woman who drinks crème brûlée."

"You drink it too," she chided.

Dylan's look confirmed what Briana had always suspected. Dylan would have preferred a real cup of coffee most days. She opted for the flavored Keurig solely to be with her.

"I was thinking." Briana touched the smooth granite countertop with one finger, a little nervous over what she was about to suggest.

"What's up?" Dylan asked over her shoulder as she reached for some mixed berries from the fridge.

Damn, she was hot. Even zipping around her kitchen with bedhead and glasses on, in a hoodie and PJ pants. Seeing this semi-vulnerable side of the smooth detective who was always so squared away gave her a chill she didn't quite expect. Dylan popped a blueberry and touched her hand. "What is it? What were you thinking?"

"New rules," she blurted.

"Okay, I'm listening." Dylan shook the small ceramic bowl and picked out a strawberry.

Briana liked the way Dylan looked so serious and committed even though she didn't know what was coming. It didn't hurt that Dylan held her hand and gave it the smallest squeeze of encouragement.

"The thing is," she started, "I still believe everything we discussed." She sipped her coffee and dug deep for her words. "The reasons we shouldn't act on what we feel. Professionalism, respect, our careers. All of those things still ring true for me."

"I know."

"But we obviously both want this right now. At least I do," she said, putting her emotions on the line.

"I do too, Bri."

The shortened name. It was a familiarity that hit her right in the gut. Coupled with Dylan's soft smile that affirmed they were a hundred percent in this together. It sent her off the deep end in the best possible way.

"That's one of the things I liked about you from the very first time we met." She channeled bluntness to echo her point. "When we met the day of the basketball game, I told you I wasn't looking for a relationship."

"I remember."

"You didn't dismiss me. Or try to convince me otherwise."

"I actually agreed with you."

"Exactly." She gripped the warm mug with both hands. "We're on the same page as far as priorities are concerned. It's almost irresponsible to ignore that."

"That's what you liked about me? My priorities?"

Briana lifted her coffee to hide her expression. "Eh, you're not hard to look at."

Dylan pumped her fist in faux celebration.

Briana shook her head and laughed. Dylan was more than she expected in so many ways. Funny. Smart. Playful. The depth of her personality was a fantastic surprise.

"What I'm trying to get at"—she reached for Dylan's hand—"is that what we've stumbled into might be perfect." Briana hoped her thought process didn't sound premeditated. She traced the lines on Dylan's palm.

"A nonlabeled but exclusive arrangement while we work on cracking the most important case of our lives. Is that what you mean?"

Briana laughed at Dylan's description even though it was on the money.

"You made a point last night." Briana brought Dylan's hand to her lips and kissed a knuckle. "You said people might talk about us anyway."

"I just think people like to talk. To gossip. Sometimes it's accurate, sometimes not. I don't think we—or anyone—should make decisions based on what might be rumored now or in the future. That's all I meant."

"I agree with you. It's such a poignant observation."

"That's me. The poignant observer." Dylan winked.

"It kind of *is* you." Briana stopped to consider for a second. "Your observation got the case off the ground. You put it together that Benji and Paul were related. You figured out that Paul was in charge. You're intelligent and intuitive."

"I try." Dylan's smile was appreciative, but her eyes were focused on Briana's mouth.

"Are you going to kiss me?" she asked even though it broke the moment.

Dylan nodded and came around the island to plant the softest, most decadent kiss on her lips. It deepened, and she didn't fight it. Instead she ran her hand up to touch Dylan's buzzed hairline and felt her legs spread open to bring Dylan closer.

"Sorry." She felt Dylan's mouth below her ear, on her neck. "You complimenting me turns me on, apparently."

"I'll have to remember that."

"I interrupted you, though." Dylan dotted her nose with a kiss, dialing back the moment and stepping away. "Tell me about the new rules. Then remind me to tell you about Trevor."

"Is everything okay with him?"

"Yep. It's nothing. Work."

"Oh, okay." She sipped her coffee and prayed her idea came out normal. "Anyway. If we both want this, it is insane to deny ourselves. I mean, look what happened last night."

"I thought last night was pretty great."

"Of course, yes." Why was she botching this? She took a deep breath and tried again. "I meant before we came here. You left the city because I was talking to Dante. I had an aneurysm when I saw you with the Starbucks girl."

"That's called jealousy, by the way." Dylan stuck her tongue out, and instead of being annoyed, she was charmed by the silly act.

"I hate you."

"You don't. But go on."

"I just think we could drive ourselves crazy by not acting on what we feel. Despite my suggestion to the contrary a few weeks ago. I now see how abstaining is actually more distracting than pursuing this."

"I agree." Dylan's brow creased. "I feel a caveat coming on."

Briana's heart sank that Dylan anticipated it and seemed perturbed. "I just think we should be discreet."

"I think that's fair." It calmed her to see Dylan's expression relax. "Not to start an argument, but I've kind of been saying that all along."

"I know." Briana was more than a little nervous, and she picked at her manicure. "Can we please be very careful in the office? No touches, no looks, no nothing."

"Yes, Boss."

"Dylan, I mean it."

"I know, babe." Dylan leaned forward to give her a quick peck. "I'm just playing because you worry too much. But yes, discretion is fine with me."

"I also think we should be cautious around here."

Dylan looked around her apartment, apparently not following.

"In the neighborhood," she clarified. "We should be careful. New York is huge, but it's also small in so many ways." She saw Dylan's face sink. "Please don't be mad. I'm not trying to hide you."

"I know." Dylan straightened her back and cracked her neck. "I know you're right. I just like holding your hand. It's stupid."

"It's not." It was so incredibly sweet and unexpected. But completely taboo for what they were considering. "Come here," she said. "Hold my hand now."

Dylan accepted the offer and let Briana guide her into an embrace. Briana rubbed her strong shoulders and peppered her face with tiny kisses. "I'm sorry and I hate even suggesting we keep this hush-hush because it just feels…well, wrong. And I'm worried that I'm coming off bossy, and I'm not trying to be." She hoped she wasn't pushing Dylan away with her request. "I just think for right now, handling it this way is for the best."

"You're right," Dylan said. Briana liked the weight of Dylan's body in her arms. "I hate that you're right. But I know you are."

"What are you doing today?" she asked, thinking some daytime togetherness might make up for the secrecy of their union.

Dylan kissed her cheek and leaned back against the counter. "Today, I am putting in a new vanity for Mrs. Lemke."

"Your tenant?"

"No." Dylan shook her head. "Rose Lemke is my neighbor across the street."

"Ugh." Briana held a hand to her forehead. "Do I even want to know?"

"She's a seventy-year-old widow." Dylan laughed.

"Are you, like, her super or something?"

Dylan stuffed her hands into the pockets of her pants. "No." She reached back for more fruit. "She told me about a problem with her bathroom sink a week or so back. I offered to take a look at it for her. It was a bad leak, and it pretty much destroyed her cabinet. Rather than just replace the pipes, I suggested buying a new unit. She was going to pay for the install, but that's a rip-off. I told her I'd do it for her today."

"Will she pay you?"

"She'll try. I'm not going to take her money." She finished her coffee. "I will, however, let her send me home with a plate of pasta and meatballs, if she offers. Because that lady can cook."

"You're nice." Briana rubbed Dylan's stomach just because she wanted to touch, and they were in a safe place where they could. "Oh, hey, what did you want to tell me about Trevor?"

"Ah, that." Dylan reached for her hand. "Trevor asked me talk to you about the case."

"Oh?"

"Apparently he thinks I have some sway with you." Dylan ran one finger up her thigh. Her expression was all devious charm. "And after last night, I think he might be right."

"Dylan." She breathed her name in the sexiest voice she could muster and let Dylan's hand reach almost to her center before stopping her cold. "Don't do that. It's not funny."

Dylan's smile was enormous. "It's a little funny," she said.

Briana shook her head but kept the vibe light. "For real, what's up with the investigation?" She pulled Dylan close, still wanting contact.

"For real he's hoping I can convince you to consider the undercover operation at the Wine Bar."

"That's simple." She guided Dylan's hand down the front of her pants, knowing she was already super wet. "Get me some real PC and I'm all in."

Dylan's groan was guttural. "Yes, ma'am."

CHAPTER FIFTEEN

"We got it."

Briana looked up to see Dylan and Trevor in her doorway. They were both beaming and breathless.

"Did you two take the stairs up here?" she asked. She stood up and moved a box of discovery off a chair so both seats were open. "Sit down. Tell me what's got you both so excited you left the plant and came up to the dreaded legal office on the tenth floor."

One look at the sparkle in Dylan's ice blue eyes and she knew it was going to be good news. She'd learned a lot about Dylan in just a short few weeks since they'd made their clandestine arrangement official. First and foremost, Dylan's eyes revealed everything. They twinkled when she was giddy. She sported a mini eleven between her brows when she was stressed. Her pupils expanded when she was ready to make her move. And, God, her eyelids dropped closed one millisecond before the rest of her body stilled as she climaxed.

Work.

She was at work and needed to compartmentalize. She could have these decadent thoughts all she wanted when she was at home. Or at Dylan's. On the subway, even. She even gave herself a little leeway for daydreaming during administrative staff meetings that had little to do with casework. But right now she needed to get a handle on herself.

"What's going on?" She made sure to look at Trevor as much as Dylan. "Enlighten me."

"We got some good stuff on Benji's phone just now." Trevor leaned all the way forward in his chair, racing through the details. "He says to Paul, we'll come up by you on Seventy-Second. That's the Wine Bar. On Seventy-Second and First Avenue. This is going to be it."

"Okay. I have a few questions," she said, hoping to slow him down a little. She looked at Dylan to fill in the gaps.

"Dom and Karrakas have been on Benji all week," Dylan said, dusting off her jeans. "He's done very little. George has been dropping off to his regulars. But when we follow them at night and on the weekends, they tend to go to college raves, frat parties. Places where it's hard for us to blend in."

"Okay."

"We think that's where they're hitting up the college crowd. Benji started to say something on the phone. He was on with Paul, and he said something about needing to restock because *the kids like to party.*" Dylan put air quotes around the phrase. "Paul shut him down right away and directed them to come up to see him at the bar on the East Side to discuss business. We're pretty sure he's referencing the Wine Bar."

"When?"

"It was going to be tonight, but it's George's grandmother's birthday."

"I love their family loyalty." Briana shook her head. "Is there a rain date?"

"Tomorrow night it looks like." Dylan's smile was so confident and proud it made her happy inside. Which stood in complete contrast to how she felt about the green light she knew she felt compelled to give.

"You want my support on the undercover operation, I assume?"

"Briana, I really think it could be good for the case." Trevor was almost pleading, but it was hardly necessary. She knew it was time.

"Nieves is going to call you. We wanted you to hear it from us first." Dylan was so sincere. She followed their rules. She never blurred the lines at work. Briana simply hated the idea of Dylan being in any kind of danger even if the chances of things going awry were slim.

"All right." Briana tried to stay positive as she reminded herself that Dylan was smart and savvy. If this was anyone else, she would be thrilled at the development. "Let's do it," she said, verbalizing her decision on the spot and avoiding the risk of allowing emotion to cloud her judgment.

"Awesome." Trevor clapped his knees in excitement. He stood quickly. "We gotta jet. We're going to meet the tech guys to see what the options are to wire up Dylan and Trish."

Ugh. Trish. She'd almost forgotten about that part. *It's just work*, she said to herself trying to block out the image of Dylan and Trish pretending to be a couple. "Great work, you two." She caught Dylan's eye as she was about to leave. "Dylan."

Dylan turned, and her expression was full of care and gratitude and something else she couldn't readily identify. It took every ounce of restraint not to step into her space just to feel the safety of her arms. "Be careful," Briana said as blandly as possible.

The smile that Dylan levied melted her on the spot.

"Always."

Briana handed a Spanish onion to Dylan. "Will you do this one when you're done?"

"Of course," Dylan said as she took it and put it next to the peppers on the chopping block. "Quick question." Dylan bumped her hip. "Are you going to look at me at all tonight?"

It was cute that she was trying to keep the mood light, but Briana knew Dylan was attuned to her energy.

"I mean, I'm happy to eat stir-fry and not talk about it, but you seem upset, and I want to allay your fears." Dylan ducked in and stole a kiss. "And I want to a-lay you later."

Dylan laughed at her own cheesy pun, but Briana could barely crack a smile.

"Wow. You are tough tonight." Dylan returned to chopping.

Briana reached for the cubed veggies and added them to the pan. "I'm sorry, Dylan." She stirred the chicken, knowing she was being ridiculous. "This whole thing just has me...stressed, I guess."

"Come here." Dylan hugged her from behind and leaned back against the island. "Babe, talk to me. Please?" Briana always loved the feel of Dylan's arms around her, but right now it didn't have its usual calming effect.

"It's not going to make a difference."

"This is because of what we talked about today. The undercover operation tomorrow night?"

Briana reached forward to lower the flame on dinner and turned to face Dylan. "I know it's stupid. I'm being irrational."

"I didn't say that."

"It's true, though."

"Can I ask you a question?"

She nodded.

"If it was Trevor or Ahmed going in, would you feel this way?"

She ran a finger along Dylan's belt, stopping an inch from her holstered firearm as she thought about her response. She was a cautious attorney. She was hands-on with all her cases. She considered every move thoroughly before making decisions.

"I would always be concerned about something with so much margin for error," she said. "When there's a chance of officers being discovered or, God forbid, getting hurt."

"I know. You care. Everyone knows that about you." Dylan hunched a little to meet her gaze. "That's not what I asked." Briana felt Dylan's hands on her hips. "If it wasn't me going in, would you be this stressed?"

"But it is you."

"Exactly." There was a second of silence and Briana knew Dylan was waiting for eye contact. She couldn't resist even if she wanted to. "Bri," Dylan said, using the nickname she loved. "I'm a better cop than Ahmed. I know that sounds obnoxious." She shrugged and looked a little embarrassed to be touting herself. "Don't get me wrong. He's great. The whole team is. But when it comes to this kind of field work, I'm good. You should trust me. Even Trevor. He's the best. But he knows I've got this. Because I do." Dylan caressed her arms. "It's going to be fine. I swear."

It was crazy that just hearing Dylan boast made her feel better. It was like her confidence was contagious, and while she wasn't totally relaxed, there was something in Dylan's words and demeanor that made her believe it was going to be all right.

A few feet away the door opened, and the backdraft sucked whatever tension remained right out into the corridor as Stef entered the apartment.

"Look at you cuties," she said, joining them for a group hug and placing a kiss on each of their cheeks. "You guys are freaking adorable," she said.

Briana raised her eyebrows. "That's funny, because we were just fighting."

"If this is how you guys fight…" Stef widened her eyes but let the sentence drop off. It didn't matter—her implication came through loud and clear. "What's for dinner?" she asked.

"Stir-fry," Briana said. She gave Dylan's butt a playful smack. "If Detective Prescott ever finishes chopping the vegetables."

The rest of the night was fine. Dinner was delicious. The company, even better. Briana loved the way Dylan had turned her mood a hundred and eighty degrees with a simple honest conversation. It was direct and refreshing and everything she always wanted in a relationship. Not that she was saying this was a relationship. What had they defined it as? An exclusive, noncommittal liaison? Damn if she could remember the label they'd settled on.

All she knew was that it felt good and right and balanced.

In the quiet of her bedroom, she heard Dylan's even breath, the sign she was out cold. Dylan was predictable like that. The second she came, she was wiped. For some reason, Briana found it endearing. Perhaps it was because she was always well taken care of by then. Or maybe it was the sheer knowledge that she was able to make Dylan lose control with her.

Briana smiled in the dark, thinking it was likely both.

She liked how selfless Dylan was, how thoughtful. She appreciated the grand gestures—the walks home, the daily case updates. But she was a sucker for the little acts too. The way Dylan made sure the work fridge never ran out of skim milk and always had some at her house these days. The fact that her cabinets were stocked with her favorite treats: pistachios and trail mix and Sour Patch Kids.

Dylan cared about her. And the feeling was mutual. Briana looked forward to morning coffee at the plant. She loved that Dylan was the last person she communicated with on the nights they spent apart. She indulged in every minute they were together in either her apartment or Dylan's, where they could be open and free to kiss and touch.

Holy shit.

She could give it any phony description she wanted. Dylan was her girlfriend. Her secret girlfriend, but most definitely her girlfriend.

It happened so naturally she could hardly pinpoint when things had moved out of the casual zone and into something more defined. More importantly, for the first time in forever, she was absolutely elated with the shift.

CHAPTER SIXTEEN

W e're spread all over out here." Trevor's voice was even, but
Dylan picked up on just the slightest bit of tension in his delivery.

She didn't have a whole lot of time to talk him off the ledge, so she gave him a sturdy "10-4," in hopes that less was more. "I'll see you on the other side, brother," she said, ending the conversation and turning to Trish.

"You ready?" Without waiting for an answer, Dylan took Trish's hand and strode into the Wine Bar.

She was full of confidence and anticipation. And honestly, there was really no reason to be nervous. Conversations intercepted over the wire had told them George and Benji were traveling together in Rivas's Maxima. Twenty minutes earlier the surveillance team had followed George's car to the location and watched both men enter the establishment.

The objective for tonight was simple. Get eyes inside. Have a drink. Anything beyond that was gravy.

Dylan had studied photos on the Wine Bar's website in addition to whatever images she could dig up on popular review forums. Even though that research had provided a good sense of the interior layout, Dylan was unprepared for how quaint and intimate the establishment was. There were a few small tables, but the bar was wide open. George and Benji were sitting at one end with Paul. Dylan went straight for an open spot in the middle of the bar.

"What do you want, babe?" she asked, playing it up.

"I don't know," Trish responded as she perused the wine list. "Are you going to do red or white? Or are you going to be boring and order a beer?"

The bartender laughed and stepped close to wait on them. "Good evening, folks. How are we tonight?"

"Good, thanks." Dylan looked around pretending to admire the ambiance as she absorbed every last detail of the space.

"Are you wine drinkers? Or would you like some suggestions?"

"I made her come in here." Trish nudged her playfully. "We were on our way home, but this place looked so cute, and I said we had to stop for a drink. It's so cozy."

The bartender smiled. "I'll be sure to tell the owner you said so." He ticked his head toward Paul. "He's sitting over there." He leaned forward and spent a decent amount of time explaining the various wines listed, finishing by saying they were free to start with a sample if they didn't want to commit. "We also have a nice selection of beer if that's more your speed," he said to Dylan.

"Nah, I'm here. When in Rome, as they say." She picked a Californian blend that was reasonably priced. She'd barely listened to his spiel because she was trying to focus on the conversation a few feet away.

Trish pointed to an Italian vintage he'd recommended, and he nodded amiably. "I'll get those right away."

As he worked, Dylan and Trish chatted like they were a regular couple. Even though they had coordinated backstories to draw upon, it wasn't necessary. And truthfully, Dylan knew it was better to keep it simple. They knew each other well enough to find common ground. Dylan steered the conversation to a singing competition show Trish's favorite contestant had just been booted from.

The banter was light and lively but bland enough that she could half listen and still make observations.

So far, there was no smoking gun. While she imagined their targets were talking business, they spoke low and in hushed tones. No money or product had exchanged hands. Trish was seated with her back to the guys, and Dylan faced her, hoping her angle created a good vantage point for the pinhole camera secreted in her clothing. She knew it wasn't much. They could be discussing sports or politics, but her gut told her this place was HQ, and they were ironing out details of their operation.

After almost fifteen minutes, the only other couple at the bar departed, leaving the Wine Bar empty, save for their subjects and them. Dylan felt her back tighten with just the tiniest amount of excitement and stress, confident this was it. The moment she'd been anxiously anticipating. An opening for Benji and George to chat them up, to gawk at them, to give it their best shot.

But it was Paul who made the move. Making eye contact, he offered a nod and the hint of a smile, slightly raising his glass in a way that signaled both appreciation for their patronage but also a kind of sovereignty over his domain. Dylan suppressed her eye roll and replaced it with an expression of eager gratitude. It was fucking perfect, and Paul couldn't resist the opportunity to play king. He hopped off his stool and headed toward them.

This was going to be interesting.

"Hello, ladies." Paul sized them up deliberately, and Dylan looked right into his dark brown eyes. An arrogant smile completed his polished look. He gestured toward the bartender, who was filling an order. "Simon tells me this is your first time here," he said. "I hope you're having a nice night. Enjoying your drinks."

"Yeah, it's great." Dylan raised her glass in support of her statement. Next to her Trish stiffened. Dylan covered her knee to convey it was all good.

"I'm Paul. The owner." He was too comfortable. "Please tell me if there's anything you need."

The notion that Paul would be the one to take an interest in them was one Dylan hadn't really anticipated, but presented with direct access, her mind raced for the best way to leverage the opportunity.

"I think we're good." Dylan looked at Trish to be sure, the way she would check in with Briana if she was on a real date.

"Did you have dinner next door?" he asked. He clearly wasn't going away, and Dylan knew that meant one thing. He was vetting them. As cops or customers, she wasn't sure.

"Is the Italian restaurant next door connected to this place?" she said answering his question with one of her own. If they were doing this, she was in.

He looked over his shoulder at the arched doorway she'd noticed in the back. "It is, yes." He grin was broad and toothy and smug as fuck. "Wine Bar operates independently. However, we also serve as Victor's service bar."

"Ah," she said. "Makes sense."

"They have a delicious menu. If you're interested, I can see if there's a table."

"We actually ate earlier. We sort of stopped here spur of the moment."

"Do you live in the neighborhood?"

"Downtown," Dylan said. "FiDi."

"The financial district. This is a trek for you."

"We like to go out to dinner." She reached for Trish's hand subtly. "Can't be taking her to the same spots over and over. Gotta keep it interesting, you know." She added a wink. "We checked out the Afghani place down the street."

"I saw it got a fantastic write-up recently. Tell me, how was it?"

"Really good." Dylan put on a good show. "I kept it simple, though. I ordered a chicken kabob dish that came with jasmine rice."

Paul focused his attention on Trish. "And what about you, dear?" *Dear.* Gag.

"Oh, I got the same thing." Trish didn't miss a beat, and Dylan squeezed her thigh in discreet praise. "It was yummy, though."

"Are you enjoying the wine?"

"It's nice," Trish said.

"Paul, we're gonna hit it," Benji called out as he stood to put on his jacket.

"Sit down," Paul ordered. "We still have some business to go over."

Fuck if Benji didn't stop dead in his tracks. "Hurry up, cuz. We want to go out."

"Relax yourself, Goldenballs." Oh my God, they got an actual *Goldenballs* reference. Dylan laughed out loud, even though Paul was obviously showing off for them.

"Let me guess," she said. "Little brother?"

"Baby cousin." Paul gave her the information she already knew, but she nodded in deference to his authority.

"So that makes him the junior partner here?"

"No." Paul shook her off. "I'm an attorney." He reached in his breast pocket and handed them a business card from his law firm. Cocky motherfucker. "This"—he looked around the Wine Bar—"is just for fun." A place to wash the drug money, more like.

"So, wait." Dylan shook her head in faux disbelief. She looked down the bar at Benji and George. "You guys are all lawyers?" Dylan wiggled her eyebrows at Trish. "Babe, I think we just hit the jackpot."

Paul laughed at her stupid humor. "Are you in need of representation?" he joked.

"Not yet, thank God." She looked at the sky, faking gratitude. "But they say everyone should have at least one lawyer on their side. I'm hoping we just scored three."

Paul clapped her shoulder jovially. She loved that he was getting comfortable with her. "Sorry to burst your bubble. But my cousin and his friend just do odd jobs for me. As far as legal advice goes, you're stuck with me."

"One's better than none, right?" She continued the spirited back and forth, hoping Paul might drop his guard even further. "Your card says you work in Princeton. Don't tell me you come all the way here from Jersey."

"It's really not so bad if you know the right time to travel. I've mastered the science of knowing when traffic flows and when the turnpike is going to be a virtual parking lot," he said with a smug laugh. Transporting narcotics across state lines. Dylan nodded, pretending to care as she mentally checked off another chargeable offense.

"What do you do for work…?" Paul paused, waiting for her to introduce herself.

"Dylan." She extended her hand. "Dylan Burke," she said, using the fake surname that matched the department-issued fictitious ID in her wallet. "This is my girlfriend, Trish."

"Whoa, whoa, whoa." George put his beer down with a thud. "You guys are, like, actual lesbians?"

"George." Paul leered at him.

"Bro. I'm not saying anything bad. I think it's cool. You guys are both hot."

Dylan saw Benji elbow him to shut up.

"Knock it off," Paul scolded. "My apologies on behalf of that Neanderthal." He rolled his eyes, but in the moment Benji had gotten up and joined them.

"Sorry about that. George can be a jerk." Benji signaled between himself and Paul. "Our aunt's a lesbian. We get it. We're allies."

The fuck was happening here?

Dylan wasn't sure she understood exactly. But one thing was clear. She and Trish were directly engaged in conversation with Paul and Benji Goldenballs Rafferty.

"I'm sorry. I'm sorry. Geez, I didn't mean it in a bad way." Enter George Rivas with semi-heartfelt goodwill that was mostly defense.

"It's cool." Dylan held her hands up to stop the circle of apology. "We're all good." She reached for Trish's hand. "We should go, though."

"Good job, Rivas. Scaring away customers. That's great for word of mouth."

"Nah, man, it's fine. Honest." Dylan waved him off like it was no big deal.

"Hold on." Paul snapped his fingers for the bartender's attention. "Simon, pass me the book." Simon handed over a big ledger. Paul started writing as he spoke. "I know you paid with a credit card before, and it's actually kind of a hassle to reverse the charges on booze. So please, take this as a token of our goodwill." Paul handed her a gift certificate. "You can use it here. Or next door at Victor's. Your choice. It's the least I can do."

Fifty bucks. She accepted the graciousness with a handshake. It was almost a nice gesture, but more important than that, it was an invite to come back. And that was a home-fucking-run.

❖

Dylan was still on a high from the success of the night and she rode the wave of adrenaline right to Briana's front door.

"Is it okay that I came by?" she asked as Briana stood aside to welcome her in. "I just really wanted to see you."

"Of course." Briana offered her a quick peck on the lips, and Dylan saw that she was wearing her NYPD T-shirt. It was enough to get her going.

"I like you in my clothes." Dylan placed her bag on the floor so she could deliver a proper hello. She held Briana's face and kissed her for real. "I like you out of my clothes too," she said with a wink.

"Oh, I know." Briana played along but took her hand and guided them to the couch in the living room.

Dylan looked around and noticed most of the lights were off. It was almost eleven. "Were you sleeping? I didn't wake you, did I?" she asked, letting one question flow right into the other.

"No." Briana shook her off with a sweet smile. "I was getting ready to go to bed, though. I figured you might be going out with everyone afterward to celebrate the success of the operation. I was secretly hoping I'd hear from you." She shrugged. It was so cute. "This is way better than a text, I have to admit."

"You heard the good news?"

Dylan wasn't sure how Nieves or Hollander had been able to bring Briana in the loop already. After all, the undercover operation had just finished. Afterward, everything was so harried between having the tech guys take off her recording device and downloading the audio and video while she and Trish debriefed their bosses and Trevor. There'd barely been time to think, let alone process and consider the next steps.

"I was there." Briana traced a finger over Dylan's favorite song lyric tattooed inside her forearm. "In the plant," she added for clarity.

"No way. Really?"

Briana nodded, and Dylan felt her heart race. It was thrilling to know Briana had witnessed her in action. Doing what she did best. Being sly and covert and collecting intel. At the same time, Briana's presence meant she was privy to every touch and term of endearment she employed to pass as a couple with Trish.

"Bri," she said, mindful not to use any of the same terminology. "The stuff with Trish...it was just for show. You know that, right?"

"I know."

Dylan touched her gorgeous face. "I know you know. But it is the truth."

"I only left the plant once I knew you were out of danger." Briana turned her face to kiss her hand. "You were really great, Dylan." She seemed genuine and supportive. "Not that I'm surprised," she added. "Still, it was impressive to watch. Nerve-racking, but impressive."

"Aw. Were you worried about me?" Dylan let her voice lilt to keep things light.

"Jerk." Briana slapped her good-naturedly. "You know I was."

"You just have to trust me," Dylan said.

"It's not you I have doubts about."

Briana's expression was suddenly serious, and Dylan wondered what percentage of her concern was over the perps they'd infiltrated, and how much had to do with the Trish charade. Either way, the topic seemed closed for the moment.

"You're going to stay, right?" Briana asked. She'd returned to caressing her forearm and outlining her tattoos. It was driving her crazy in the best way. But the question threw her a little.

"Is that okay?" Dylan stilled her hand and intertwined their fingers. "I want to."

Briana rested her head on the back of the couch. Her eyes were beautiful and inviting when she nodded assent. "I want you to stay. I'm never sure if you need to be at home since you're the landlord and all. I didn't want to get my hopes up if this was just a pop in."

"You're stuck with me." She tilted her head to copy Briana's position on the sofa so they were more or less eye to eye.

"Good." Briana shifted her stare to the kitchen behind them. "Are you hungry or anything?"

"I'm fine," Dylan said, oddly touched by the simple offer.

"Come, then." Briana stood and led the way to her bedroom. "Even though I'm up to speed, I still want to hear all the details."

Could this really get any better? Briana was hot and smart and thoughtful. She cared about Dylan, and she was interested in the case. She asked pertinent questions. The best part was that Dylan was free to answer them. If she had been lying next to anyone else, she would have been compelled to gloss over the facts and give a redacted version of the events.

In a tank and boxers, Dylan stared at the ceiling, picturing everything, as she gave a thorough play-by-play. She included details about how the three guys were dressed and where they were sitting when she arrived. She heard excitement in her own voice when she went over the Wine Bar's layout and lighting and where she thought might be an effective place to put a stationary eavesdropping device.

"You'll have to go back in." Briana didn't sound entirely thrilled at the prospect as her fingers made absentminded squares over her abs. "Your intel is great, but it's not quite enough for a bug yet."

Dylan hoped that Briana's resistance came solely from a legal perspective and nothing else. "We did get an invite." She winced in anticipation of Briana's reaction to yet another fake date with Detective Trish Suarez.

"Ugh. Don't remind me." Briana rolled on top of her and sat up in a straddle, smirking and writhing on top of her. "Try not to propose to Trish at the Wine Bar if you can help it."

"Anything for you." Dylan moved with her even though she wasn't ready for action just yet. "I'll only buy a ring if it's absolutely necessary."

"Not funny," Briana said. But she was giggling in spite of her words, and Dylan loved that they could joke like this.

Dylan flipped them, so she was on top. She covered Briana's face with kisses. "I'll be right back," she said, bouncing up to hit the bathroom before things got good.

"Don't be too long," Briana called after her. "Or I'll be forced to start without you."

Dylan swallowed her laugh as she headed down the hall. After a quick pit stop, she breezed into the kitchen and reached into the fridge for two waters, thinking about her spirited repartee with Briana and the fun they were about to have.

"Whoa, my bad."

The voice surprised her, but mostly because it was too deep to belong to Briana or Stef. She turned around and shut the refrigerator door, using the water as a pathetic modesty shield.

"Holy shit."

There was no amount of warning that would have prepared Dylan to see her old friend. Because truthfully any kind of heads-up would have led to her avoiding this situation altogether. But right now, in her semi-compromised condition in Briana's apartment, there was no way out.

"JJ." She stood ramrod straight. "This is...not where I expected to bump into you," she said, trying to sound chill.

"Yeah, same." JJ gave her a full once-over and nodded as though she was evaluating some kind of invisible progress. She rested her elbows on the kitchen island, clearly ready for some bro time, apparently not giving one shit that they were both in their underwear. "You look good. Tell me, how have you been, Junior?"

Junior. Jill Jessup couldn't resist being a dick for two seconds.

"Good." Dylan nodded with her chin. "I was, uh…just, um…" She pointed to Briana's room with one water bottle, furious that JJ was killing her vibe.

"I see that." JJ picked a pistachio from a bowl on the counter and shelled it, popping the nut into her mouth. "Briana Logan," she said with a disgusting amount of shock-infused pride. "That's a score for you. I'm impressed."

"Still the same JJ."

Over the years, Dylan had spent enough time with Jill Jessup to know what she was all about. JJ was…something. Brilliant, suave, funny. Women practically threw themselves at her. And she could be fun to hang with. Always ready with a killer story and an open tab. Dylan got it. More than once she'd reaped the benefits of JJ's generosity. Everyone loved the life of the party.

But after the lights came up, JJ could also be rude, elitist, and insufferably arrogant. To her, in particular. In the end Dylan drifted away, deciding free drinks and funny anecdotes weren't worth a lifetime of condescension.

"I went for the roommate. Stef," JJ added, as though she'd had a choice between the two women. Her sense of entitlement was infuriating. "Anyway, I should get back in there. Any chance you could snag me a few waters?"

"You can take these," Dylan said, mostly to end the interaction.

JJ swiped them readily. "Thanks, Dylan. See you in the morning, kid," she said as she walked away and waved over her head with one of the bottles.

Dylan was so stunned she forgot to get replacement waters before hightailing it back to Briana's bedroom.

"I was getting ready to send out a search party. Everything okay?"

Briana held the sheet over her naked torso as she sat up in bed. Dylan resisted the urge to kiss her beautiful chest.

"I don't know how to say this, so I'm just going to say it." Dylan sat on the side of the bed with her back to Briana, mostly to resist temptation.

Briana leaned over and switched on the bedside lamp, clearly sensing the urgency. Dylan relaxed into her body pressed up against her back. She felt Briana place a kiss on her bare shoulder. "What's wrong?"

"I ran into Stef's new girlfriend, or whatever they are." Dylan actually had no idea if JJ and Stef were exclusively dating or just casually hooking up. She only knew how much Briana worried about Stef's tendency to fall too fast, to trust too readily, and Dylan felt an obligation to be forthcoming. "This person she's seeing." She felt Briana's arm drape across her shoulders, and she shifted so she could face her. "Bri, she's a total player. Like a real heartbreaker. A stud. A dog. Whatever term you want to use."

Briana smiled and kissed her. It was not the reaction she was expecting. "I guess you know JJ."

"You're not surprised," Dylan said.

"I'm not." Briana scrunched her nose. "I introduced them."

Her head was going to explode. "Wait. You know JJ?"

"I've known Jill Jessup for a long time." Briana shut the light off and scooted over on the bed to make room. "Lie down with me." She patted the mattress lightly, and Dylan took the invitation to be close. "JJ was a seasoned AUSA when I was first on staff at the office. She was somewhat of a mentor to me. Our paths have crossed over the years since then."

Dylan felt her heart drop into her stomach.

"Professionally," Briana clarified. "Trust me, I know how JJ is."

"And yet, you want this to happen?" Dylan's head was still spinning.

Briana kissed the corner of her mouth. "Stef's a big girl. She knows what she's getting into with JJ." Dylan felt Briana's hand brush over her chest, and her pulse regulated at the smooth touch. "I have more concerns when she goes in blind and expects true love."

"Whew." Dylan let her concerns go with a full exhale. "That was easier than I thought."

"You're sweet to be worried about Stef." Dylan felt Briana's hand slide over her boxers. "How did I get so lucky?" Briana teased. "Landing the ace detective with the heart of gold."

Briana straddled her again and Dylan throbbed in response. "I'm still not shipping them as hard as you are," she said. "But if you say all's good"—she held her palms up in surrender—"who am I to argue?"

"Baby," Briana breathed out the word, and her sexy whisper combined with the way she was moving sent Dylan into a different kind of tailspin, "is there a reason we're still talking about them?"

Nope. There was no good reason at all.

CHAPTER SEVENTEEN

It's dead here.

Dylan sent the text to Briana as she swiveled in her chair to look around at the empty plant. She knew Briana was busy with her family and didn't expect an immediate response, but she was happy when one came.

When will you get to your mom's?

Nieves wants the phones monitored until 12, just to be sure there's no makeup session this am.

Last night had been a complete bust.

All week the three stooges had talked on the phone about a Wednesday night meeting at the Wine Bar to discuss business before the holiday weekend. The team was amped. Dylan and Trish were ready to use their gift certificate, backed by the excuse of treating themselves to a pre-Thanksgiving night out. They figured it was totally plausible a couple might want a date night before a weekend traditionally loaded with family. But then in the eleventh hour, just before they were set to head to the Wine Bar, Paul called off the meeting with Benji and George, citing a last-minute family emergency. Something about having to pick up his wife's cousin from the airport.

With the undercover mission aborted, the team went for drinks together to pay tribute to each other and months of hard work. Even though Dylan had only been with the investigation for part of that time, she felt like an integral part of the family.

When Briana showed, Dylan knew it was to see her.

Despite not being able to really be together, they still connected. Dylan stole glances, and her fingertips tingled when she discreetly touched Briana's back. She knew Briana could feel it. Even apart they were fire. The only problem was that Trish wanted to stay in character with Dylan. Even though it was just for a laugh, Dylan wanted no part of it. But the guys played along with Trish, yukking it up and making jokes. Dylan's spirit sank when she registered Briana's anguish over the farce. The problem was she felt powerless to nix it completely without making it a huge deal. Instead she downplayed it as much as possible and hoped her good intentions counted for something. There was no way to know really because when Briana left early to catch the Long Island Railroad to her parents' house, there was no opportunity for a personal good-bye of any kind.

It's almost 12. Briana's message came through with a series of celebratory emojis and one heart. *I can't wait to see you. Rush through dinner with your family, please. LOL.*

Briana missed her. She could tell. Or maybe that was her own emotion she was tapping into so strongly right now. Less than twenty-four hours had passed, but she couldn't wait to see Briana. She almost wished she could bypass Cynthia and Kevin altogether.

I'll hurry, she typed back, knowing it was the truth.

Earlier in the week she and Briana had made a plan to travel back from their respective Thanksgiving dinners together, after everyone had put in ample face time with their relatives. At the time, Briana had insisted that Dylan agree to stop in for a bit to meet her family and have a piece of her mom's famous pumpkin pie. She didn't need convincing. Any time with Briana was a bonus in her opinion.

Now sitting at the Logan family dining room table with Briana's hand on her thigh beneath the tabletop, she was still in no rush to get home. The pumpkin pie was awesome, the company delightful. Briana's family sat around drinking coffee and wine and talked about New York, politics, work, and pop culture. Her mom and dad asked questions and told stories about Briana and her younger sister, Brittany. It was warm and welcoming. Honestly, amazing.

It was almost eight o'clock when Briana stood to get their jackets.

"Are you girls really going to drive back to Brooklyn tonight?" Briana's dad seemed genuinely dismayed at the thought. "Why don't you stay? Brittany and Ted are staying. Come on," he said, trying to coax them. "We can play Left, Right, Center or Thirty-one."

"Pete. Give the girls a break. If they want to go back, let them go back." Mrs. Logan waved her husband off and smiled. Dylan caught her look at Briana. "Do what you want, honey. Your dad just misses you." She signaled Mr. Logan to help her in the kitchen.

"Come on, Briana, stay." Brittany was positively enthusiastic. "It'll be fun." Even her boyfriend Ted got in on the push with two spirited thumbs-up.

Dylan looked at Briana and suddenly felt like the sole holdout. She squeezed Briana's hand. "Bri, do you want to stay?"

"No, baby. I feel bad. I hadn't thought of it before, and you probably want to get home. It's fine."

"I'll do whatever you want." It wasn't just that Briana called her *baby*, which made her swoon. She was happy to spend time with Briana anywhere, and if this was where she wanted to be tonight, that was just fine with her.

"Really?" Briana pulled them into the pseudo-privacy of the front foyer to study her face. "Are you sure?"

"Yes."

Briana's expression was exuberant, and Dylan was pleased to be partially responsible. "Do you have to work tomorrow?" Briana asked.

"No." Dylan smiled. "That's the trade-off for working the holiday. Do you?"

"Nope."

"So it's settled, then."

"And you're sure you're okay with this?" Briana was so sincere it melted her.

"I am," she said honestly. "I like seeing you happy. And I like being with you." She shrugged. "If I have to sacrifice one night of sleeping next to you, it's worth it."

"Who's sacrificing that?" Briana seemed legit confused by her statement.

"I just meant...you know, being here at your parents' house—"

Briana cut her off with a kiss. "Dylan, I'm thirty-two years old. My parents aren't naive. We're sharing a room. And a bed." She bit her lip seductively. "What happens beyond that"—she raised one eyebrow in a sort of taunt—"well, that's entirely up to you."

❖

Everything about the night was perfect in ways Dylan didn't expect. She laughed her head off playing dice and cards with the Logan clan. She ate second round turkey at ten p.m. Mr. and Mrs. Logan asked her about her life and her job, and Briana bragged about her investigative prowess and how she could fix just about anything. Briana's family was fun and nice, but the best part was Briana never stopped touching her. Right up to and including the hushed, yet oddly intimate sex they had in the guest bedroom when everyone had called it a night.

It was all wonderful and sweet and charming and fun, and the awesome vibe carried right into midmorning, as Dylan sipped coffee in the unseasonably warm weather on the Logans' back deck. Briana sat next to her in an oversized hoodie, her hair a touch wild and sexy as hell.

"Are you itching to get home?" Briana broke off a piece of croissant and offered it to her.

"Not really," Dylan said. She looked down at yesterday's jeans. "Only to be in clean clothes," she said with a shrug. "Other than that, I'm in no rush."

"I could see if my dad has something that fits you. Or Ted."

It was a thoughtful gesture, but unnecessary. And it wouldn't work anyway. She was taller than Ted and skinnier than Mr. Logan. "It's cool." She kissed Briana's temple. "If you can deal with looking at recycled me, I can deal for a while longer."

"I can't ever stop looking at you." Briana hooked her arm and scooched closer. "It's sort of a problem." Briana widened her eyes in a kind of playful self-scolding. She ran her hands through Dylan's hair and pulled it gently in the way she loved. She was looking right at her. Studying her. Gratuitously, it seemed. Dylan didn't mind. In fact, she loved that they were outside in the light of day, under a gorgeous blue sky, and were able to be together. It was refreshing.

As if Briana read her mind she asked, "Would you be up for a walk on the boardwalk?"

"Definitely," Dylan said. "What were you thinking? Long Beach?"

Briana smiled and nodded. "It's only a fifteen-minute drive from here. And it's so warm out. Seems crazy not to take advantage."

"Sounds perfect." Dylan looked at her mouth and was tempted to lean in for a kiss but resisted since they were in her parents' backyard.

"You want to kiss me," Briana said, reading her thoughts again.

"Always." There seemed no point in pretending it wasn't the truth.

Briana didn't smile or tease. She simply touched her face and brought their lips together with the softest, most delicate touch.

On the surface the moment was small, inconsequential. But inside Dylan felt the shift. It wasn't scary or stressful like she'd always expected it to be. On the contrary, she felt light and free and complete, and she didn't fight it or try to talk herself out of it. She simply held Briana's hand and let her heart go completely.

Ninety minutes later, they strolled the Long Beach boardwalk hand in hand, both in awe of the balmy sea air so late in the season.

"How was your mom's yesterday?" Briana said. "I never really asked."

"It was fine. Cynthia was very...Cynthia." Dylan laughed, knowing her bizarre response would elicit questions.

"Wait. Do you call your mom Cynthia?"

"Sometimes. It drives her crazy. I sorta do it to tease her."

"Does she get mad?"

"Not mad, really. She knows I'm mostly playing."

"Mostly?"

"She was a kid when she had me." Dylan shrugged. "My grandparents were really the ones who raised me. It's not a secret for either of us." Dylan loved her mom, but their relationship had never felt maternal. "Cynthia and I"—she paused to select her words carefully— "we have a nice bond. She feels more like an older sister than anything else. It's nice. Special, even. Just not mom-ish, if that makes sense."

"What about your dad? Do you talk to him?"

"He passed away," she said.

"Dylan, I'm so sorry. I didn't know."

"It's okay. I didn't really know him that well."

"What happened? Can I ask?"

"You can ask me anything," Dylan said. It was crazy, but she didn't think there was anything she wouldn't be willing to share with Briana. "Bobby Prescott," she said, recognizing an unusual nostalgia in her tone. "He was around a bit when I was a baby. But I think I more remember pictures of him, than actually him. Do you know what I mean?"

"I can understand that." Briana squeezed her hand, and maybe Dylan imagined it, but she felt the support stream through her body.

"I remember once when I was in high school. He had gotten clean. He wanted to see me. To connect. He came by the house. It was nice. He was nice."

"He had a problem with drugs?"

Dylan nodded. She'd never told anyone. Not her friends. Not coworkers. No one she'd ever dated. It wasn't that she was embarrassed. It was simply that she'd never felt close enough to anyone to really share the complicated mix of shame, pity, and love she felt for a man she'd hardly known.

"He and my mom continued to date after I was born. He even lived with us for a bit." She chewed her lip, remembering the narrative she'd been told. "When I was around three, he fell in with a bad crowd." She hunched her shoulders. "It was all downhill from there."

"Baby, I am so sorry." Briana kissed her shoulder.

"It's okay," she said. It felt good to talk about her father with Briana. Cathartic and respectful at the same time. "I think his life was a roller coaster. In and out of rehab. Relapse, recovery. Ultimately, he died of an overdose. He tried, though. Multiple times. Gotta give him credit for that."

"He made you. I'd like to say his life was of value if only for that. And yeah, I mean that selfishly for me." Briana stopped walking and Dylan paused with her.

"This was his." Dylan pulled out the St. Michael medal she never took off. "He was wearing it when he died."

"It's lovely." Briana's hand brushed hers as she touched the medallion. "Are you religious?"

"Not at all, actually." Dylan didn't really know what she believed in, but she hadn't set foot in a church since her grandparents stopped forcing her to go to mass during high school. "I guess I'd say I'm more spiritual than anything else. As far as my dad is concerned, I don't know if he was religious or not," she said. "But St. Michael is known as the Protector, the patron saint of police."

"Oh my." It seemed Briana understood the significance, and Dylan choked up when she covered her heart with her hand. "He was wearing it for you. A prayer to keep you safe." The emotion on Briana's face touched her more than it should.

"I don't know. Maybe." Dylan started to walk, but Briana reached for her hand and stopped her.

"He'd be proud of you."

"You think?"

Briana laced their hands together and looked more sincere than she'd ever seen. "You're an unbelievable detective. An even better human being. You're going to dismantle a drug network that's responsible for at least one overdose, probably countless more. That's the impact you have on the universe. Pretty incredible, if I do say so myself." Briana held her face and pulled her close for a kiss. "I can't even get into the effect you have on me. I think you know, but in case you don't. I'm breaking all my own rules. I can't seem to stop myself. I don't even want to."

Dylan kissed her over and over, forgetting for a second they were outside on the semi-crowded boardwalk.

"Come on, we should walk more." Breaking from the kiss, Dylan took Briana's hand and led the way. "It's not every day we get to do this. We should live it up. I don't know about you, but it feels like the hiding is getting harder."

"Ugh. I know what you mean." Briana rested her head against Dylan's biceps as they strolled. "I have to remind myself not to touch you constantly. I force myself to make equal eye contact with the other detectives in the plant."

"Do you?" Dylan smiled. It was nice to know she wasn't the only one having trouble compartmentalizing these days.

"Yes." Briana squeezed her hand. "Except for Trish. There's not enough good karma in the world for me to be anything beyond civil to her. Not while she throws herself at you. Screw that."

"I'm sorry about the other night. At the bar. I really didn't know what to do during Trish's antics. I don't egg her on—I swear."

"I know. It's just…seeing it unfold in the Wine Bar while you two were undercover was one thing. And I know it'll be even harder the next time. The fact that Trish wants you for real and is so blatant about it. Ugh. Plus, she gets to touch you publicly. It's not fair." She tilted her head to the sky, and Dylan imagined she was envisioning it all over. "It's a lot."

"It'll be over soon." Dylan hoped Briana found comfort in her sentiment because the truth was the investigation still had a long road ahead before a takedown was in sight.

"We'll see," Briana said, seeming to acknowledge the end was still a ways off. "Until then, I just have to deal with being your closet girlfriend."

"Girlfriend." Dylan covered her chest with both hands, feigning a heart attack. "Oh my God. Briana Logan, are you okay?" She leaned in close. "I know commitment is hard for you. Are you sure you want to put the GF label on it?" She winced to add dramatic effect.

"I'd better be your girlfriend." Briana took her by both hands and backed them to the boardwalk railing. "Especially if I have to watch Trish Suarez manhandle you." She added a fake gag. "I'd better be the only one you come home to."

Dylan looped her arms around her waist, kissed her neck, and whispered in her ear, "I can live with that."

"I'm serious, Dylan."

Dylan stopped teasing and looked her in the eye. "I know." She smiled and felt herself channel the significance of the exchange. "I feel the same way." Gone was the playfulness of the previous moment. In its place were feelings. Mutual and real and fucking deep. "Bri, I know I joke and tease sometimes. The truth is…" Fuck, she was going for it. She looked past Briana at the ocean in the distance. "I care about you. Like, deeply."

"Good." With the lightest caress, Briana guided her face back toward her. The emotion in her rich, expressive eyes said it all, but she spoke anyway. "I care about you too. Deeply," she added, copying her specific awkward phrasing.

The breeze blew warm and salty around them, marking the moment Dylan knew she would never forget. Their words might have fallen slightly short of the big *L*, but one thing was clear—they might not be ready to say it, but Dylan was pretty sure they both felt it. And for now, that was enough.

CHAPTER EIGHTEEN

In mid-December, Dylan and Trish went back to the Wine Bar and acted thrilled that Paul remembered them. Benji raced over to say hello and showed them pics on his phone of Aunt Debbie and her partner Angie from a recent family gathering to prove his endorsement of the gay agenda. They engaged in some brief conversation with the guys, but Dylan cut it short, citing work the next day and promising to come back again soon.

After that, the team let a few meetups pass, opting not to do any undercover inside. They didn't want the trio to become suspicious, and surveilling them from the outside was enough to establish the Wine Bar was the central hub of the operation. It didn't take any further convincing to get Briana to agree to write for a warrant to put a bug inside the business. But getting the paperwork up the legal chain during the holiday season was a different story.

The month was filled with soirees, office parties, and vacation. So many distractions meant not only couldn't they get the authorization needed to move forward in a timely manner, but Dylan was forced to attend several work functions where men and women openly ogled Briana. It killed her to not be able to stand by her side, hold her hand. She knew it bothered Briana too, and when they talked about it at night, Briana reassured her of what she already knew: They were only keeping things secret because of the case. Their careers took precedence, but only for now. It would all be worth it in the end.

Dylan didn't mind when they spent a quiet romantic New Year's Eve alone in her apartment, climbing up to the roof to watch local fireworks and kiss at midnight. But on this bitter cold January night, it felt like they were missing out when they passed on dinner with Stef and JJ. Not that Dylan was dying to spend time with her old compadre, but an authentic double date in a legit restaurant with her girlfriend sounded pretty fucking great right about now.

"Want to order tacos?" Briana straddled her lap and kissed her neck. "Or did you want to work up an appetite first?"

She knew Briana was trying to cheer her up, and she appreciated it. Dylan channeled every bit of positivity she could. Kissing her generously, she said, "Whatever you want. I leave it up to you."

"I always want you." Briana dotted a kiss on her nose. "But I can tell you're bummed right now. So let's eat. We'll talk it out, okay?"

"I'm sorry." Dylan let her forehead rest on Briana's soft chest. "I don't mean to be a downer."

"You're not." Briana went to the kitchen and took down two tumblers. "I know it's the dead of winter, but I'm making us margaritas."

"You are?"

"I am."

Dylan watched Briana pull a stepstool over to get the tequila stored on the highest shelf. She stood up and went to the kitchen, reaching to grab it with ease.

"Thank you, baby."

"I love when you call me that."

"I know you do." Briana cut up a lime. "I have to be so careful at work. I've almost slipped and called you *baby* a hundred times."

Dylan stretched her arms across the counter and watched Briana work. "Why is this so hard?" she said rhetorically.

"It's just for now. We just have to get through it. And we will." Briana smiled at her, and her good cheer was contagious. "Will you get the triple sec down too? It's on that same shelf."

Dylan handed it over. "I don't even know why I'm being a baby about dinner tonight. It's not like I'm dying to hang out with JJ. It just got to me for some reason."

"Why don't you like her? JJ, I mean. You never really said."

"It's not that I don't like her." Dylan didn't quite know how to properly convey how she felt about JJ. Their friendship had been all highs and lows. In the past there'd been times she felt like JJ had looked out for her, but then on a dime, things would turn, and it was as though she was left blowing in the breeze. In the end, Dylan decided friendship wasn't worth that kind of emotional whiplash. But even hearing the explanation in her head made her feel responsible for their dissolution, and she didn't think that was an accurate representation. "I'm shocked that she and Stef are still going strong," Dylan said instead, steering the conversation to less complicated terrain.

"You and me both," Briana said, filling their glasses with ice. "But hey, who are we to judge, right?"

"No, you're right. If Stef's happy, that's all that matters."

"And JJ. I'd venture so far as to say she's happy too."

"JJ's always happy when she's getting attention."

"There it is." Briana bumped her hip. "I knew there was a story."

"There's not. Not really." Dylan laughed at Briana calling her out. "She just...when we used to hang, she would get mad if I got more attention than she did."

"Oh my God, I bet it drove her crazy when girls went for you over her."

"That rarely happened."

"I do not believe that."

"You should. It's the truth." Dylan was being honest. Because even when there was a chance of her winning the one-sided competition JJ was always intent on having, Dylan typically threw up a white flag. She learned fast that getting the girl wasn't worth dealing with JJ's bruised ego. "Losing makes JJ vicious. She can be mean."

"That, I believe." Briana widened her eyes. "I've seen her in court."

"I'm sure she's no picnic to be around when the verdict doesn't go in her favor."

"I wouldn't know," Briana said. "She doesn't lose." Of course she didn't. How annoying. Briana gave their drinks a final stir. "JJ's a brilliant attorney. She's thorough. Compelling. Persuasive," she said, still singing her praise.

"I'm sure."

"But that doesn't give her the right to treat anyone badly." Briana handed over her drink. "Taste that."

Dylan took one sip and almost melted. "This is delicious. Thank you." She took another hefty swig, blown away by how good it was. "Where did you learn to make amazing margaritas?" she asked.

"I worked as a bartender for many years."

"No. Really?"

Briana's gorgeous smile was coupled with a nod. "True story."

"When?"

"Well, in high school I waited tables at the local Houlihan's. But there was a bartender there who taught me how to make drinks. In college and law school I leveraged that skill to get bartending jobs. It was pretty lucrative."

"After tasting this"—Dylan raised her glass—"I don't doubt it." She leaned in to kiss her. "Your beautiful face and amazing personality probably helped you score mega tips too." She didn't want Briana to think she was minimizing her mixology skills. "Really, though, this is amazing. Is there anything you can't do?"

"God, so many things," Briana said almost under her breath. "Can I ask you a question?"

"Of course." Her response was a reflex even though the fact that Briana asked permission to ask a question made her a little unsettled.

"Was JJ mean to you?"

Goddamn JJ. All these years later, she still managed to steal the spotlight. Dylan reminded herself she didn't care. She hadn't in the past, and she didn't now. The simple fact was JJ had a way of making her feel inferior. Like nothing but a lowly cop to her powerful attorney. But that was years ago when Dylan was younger, more sensitive. In retrospect she considered it possible her own insecurities played a factor in the imbalance of their bromance.

"Look. It's in the past. We all change. Evolve." She didn't want to overdramatize events so far behind them. "I'm fine. JJ's fine. S'all good."

"That's all I really care about." Briana snuggled into her. "I want to make sure my baby is okay. Happy."

"I'm happy. Right now. Here." She looked around Briana's lovely apartment and heard the wind whipping outside the window. "I have you." She kissed her forehead. "This amazing margarita. What more could I need?"

"Tacos. But don't worry, they're on the way."

❖

"Wait. We're getting two new detectives, and I still don't get to leave the plant?"

Dylan was going stir-crazy listening to calls but not seeing any of the action.

"Buddy, it's not about staffing." Trevor chewed his nails. "I mean, it is, partially. We need all the help we can get. In the field and in here. But we can't risk you being spotted on surveillance by these guys. It would blow everything up, and you know it."

She did know it. But there was part of her that hoped, at least a little, that she could fall into the rear and keep a loose tail on their subjects. Even in her head it sounded like a bad idea. But after weeks of being inside monitoring the phones, she was ready to climb the walls.

"I'm just ready to get back out there," she said.

"I get it." He nodded at the phones. "They're going to the Wine Bar on Friday, right?"

"So they say." She shrugged. "We'll see if it really happens."

"You and Trish should go. See if we can tickle the wire a bit."

"Do you think Nieves will go for it?"

"I don't see why he wouldn't. It's been a while since we sent you in." Trevor reached across the workstation to a box of doughnut holes someone had brought in. "I'll run it by him. Anyway, one of the new guys is going to be in here with you and Trish full-time. We'll take the other one in the field with us."

"They're not flip-flopping?"

"We're borrowing them from Team 4." He shrugged. "Their roles are already established. Shawn's an inside guy. Chris likes the street better."

"Cool." She really didn't care about the logistics. She was happy for the added help. "When do they start?"

"Next week they'll swing into the rotation." He popped another Munchkin. "I'm going to go upstairs and touch base with Briana. I want to tell her about the new guys. Plus, it wouldn't hurt to have her endorsement before I talk to Nieves about Friday." Trevor looked around the room. "I could wait for Trish to come back if you want to tag along."

Of course she wanted to go with him. She relished any and all face time with Briana. But something about seeing AUSA Logan in action held a special appeal. In a sharp business suit behind her stern desk, taking notes and making decisions, professional Briana gave her serious wood.

But Trish had just left for lunch. And she knew Briana hated when she and Trish faked being a couple, even if it was good for the case. There was no need to throw it in her face by excitedly breaking the news. She could at least allow her space to process.

"Nah. Trish just went to grab food. You know how long that can take."

"You sure?"

"I'm stuck with these bozos for now." Dylan thumbed at the wire monitoring setup. "I'm afraid you're on your own, my friend."

"You'll be missed," he said, backing away.

"Give the good prosecutor my regards."

"Oh, I will." He raised his eyebrows. "Not the same way you would, I'm sure." Trevor waved and winked as he exited.

Dylan literally gulped at the thought Trevor might be on to them, but rather than wasting her energy on something she couldn't control, she coasted through her shift, listening to calls and blocking it out. It wasn't until she was in her apartment hours later making dinner for herself and Brianna that she even gave it a second thought.

"You didn't come to see me today with Trevor." Briana pouted a little as she sat on a stool at the breakfast bar that separated Dylan's kitchen from her living space.

"About that..." Dylan grated cheese over the pasta she was prepping. "I think he might know."

"Know what?"

Dylan winced. "About you and me."

There was a slight stutter in Briana's movement as she sipped her seltzer. "Okay," she said, swallowing her drink.

"Okay?" Dylan placed a bowl of penne and broccoli on the counter for each of them. "That's it? Just okay?" She didn't want to create a stir, but she was expecting more of a reaction.

"I don't know what to say, really." Briana picked up her fork. "I guess I'm curious why you think he knows."

"He said something today in the plant. Just teasing. But..." She thought back on the interaction. "Even though we've been careful, Trevor's a pretty perceptive guy."

"Sometimes people just pick up on energy." Briana shrugged. "Not much we can do about that."

"Did he say anything to you?" Dylan asked.

"No. He told me that some new people were being added to the team. And that you and Trish were doing a UC op on Friday. We discussed the administrative and legal aspects that go along with those developments."

"Oh." Maybe she'd been hypersensitive to Trevor's remarks this afternoon. "Do you want me to talk to him about it?" Dylan asked.

"If you want."

"I definitely thought you'd be more upset about this."

Briana speared a tube of penne. "It's not that I don't care. Obviously, we've gone out of our way to be discreet." She was quiet as she moved her dinner around. "You seem unsure if he knows or not. I suppose what I'm saying is that I trust you to handle it in whatever way you think is best. I support whatever decision you make." Briana gave her a soft smile, and it made her absolutely weak.

Dylan wasn't sure what approach she was going to take, but knowing that Briana had confidence in her was assurance enough that it would all be okay.

"I'm more concerned about Friday," Briana said with a defeated sigh.

"Hey." Dylan put her fork down and took Briana's hand. "I know it's hard. I hate putting you through it." With the new fixed cameras and mics finally installed inside the Wine Bar, Dylan knew there were multiple angles to watch and listen to the interaction. It gave a fuller picture. Of everything. "You don't have to stay at the plant and observe. You could make an excuse. I'm sure Nieves or Miri would fill you in."

"I know I could do that." She frowned. "That's not who I am, Dylan. I wouldn't do that for any other active case. Plus"—Briana covered her hand—"aside from the gagfest of having to watch Trish paw you constantly, I worry about your safety. I need to know you're okay. Every minute you're in there."

"I get it."

"I doubt that."

"Ouch." Dylan knew it had to be difficult for Briana, but she didn't think the shot was necessary. She was just doing her job, after all. "Look, Bri…" she started, but she really didn't know what to say to make it better, so she let her sentence flounder.

"I'm sorry, baby." Briana seemed to read her. "It's just hard for me. And I don't think you get what it's like to have the person you care about be both in danger and pretend to be interested in someone else. Quite honestly, it sucks. I know I signed on for this, but that doesn't make it any easier."

"I am sorry."

Dylan knew the phrase fell short, but she didn't really know how to capture the complexity of emotions she felt over the whole situation. The truth was she found the undercover assignment invigorating. Not the Trish part, but she barely paid attention to that. The fact that she was so close, so instrumental in the investigation was thrilling and satisfying in ways she couldn't seem to make Briana understand without causing her stress.

"I know you are." Briana's expression was kind, her tone full of affection. Dylan knew she wasn't angry as much as she was tense over their situation. Briana put her fork down and pulled her close. "Promise me something?"

"Anything."

"Do not fall for Trish Suarez."

Dylan couldn't help but laugh and Briana whacked her arm. "I'm not kidding. And I'm feeling vulnerable. So be nice."

"I will not fall for Trish Suarez." Dylan squared her shoulders and stood tall as she spoke like she was reciting a pledge. "Anything else?" she asked.

"Yes, as a matter of fact." Briana hooked her belt loops and led her in for a kiss. "Don't get killed."

"Check," Dylan said, meeting her lips. "How easy was that?"

CHAPTER NINETEEN

"How's your view, Briana? Can you see okay from there?"

It was nice that Miri Hollander was looking out for her, but Briana could see everything from her spot in the center of the wire room, her eyes glued to the sixty-inch monitor feeding the details of the undercover operation at the Wine Bar. Whether or not her heart and blood pressure could withstand the visual of Dylan with Trish talking to bona fide drug dealers was a different story altogether.

"Why don't you sit? Ahmed, wheel over a comfortable chair for Briana."

"I'm fine, Miri." Briana waved her off. "Thank you anyway, Ahmed." Briana couldn't even think about sitting. She needed to be able to stand and shuffle and fidget just to work through some of her anxiety.

"Here they come."

The plant fell silent as Dylan and Trish entered the frame. Briana tried not to focus on their joined hands or the way Dylan pulled out a stool for Trish to sit down. Dylan stood next to her, and Briana knew it was because standing made her feel more in control of the situation. She could do without Trish caressing the small of Dylan's back, though. *It's just work. Block it out.*

Paul approached them, and they hugged hello like they were all old friends.

"Why can't I hear them?" Briana asked.

"Hold on a second." Ahmed threw on a headset, and one of the detectives from the tech unit fiddled with a series of gadgets before he typed furiously at the computer controlling the equipment. "We're getting it. It's recording," Ahmed said. "There seems to be a problem with the audio feed to the monitor," he said, pointing to the big screen. "But it is coming through. Looks to be about a half a minute behind—is that what you're getting, Tony?"

Tony the tech guy agreed. "I could mess around with it to see if we can hear it through the speakers, but we risk losing it altogether."

"Don't do it," Nieves ordered from his perch in the back. "Ahmed, for now just listen and give us the play-by-play. You tech gurus can work out the kinks later."

In a way, Briana was happy not to hear the cutesy dialogue she was sure was being exchanged and, in Trish's case, laid on way too thick. But absent sound, her mind filled in the blanks anyway.

"Oh, shit," Ahmed said. But he sounded excited, not worried, so her pressure didn't spike too bad. "Look." He pointed at the monitor and pulled one earmuff to the side. "You saw how Dylan just stretched her back?"

They all nodded.

"Paul must have thought it was bothering her, so he asked if she was okay." On the screen Paul was signaling Benji and George to join them from the end of the bar. "Fucking Dylan, man, she went with it. Gave him a whole story about how she works for her uncle who's a contractor and she got hurt on a job." Ahmed was talking so fast it was almost hard to follow. "He just asked if she was taking anything for the pain, and she said Motrin or some shit and he just fucking offered her Percocet."

Nieves jumped out of his chair. "Are you serious?"

"I'm telling you, Boss. Look, look." He pointed at the screen where Benji stood next to her, blocking the camera's view a little. "I know you can't see it. Fuck. Oh, good, good. Paul wanted her to take it, but she told him she just took a Motrin 800."

"Good job, Dylan." Miri breathed a sigh of relief, and Briana felt it to her core.

Ahmed covered both ears with the heavy-duty headset. His voice was loud as he continued to keep them updated. "Okay, okay. He told her to take it at home. She offered him cash, but he declined."

Even though she had complete faith in Dylan, Briana could feel herself start to sweat.

"Paul's asking her details about the injury." Ahmed shook his head. "Holy fuck, she's insanely good. Kid does not miss a beat. Now they're talking about how great Trish is to be there for support, yadda-yadda."

She watched a soundless Dylan work the room. She divided her attention between Paul and Benji and Trish, animated but reserved at the same time. Trish rubbed her back and dropped a kiss on her shoulder. Gross. But they were making real progress, and Briana had to remind herself of the endgame.

Onscreen, Dylan hung her head in laughter the way she did when Briana teased her. Trish was hanging all over Dylan, and it made her stomach turn. Briana almost looked away, and if she had, it probably would have been for the best. But it was like watching a train wreck. She simply couldn't tear her eyes away. And then Dylan did the unthinkable. She faced Trish, and holy crap, she kissed her. It was just a peck on the lips, but it was enough to make the bile rise in her throat.

"Yowza." Ahmed fanned himself. "That was definitely for show. But those guys ate it up. You should hear them talking about what a great couple they are."

The action portrayed on the TV indicated that the conversation had changed, and only then did Briana remember the audio lag.

"Oh, oh." Ahmed nodded. "This is good, people. Paul just said if Dylan likes the Percocet, he can get her more. He told her to stay in touch with Benji."

Miri and Ahmed high-fived.

Nieves fist-pumped.

Briana's heart sank.

She knew what had just happened was monumental for the investigation. But all she could see was her girlfriend kissing someone else.

Everything else seemed a blur as the action wrapped up, and Dylan and Trish exited the Wine Bar without incident. They were headed back to the plant, and Miri suggested Briana stick around for the debrief and a ride home, but she knew she needed to leave. She needed the rumble of the subway and frigid temperature to steel her and calm her and talk her off the ledge.

As Briana exited the F train she saw a text from Dylan. *I'm coming over.*

Don't, she typed back.

Barely a second passed before Dylan responded. *Bri, please. I need you.*

God, she needed Dylan too. She was mad and hurt and upset, warranted or not. Instinct told her the only person who would make her feel even marginally okay was Dylan. She needed her, she wanted her, she was thankful she was okay, she was furious with her. It was…a mess.

Briana looked up and realized she was on the corner of Dylan's street. It was as though her body knew the answer it had taken her mind some time to come around to.

I'll meet you at your apartment, she typed, not bothering to mention that she was basically already there.

Dylan responded with a giant red heart.

Briana walked for another twenty minutes, knowing it would be a while before Dylan made it home. The cold air was cleansing. It relaxed her and helped her see things for what they were. At first, she'd contemplated breaking things off with Dylan. It was simple enough to do. One conversation could put a stop to everything. But the thought of not being with Dylan the way she was right now immediately made her eyes water and her hands shake. And for what? There wasn't anything real between Dylan and Trish. Dylan cared about her. She saw it in her eyes—she felt it in her soul.

The kiss was just part of the act.

Repeating that mantra in her head made her feel better. Comforted by the thought and healed by the words, Briana paced the streets, coming down with each step until she stood shivering outside Dylan's brownstone.

She thought she was fine. She felt better.

But then Dylan pulled up and stepped out of her car. Across the short dark distance, Dylan's eyes stood out, bright and deep and full of emotion against the night sky. Without any kind of internal warning she was completely overwhelmed with emotion.

In a second, Dylan was next to her, holding her close and kissing her face. "You're crying." She seemed surprised and distressed at the realization. She hugged her tighter. "Oh my God, you're so cold," Dylan whispered as she walked them to the door and ushered them upstairs. "I didn't know you were here. I would've had Marie let you in."

Briana didn't say anything. She couldn't even form words.

Instead, she let Dylan take her coat and hold her hands, rubbing them for warmth while her tears flowed in a steady stream.

If the emotional display unnerved Dylan, she didn't let it show. In fact, she kept an arm around her, holding her close, as she turned on lights and flipped a switch on the wall that ignited the fireplace.

"Stay here for a minute." Dylan urged her to sit by the fire. "You'll warm up quick. I can make tea. Or would you prefer wine?"

Briana wiped away her tears. "I still can't believe you have a real fireplace." She laughed through a sniffle.

"Well, gas." Dylan shifted her eyes. "I don't know if that counts as real."

"Sit with me," Briana said as she hovered near the hearth.

Dylan sat and held her hands, seeming unable or unwilling to let them go. Her expression was remorse and pain, and it broke Briana's heart just the tiniest little bit.

"I am so sorry," Dylan said. Dylan brought her hands to her lips. "I didn't mean to hurt you. I swear. I hate seeing you like this. Even more I hate that I did this to you. I don't know what to say." Her throat scratched and she looked up at the ceiling. Briana wondered if she was trying to stanch her own tears as she continued, "I want to tell you that I felt like I had to do it in the moment. That it seemed, I don't know, expected." She looked at the blue and yellow flame behind the tempered glass. "It feels kind of pathetic hearing it out loud. But, Bri"—Dylan looked right at her—"you have to believe the kiss meant nothing to me."

"It killed me." Briana felt a tear roll down her cheek.

"I know." Dylan wiped it away and kissed the trail of wetness left behind. Briana saw Dylan look at her mouth and hesitate like she was unsure if a genuine kiss would be welcome.

She swallowed hard, truly not ready for what she knew she was going to say. "Dylan," she started, still fighting off tears. "This is so hard."

"I know." Dylan dropped her head in her lap and Briana touched her neck, petting her softly.

"Look at me. Please?" Briana was nervous. More nervous than she ever remembered feeling. She needed the strength she always found in Dylan's clear blue eyes, and when Dylan looked up at her, she refused to think or filter anymore. She simply said what she felt in every part of her being.

"I'm in love with you."

Dylan's whole face softened. "Wait. What?"

"I know," Briana said, laughing and crying at the same time. "No one is more surprised than me."

"I should probably be offended by that." Dylan kissed her. "But I'm just so happy you're not breaking up with me."

"I'm not breaking up with you." Briana held her face and kissed her over and over. "I just didn't want it to be true, you know?"

"Again with the smooth talk," Dylan said through a smile.

Briana laughed at her own ability to butcher the moment, and thank God, Dylan was laughing with her, so she knew it was all okay.

"I just mean, this, us"—she covered Dylan's heart with her hand—"it was supposed to be fun, exciting, sexy." She saw Dylan's eyebrows shift in playful challenge. "It is." Briana leaned forward and kissed her again. "But it's so much more. I can't help it." She smiled against Dylan's mouth. "I fell. So freaking hard."

"Is that right?" Dylan was teasing her. She knew the tone so well.

"I'm still upset about tonight," she said, not ready to completely brush over the incident. "It destroyed me to see you kiss Trish." Even saying the words hurt. "But it also made me realize how much I need you. How much you're mine. How I want to be yours." She looked down at her hands in her lap, feeling so vulnerable at baring her heart. "I've never felt this way. Ever."

"Briana." With one finger under her chin, Dylan made sure they were eye to eye. "I love you too. So much it hurts. I want to be with you, like, all the time."

"Yeah?"

"Yes." Dylan held her hand and kissed her. "Do you realize how hard it is not to beg you to come for coffee every morning? Or have lunch with me in the plant?" She looked down and seemed uncharacteristically sheepish. "To stay here with me every night."

"I want those things too." Dylan narrowed her eyes in response. "I already sneak down for coffee whenever I can," she said as proof. She touched her forehead to Dylan's. "I barely even break for lunch most days. I rush through my work so I don't have to stay late. So I can see you." It was the truth. Even though they didn't see each other every night, almost all of Briana's planning was done with Dylan in mind. Seeing her as much as possible had become the constant goal she was consciously striving for. "You have to promise me something."

"What is it?"

"It has to be just me. No one else."

"Of course." Dylan was so serious, it made her stomach flutter.

"Not even Trish for pretense."

"It's only you," Dylan said, leaning forward to kiss her. She pulled back for a second. "I hate even having to talk about this right now, but as far as the Trish stuff goes, I don't think it would happen again. Tonight was just because of the way it went down." She seemed so unbelievably sincere that Briana knew she was telling the truth. "Honestly, I think when I go back, for more painkillers obviously"—she seemed to be analyzing on the spot—"I don't even think she should come."

Briana caressed her face and scratched at her short hair. "I hate to admit this, baby." She kissed Dylan's perfect lips. "You were amazing tonight. You always are. It's insanely daunting and incredibly impressive to watch." Briana stood and held her hand out to Dylan. She was more than ready for what came next. "Come. Be amazing with me."

Dylan responded with her signature smirk, but it was founded in something deeper this time, and seeing the sentiment in her eyes moved Briana in a way that surpassed even the words they'd just spoken.

She smiled and held Dylan's hand the length of the hallway to the bedroom. Button by button, she took off her top, loving the way Dylan kissed her face and her neck, her shoulders, her breasts. Briana pulled Dylan's shirt off, dying for skin to skin contact. She unbuckled Dylan's belt and unzipped her pants, stepping back for the briefest moment so Dylan could put her gun away.

Briana kissed Dylan's chest and slid her hand down the front of her boxers. She moaned at how wet Dylan was already. Dylan grinned and found her mouth, kissing her possessively. She couldn't take it. Not for another second. Without a word, Briana kissed a straight line down Dylan's body.

Good God, she could get lost in Dylan Prescott.

Briana didn't rush. She took her time savoring every second as her body seemed to throb in time with her heart. She loved the way Dylan tasted, her scent, the way her hands felt in her hair, and knowing her eyes were on her. In a second Dylan would take over, guide them to the bed, touch her and taste her and move on top of her, inside her. But in this small moment she was also keenly aware that if for some crazy reason the world ended in the next thirty seconds, she'd die happy right here, on her knees in front of the person she was so deeply, so completely in love with.

"Bri." Dylan's voice was low and husky. "I need you."

Briana needed her too. She needed all of her.

She stood up and kissed Dylan with everything she had, surrendering her heart along with her body. They moved together under the covers, knowing each other so well by now. But as they kissed and touched and whispered, it felt different. Lighter and heavier at the same time. The contrast making sense and working together even though it shouldn't. It was honest and genuine and so unlike anything she'd ever experienced. When Briana came, of course it was amazing, it was always amazing. But this time it was steeped in love. True, deep, passionate, real, forever love.

And that was a complete game changer.

CHAPTER TWENTY

I can't believe they're saying twelve to fifteen inches in the city." Briana watched Stef pull back the curtain and peer out the living room window into the courtyard below. She idly wondered when Dylan would arrive as her roommate waxed on about the weather. "To think we got all the way to the end of February with no snow. I really thought we were going to make it this time."

"Well I, for one, am excited about this nor'easter," Briana said from the kitchen as she searched the fridge to see what they had in the way of sustenance. "Although we probably should've done a bread and milk run beforehand."

"Eh. We have wine and cheese. I'd say that's winning." Stef flopped on the sofa. "I am curious, though. You hate snow. Why the sudden change of heart?"

Briana didn't really need to go into detail. She could coast on the theory her elation was all anticipation of a snowy Friday night hunkered down in her cozy apartment with her bestie, but it was more than that, and she might feel better if she just got it out. "If I'm being honest," she said, reaching for two wineglasses, "I'm thrilled that the weather report trumped the undercover op Dylan was scheduled for tonight."

"I didn't realize she was still involved in that. This is the thing where she goes into a bar with some other female detective, right?" Stef knew only the bare bones, and she knew better than to ask for details, so Briana had used her as a sounding board on the nights Dylan had infiltrated the Wine Bar with Trish. The nights she needed to talk herself down and not feel like a crazy jealous girlfriend.

"Still involved." She sighed. "The part where the other detective goes with her has petered out," she said, even though tonight was the first night Dylan had been slated to go inside alone.

"Well, that's good. I mean that the chick who's into her is off the case." Trish wasn't off the case, but Briana didn't bother to correct Stef. Her friend was being supportive, and she wasn't going to divulge details anyway.

"It is good," she said. "It probably should make me feel better than I do, but...nope."

"Don't beat yourself up, Briana." Stef grabbed the remote and scanned through some options. "If my girlfriend was putting herself in danger on the daily *and* with other hot babes...no thanks. I'm out," she added with a laugh.

"How are things with JJ? I've been meaning to check in." Briana compared the labels of a bottle of red and white before holding them up to get Stef's input. "What are you feeling?"

"Snowy night. I vote red all the way." Briana agreed with a nod as Stef got comfy on the couch, taking her time answering the real question.

"Come on. Out with it," Briana prodded. "Give me all the dirty details."

"Okay, okay." Stef smiled, and even across the room Briana could see there was something deeper behind it. "I don't know, Bri. What can I say? JJ's good. She's nice, she's funny. I'm enjoying myself." Stef shrugged. "Am I slightly nervous she's out of town on business? Yeah." She combed her fingers through her long black hair the way she did when she was anxious. "We don't have anything set up. No rules. No agreements."

Briana winced before she could stop herself.

"I know." Stef read her immediately. "I'm just going to ride this wave and see where it takes me."

"And you're good with that?" she asked, but when she looked over she could see Stef was actually okay. Calm even.

"I kind of am." Stef hooked her hair into a loose bun on top of her head. "I guess I'm taking a page out of your book for a change." She tossed a friendly wink at Briana. "Speaking of, is the good detective going to join us for a snow party? Or are you going there?"

"She's coming here if that's okay."

"Of course it's okay. I love Dylan. I just don't want you to feel like you have to keep me company."

"You're the best, Stef."

"You are." Stef rose from the couch to get the glass of red Briana had poured for her. "So, it's been a minute," she asked as she took the first sip. "How goes it with you two? Is everyone good and happy?"

Good and happy fell so far short of how she felt. In the few weeks since they'd said their actual *I love you*s, Briana had never felt so alive. She was simply blown away that she had it all. Full attraction. Equal career aspirations. Deep feelings. It seemed foolish now, her previous assumption that something always had to be sacrificed. Suddenly with Dylan, everything was within reach.

Briana touched the base of her wineglass, a hundred percent sure she was glowing even as she thought about Dylan. "Stef," she started, "the thing is—"

"Delivery!" Dylan's muffled voice cut her off and was accompanied by three heavy knocks on the other side of the apartment door.

Uncontrollably, Briana felt her heart speed up as she opened the door.

"Somebody order a pizza?" Dylan asked. Her cheeks and nose were weather chapped, and a layer of fresh snow capped her thick dark hair.

"How did you get up here without buzzing?" She pulled Dylan inside and dusted her off.

"Your downstairs neighbor was on his way out."

"Holy shit, you really brought pizza." Briana was still catching up to the surprise visit. Well, not surprise. But Dylan had said she had a few things to take care of before coming over. She hadn't expected her for at least an hour. This extra time together was a bonus.

"Let me take this," she said, setting the pizza on the counter. "Hold on one second." Briana froze in place as she read the custom label on the cardboard box. "You did not!" she exclaimed, mouth agape. To confirm what was obviously the case, Briana opened the box the tiniest smidge and peered in at the specialty Sicilian pizza. Thick crust with sauce over cheese, the pie was the signature staple of her favorite pizza joint in all of Brooklyn. "Dylan." She covered her heart with both hands. "You went all the way to Spumoni Gardens for L&B style?"

"It's your favorite."

"I know, but the snow." She gestured at the window.

"It's only starting now. And my snow removal guy lives over in Bensonhurst anyway. I wanted to stop by and settle up with him. This way he's guaranteed to show tomorrow."

"You have a snow removal guy?" Stef asked.

"My girlfriend is a fancy homeowner, Stef." Briana hung on Dylan, playfully bragging as she doted on her. "She can't take chances."

"It's a service. They have equipment," Dylan explained. "I pay them so I can spend the day holed up with you two instead of breaking my back shoveling."

"Money well spent." Stef raised her wineglass in support.

"I agree," Briana said, dropping a kiss on her shoulder "What's all this?" she asked, nodding at a different box Dylan carried.

"Storm provisions." Dylan rested the box on a stool and lifted out a bottle of red, a jar of Orville Redenbacher's popcorn, and a few packages of Sour Patch Kids. "Who knows how long we'll be cooped up," she said with a shrug. She set the box in a corner with the remaining contents inside. "There's flashlights and candles in there too, just in case."

"You are incredible." Briana kissed her, not even caring that Stef was right there. "Wait." She looked around in a slight panic. "Where's your overnight bag?"

"I still need to run home. I didn't want the pizza to get cold." Dylan smiled, and Christ, she could fucking melt. "I just have to drop off milk and stuff for Mrs. Lemke. And tell her not to attempt shoveling in the morning. Then I'll grab my things and head back here."

"That's why you went all the way to Bensonhurst." Briana hugged her tight, not even caring that her shirt got damp from the precipitation on Dylan's jacket. "You wanted to give the snow guy money up front to take care of Mrs. Lemke's property."

Dylan answered with a kiss to her nose. "She's a sweet old lady. But stubborn as a mule. If her path isn't cleared five minutes after the snow stops, she'll be out there doing it herself—I know it. I wanted to make sure these guys put her high on their list."

"You're unbelievable." She kissed Dylan again. "Go. Get your things. Hurry back." Briana ushered her out the door with a final taunt. "If you take forever, we're eating that whole pie without you."

She watched Dylan retreat with a smile. There was so much love in her eyes she knew she was swooning in her own doorway before she closed the door and faced Stef.

"Girl. You are in it." Stef took a long, indulgent sip of her wine.

"Ugh." Briana reached for her own drink, not even bothering to mount a defense. "You have no idea."

"I beg to differ." Stef tapped the pizza box. "This is beyond cute girlfriend shit. This"—she made a circle with one finger inclusive of Dylan's entire aura—"this is the real deal."

"I know."

Stef's jaw dropped with flair. "Briana Adele Logan. Get the fuck out." She shook her head and looked around, making no secret of marking this precise moment. "You're not even fighting me. Making excuses. Reasoning. Rationalizing."

"What's to fight? Or rationalize. Or whatever." She held her palms up in surrender. "I'm in love with her. Totally and completely."

"Look at you." Stef put her wine down, scooted around the island, and did a happy dance. She hugged Briana and kissed her cheek. "My baby is all grown up. I'm so proud of you."

"You're such a jerk." Briana whacked her forearm. "We're the same age."

"I'm teasing." Stef took a step back, still clearly assessing.

"Stop it. You're creeping me out," she said with a laugh.

Briana couldn't help but notice the genuine affection in Stef's eyes. It was reinforced by the sentiment in her tone when she said, "I'm just so happy for you."

"Thanks, Stef."

"I mean it, though. You deserve this."

"You do too, you know. With JJ…or someone else."

"We shall see." Stef raised her eyebrows and her glass in a toast to the unforeseeable future, before shifting her gaze to the pizza between them. "Can we eat this?"

"Yes. Of course." Briana grabbed some plates from the cupboard and hooked them up with napkins as Stef placed a slice on each plate. "There is something on my mind," Briana said.

"Is it how we've completely switched roles, and now I'm all, oh love, whatever, who needs it?" Stef said before taking a bite of pizza.

"And you're over there with heart eyes over the pizza your girlfriend dropped off."

"No," Briana said through a chuckle. "Although, and I know I'm making a big deal out of it..." She loved Dylan so much she couldn't help but swoon even in absentia. "But how great is she?"

"She is great. I'm teasing you. I might be the tiniest bit jealous."

"Stop." Briana waved Stef off with her napkin.

"I will." Stef nodded as she eyed the next bite to devour. "What were you really going to say? What's on your mind?"

Was she really considering this? Briana put her slice down and wiped each finger with precision, second-guessing herself for the millionth time as she said, "I'm thinking about leaving the US Attorney's Office."

"Oh, good. So, nothing drastic, then?"

God, she loved the way Stef could make anything seem not dour. Here she was talking about upending her career path, and off the bat Stef made her laugh about it. "It's not for the reason you're thinking."

"It's not because you're in love with the lead case detective?"

"Dylan's not the lead."

"Irrelevant. Move to strike." Stef pretended to wait for a ruling from the imaginary judge before turning back to Briana. "I'd win this case, but go on."

"You wouldn't. I'm amazing in court." Briana rarely bragged about herself. But when it came to her job, she was in a league of her own, and she knew it. "Which is kind of my point, though." She toyed with a bit of crust on her plate. "Look. I can't pretend Dylan doesn't factor into my thought process. Of course her role in the investigation plays a part." She took a sip of wine, still struggling to wrap her own head around what she was considering. "It's more than that, though."

"Talk to me. Tell me what you're thinking."

"I've worked for the federal government for most of my career. I've prosecuted a lot of cases. Learned a ton. Worked with some excellent attorneys."

"You think you've reached a point of diminishing returns?"

"I don't know that I'd go that far. I love my job. I think I could be great running that office someday. It's still my career aspiration." She swirled her wine. "I'm starting to think some varied experience might help me attain that goal. And make me a better attorney when I get that coveted spot."

Stef nodded, and Briana knew her brain was churning the info. She could almost hear the thought process.

"Look, Stef. Obviously sleeping with Dylan was not the brightest move, as far as my career goes. And yes, I'm concerned it could be exposed at trial and color the perception of the investigation. But honestly, that's not even my main motivator right now. Men sleep with opposing counsel, investigators, victims, defendants." She rolled her eyes remembering a huge news story from two years back. "It doesn't derail entire cases or end their careers. There's no reason it should have that effect on mine."

"The rules are different for women, and you know it."

"I know," she said, taking a minute to let the impact of injustice sink in. "I refuse to let archaic rules dictate my behavior." She took a bite of pizza to punctuate her defiance. But even as she chewed, she knew her feelings went beyond proving a point. "I keep coming back to the same thing, though."

"Which is?"

"If we were only sleeping together, it would be different." There was no way to make this sound like anything other than what it was. "If that was the situation, I could justify it. Or stop it," she added almost as an afterthought.

"You're past that point." Stef understood her.

"I'm afraid being in love with her will affect my judgment. It hasn't yet. Mostly because I'm compartmentalizing the hell out of my life. But it's a challenge. And what if I fuck up this case?"

"You won't."

"I'm glad *you're* sure."

"Bri, I've known you since we were first year law students together. I've seen you ace killer classes, win impossible trials, and date difficult people. I'm not saying Dylan is difficult," she said, modifying her response. "It's just, I know you can handle this. The question is whether or not you want to."

"I just don't know if it's the right thing to be doing."

"Have you talked to Dylan about this?"

Briana dropped her head onto the counter. "No," she muttered into her shirt sleeves.

"Why don't you talk to her?" Stef petted her head like a child. "Get her take?"

"She's not going to be happy."

Briana stood upright and took a sip of wine, for a moment mulling the argument to stay on board. "Changing AUSAs mid-investigation"— she widened her eyes—"isn't optimal. The detective team will have to bring whoever takes over up to speed. Not everyone is like me. Living and breathing my job twenty-four seven. AUSAs come with varied levels of competency and dedication." That was all true. But it wasn't the reason she hadn't talked about it with Dylan yet. "I think she's going to take it personally."

"But it's not personal."

"This case means a lot to her. To her career. I'm aggressive. More so than some of my colleagues. I let her do a lot because I trust her. We have an established rapport."

"Yeah. And established positions. I'm talking, like, reverse cowgirl."

Briana almost spit her wine out.

"I'm kidding, but I'm not," Stef said. "My point is, you two are entangled. On multiple levels. There's a physical connection. An emotional connection. It's a lot to manage." She reached out and touched Briana's hand. "Talk to her. Tell her how you feel, what your concerns are. Be honest. She'll listen. I really believe that."

Briana let out a heavy sigh, knowing Stef was right. "Don't say anything this weekend, okay?" She was still so conflicted. "I still don't know what I'm going to do."

"I'm not going to say anything. You have my word." Stef opened the pizza box like she was thinking about another slice. "You put any feelers out yet?"

"No." Briana reached for a kitchen knife and sliced an end piece down the middle, giving half to Stef.

"You should talk to JJ," Stef said, reaching for the grated cheese. "She'd hire you in a second. I know that for a fact." Stef topped off their wine. "I know you make fun of her for going into the private sector and all that, but her firm is doing some really good stuff."

"I know they are. I just read that article in *The New York Law Journal* about the class action matter they pursued where the victims were all minorities." It was a good case involving politics, discrimination, and advocacy. She'd been proud to know the attorney brave enough to take it on. "I tease JJ, but the truth is she's an outstanding litigator doing some great work."

"Talk to her when she gets back," Stef urged.

"Maybe," Briana said. It was nice to know she had an option even though she was still on the fence herself. "I reserve the right to not make a decision today." She nodded resolutely.

Stef lifted her wine in the air. "To snowstorms and indecision."

"To great pizza and hot girlfriends." Briana seconded the toast with a raised glass and a smile. The second Dylan passed through her mind, she couldn't keep her joy hidden. In that instant she knew, no matter what decision she came to, everything would be okay.

CHAPTER TWENTY-ONE

The end of February was a beast, and March wasn't looking much better. Constant snowfall and single-digit temps virtually stalled the investigation. The weather was screwing with everyone's schedule—even the bad guys didn't want to brave the elements, it seemed. The team couldn't catch a break on surveillance. But at least Dylan had made two more undercover oxycodone purchases from Benji, and that was enough to keep some forward momentum. On the upside, Dylan chose to leverage every spare minute she could steal with Briana. Even if it meant grocery shopping on a Sunday morning.

Dylan jacked up the heat as she navigated slowly along the cobblestone streets of Red Hook to Briana's favorite supermarket. The parking lot was a ghost town, and she pulled into a space right in the front row.

"Look at that." Across the console Dylan touched Briana's arm and pointed at the tiny Statue of Liberty visible in the harbor. "I can't believe what a clear view there is from here."

"Kind of beautiful, right?"

"It is."

When Briana turned back to face her, Dylan was so caught up in the moment she almost went for a kiss, forgetting they were in public.

"Soon, baby." Briana touched her face softly, answering the unspoken desire. The gesture was thoughtful and exactly what Dylan needed for reassurance they were on the same page. "Come on—let's face the cold, stock up on some essentials, then go home and I'll make us brunch. Sound good?"

It sounded fantastic. "What's special about this store?" Dylan asked. She wasn't complaining so much as curious to know why Briana loved it so much.

"I guess nothing, really." Briana laughed as she hugged herself against the cold. "I like the layout. Reasonable prices. Everything's all in one place. No running from one specialty store to the other, like our neighborhood. And they have an amazing coffee selection. Wait until you see it."

Dylan leaned in close to touch their shoulders together. "Don't tell me. It's all boxes of flavored Keurig?" she teased.

"Ha." Briana scrunched her nose the way Dylan loved and hooked her elbow. "Now that you're my girlfriend, I don't have to pretend that's the only coffee I'll drink."

"I knew it was a farce."

"From minute one, I suspect."

"Not really. I will admit I had a sneaking suspicion you were coming to the plant to see me as much as for the coffee." Dylan leaned in close and kissed her cheek.

Briana didn't pull back. "We still have to be careful," she said as she reached for a shopping cart.

"Pshh." Dylan took control of the handle so she could steer. "Kisses should be one of the perks of having to go shopping at the end of the earth."

"The perks are going to be French toast made from the amazing baguettes that are baked on-site. And I'm going to top it with fresh strawberries and bananas."

Dylan pinched her waist. "I'm going to top you with fresh strawberries and bananas."

Briana placed a bunch of bananas into the wagon. "Ooh, we should get whipped cream."

"You are a tease," Dylan whined as she cocked her head back.

Briana touched her belly. "It's not teasing if there's follow-through." She bit her lip and wiggled her eyebrows, and Dylan couldn't resist. She reached for Briana's hand and held it.

"I love you," she said.

"I know." Briana's voice was low and soft as she squeezed her hand and blew a small kiss. It was a trifle of a moment, but Dylan felt it everywhere.

"Hey, guys. Cold enough out there for ya?"

Dylan turned and dropped Briana's hand in a flash. She had been so lost in her own world that she hadn't even noticed the arrival of a scruffy hipster nearby. But sure enough, Shawn Fisher was not two feet away, comparing apples for ripeness.

"Yo, Shawn, what's up?" Dylan tried to sound like she hadn't just been caught with her hand in the cookie jar. "I thought you were on the wire today," she said, even though she knew the plant schedule inside out.

"Trish and Ahmed today," he said as he rested his basket next to some Granny Smiths. "Hello." Shawn smiled at Briana.

"Oh." Dylan snapped into action. "You know Briana, right? She's the AUSA on our case," she said, then rounded out the introductions. "Shawn's one of the new detectives we stole from Team 4 a little while back."

"Yes, I remember." Briana smiled at Shawn, but Dylan saw her guard go up. "We had a mini meeting when he first transferred in. To take care of the paperwork," Briana explained to Dylan.

"Right. Of course." Dylan smacked her forehead with the base of her hand, mortified that she was overtalking and making things awkward. "What am I saying?" She leaned her weight on the cart and nodded at the milk and bread in Shawn's basket. "You live around here?"

"Yeah. Right over on Wolcott." He pointed in the direction of the entrance. "What about you guys?"

Dylan ticked her head toward Briana. "We're neighbors up in Carroll Gardens. Briana's a sucker for the baguettes here."

"They are amazing."

"I'm excited to see for myself." Dylan rubbed her hands together in anticipation. "Anyway. Good to see you, Shawn. Catch you tomorrow."

"Have a good one," he said with a wave.

They were quiet for a few seconds, and Dylan made sure they were out of earshot when she asked, "Are you okay?"

"I'm not great." Briana's tone was all stress as she placed some agave sweetener in the bed of the cart.

Dylan wanted to comfort her. She wanted to stop everything and take Briana in her arms and hug her. Kiss her forehead, tell her everything was fine. But there was no way that would go over, so she wheeled along in silence until they reached the bakery section. "I know you're freaking out, but I really think it's going to be fine."

"I know you do." Briana examined the baguettes with care before selecting one and placing it down gingerly. "Whatever happened with Trevor?"

When Briana finally made eye contact her expression was steel, and Dylan had no idea what she was talking about.

"A while back, you said you thought he knew. Did you ever talk to him?"

"No." She frowned. "It never came up again, and I let it go. It felt like the best way to handle it." Dylan really believed it was no big deal. She thought the same about Shawn. Everyone was too busy with their own lives to really be invested in things that had no bearing on them. "As far as Shawn is concerned, think about it for a minute. It is completely plausible for us to shop together here. I have a car. You live around the block from me."

"Dylan, it's nine a.m. on a Sunday morning."

She shrugged. "It's only weird if we make it weird."

Briana answered her with an eye roll.

"Shawn isn't going to say a word. I feel confident in that."

"You feel confident in everything." Briana's tone was soft, but it carried a touch of bitterness.

"Listen to me." Dylan moved just slightly closer so she could lower her voice. "Shawn has his own shit going on. He's trans, did you know that?"

"I know," Briana admitted.

"Did you also know that the guys on Team 4 are complete assholes?" It drove her crazy to have to dignify their behavior by giving it a forum. "Like, they don't technically *harass* him." She threw air quotes around the word. "But they're not nice to him either."

"That's terrible."

"He's happy with us on Team 2. And he's a good detective. He uncovered the Medicaid scam Paul's running under the umbrella of his law practice, and the Social Security stuff he's involved in." She waved it off. "My point is...he's a good fit with us. We want him to stay. I think he wants that too."

"And you think that means he's not going to say anything."

"Well that, and he's just not that kind of guy. He's not a gossip. He's just…nice."

"Okay," Briana said, but she didn't seem as relaxed as Dylan had hoped, and she wasn't willing to leave it be.

"I see you stewing over there," she said as she pushed the cart along. "Talk to me. Tell me what you're thinking. Let me help you."

Briana stopped dead in the potato chip aisle.

"There is something I want to talk to you about."

She'd never seen Briana look so serious. Dylan's heart raced with slight apprehension. She swallowed hard, trying to prep—for what, she wasn't sure.

"What is it?"

Briana tilted her head to the fluorescent lights overhead, her shoulders dropping in a kind of surrender. "I'm thinking about leaving the US Attorney's Office."

Dylan let out a full breath in relief. A job change she could handle. Support, even. "Where would you go, private practice?"

"I don't have it all figured out yet. But that is what I'm thinking, yes."

"Well, you have time to figure our something." Dylan squeezed her shoulder with a touch that could easily be platonic. "Nieves was just saying it would be at least spring before we take the case down."

"No, Dylan." Briana's knuckles went white as she clutched the edge of the cart. "I'm considering leaving now. Midcase."

"Wait. Now?" Dylan's heart pounded fiercely. Why was Briana sabotaging them? "You're going to leave over Shawn Fisher? That's insane." Dylan was hurt that Briana didn't trust her enough not to give up.

"It's not because of him. It's all of this." She held her arms out and half spun around. "The sneaking around. The hiding. I hate it. I want to be with you anywhere I want. Not look over my shoulder the whole time."

God, she felt the same way. It was a constant struggle to not act on her feelings all the time. Even in the parking lot, she'd forced her hands in her pockets to keep her instincts at bay.

"It's getting harder," Briana said. "I know you feel it too."

"But is this really the only solution?" She was just shy of begging, but she wanted more of Briana, not less. "What if we went away? For a weekend. We could take a ride out to Montauk or Mystic?"

"Honestly? I would love that. But when?" Briana's expression was almost pleading. "Think about it. This case has us constantly on call. There's hardly been a weekend when one of us hasn't run into the office—you to listen to a call, me to amend the warrant. Going away right now…it's just not feasible."

"But the case won't last forever." Dylan knew Briana was making sense, but she fought the logic anyway. "I don't want to lose you. In any capacity," she said.

"You wouldn't be losing me, though." Briana uncrossed her arms and reached out to her. It was a simple touch but it felt so nice. Why was she resisting this?

"It's just…" She stopped herself. Not because she didn't think Briana would listen. More because she didn't know how to put into words that she'd never been in a relationship that was even remotely close to this. In the past, she'd only ever revealed an edited version of herself. With Briana she'd put it all on the line. She'd been unable to stop herself. The result was a union that was equal and honest and balanced and so full of love. What if even the smallest change messed with that dynamic? "Is your mind made up?" she finally asked.

"No." Briana looked right at her, and all Dylan wanted to do was kiss her.

"Would you think about it a little longer?" Maybe it was selfish to even ask, but she needed to know she was doing everything to maintain their perfect status quo. Or maybe she just needed a minute to wrap her head around the idea. She wasn't even sure. "Not forever. Just give it a bit more time?"

"Of course." Briana rubbed her forearm and coupled the gesture with a shrug that was submissive and sweet. "I would do anything for you." She moved away and pulled the wagon along with her, advancing them down the row. "Come on. Let's finish up and get out of here." She dropped her voice to a whisper and added, "I literally don't know how much longer I can keep my hands off you."

It was precisely what Dylan needed to hear.

❖

Dylan secured the envelope and scribbled her initials and shield number across the seal at the top. The phones were quiet, and even activity in the field was sparse. While Shawn was busy scouring the financials of the Wine Bar and Paul Rafferty's bank accounts, she tackled transcripts.

She placed her work in two neat piles ready to be filed away for future reference and evidentiary purposes.

"That's all she wrote," Dylan said as she capped her pen with finality.

"All caught up?" Shawn asked without taking his eyes off his own busywork.

"For the moment." She laughed. "Cut to an hour from now when George starts his rounds, making calls and dropping off drugs to his clients."

"Enjoy the peace, I say." He leaned back in his chair and crossed his ankles up on the counter.

He wasn't in position two seconds before Detective Chris Conroy burst into the room, knocking his feet down and playfully teasing, "Where's your manners, bro?"

Trevor was a half-step behind. "Oh, cool, you're both here. We want to pick your brains on something."

"What's up?" she asked, looking back and forth between them.

Trevor looked at Dylan. "You know how you've been texting with Benji? And meeting up to buy more oxy?" He shifted his focus to Shawn. "And you zeroed in on some intel you think is related to a heavy hitter that Paul deals with. Like a real drug trafficker?"

"Yes." Shawn thumped his hand on a thick stack of papers. "Fernando Rojas. There's definitely a link there. He contacts Paul a lot, but they never really say much on the phone. I did some digging, though, and Rojas's name is on some of the paperwork used to open the Wine Bar. There's some fugazi money transactions between them, I'm sure of it. I just don't have it figured out yet."

Trevor nodded, taking it all in. "So what we were thinking…" He kneaded his hands together the way he did when he was gearing up for something big. "Dylan, you know how you told Benji you might have a friend interested in purchasing?"

"I'm trying to get him to sell me more. Bigger quantity. Just to make the charges better, when it comes time to arrest."

"I know. It's perfect." He clapped Chris on the shoulder. "Next time, you're going to bring Chris with you." Dylan was about ready to protest but Trevor stopped her. "Hear me out." He scratched his five o'clock shadow. "We have these guys dealing pills. On the phone, directly to you. And we know they're into heroin. Fentanyl. Coke. But our initial victim was DOA on a heroin overdose. That is the predicate crime for this whole case. Dylan, remember the female student we interviewed in Jersey?" She nodded even though he was mostly just verbalizing a list. "She OD'd on heroin as well. It would be money if we could get an actual heroin sale. Bring everything full circle, lock it up real tight."

"I'm getting there, bro. Give me some time to develop my opioid habit, and I'll go in for the quick cheap hit."

"I know. But do we really have time?" he asked. "Every day these guys are in business more drugs hit the streets. The risk of addiction increases. Lives get destroyed. People die. I hate the thought of that."

Dylan did too. It was something that kept her up at night.

"Honestly, Dylan, and I mean no offense here." Who fucking started a conversation like that? A know-it-all like Chris Conroy, that's who. Dylan tried to control her irritated expression when she gave him her attention. "You don't really pass as a heroin user."

"And you do?" She hated that she was being so defensive, but as far as this case was concerned, Chris Conroy was the newbie, not her.

"I did seven years as a narcotics undercover." Chris folded his arms across his chest, arrogant as fuck. "I got this."

"And we don't think this is going to blow the case up?" Dylan wondered aloud. "What if they make us as cops when I walk in there out of the blue with a complete and total stranger?"

"It's a risk, for sure," Trevor piped up. "But Benji's sold to you a bunch already. And we need to do something to get to the next level." He shrugged. "Obviously, we'll be prepared if shit goes sideways. Pull the plug right on the spot. Make collars and hope one of 'em flips."

"That's not going to happen anyway," Chris said. "I know my stuff. I can do this."

"What's the angle?" Shawn asked, beating her to the question.

"I contacted one of my old confidential informants." Chris rubbed his biceps as he talked. He was a little too in love with his own physique.

"There was a turf war about a year and a half ago. Since then, Fernando Rojas has been trying to regain some territory in Washington Heights. I'll go in with a backstory, casually drop some deets about living with my girlfriend up on Saint Nicholas Ave. I'm telling you, Paul's greed will take over from there. We're gonna see dollar signs in his eyes. Trust me, I know how this plays out."

He seemed so certain that Dylan was inclined to believe his instincts were correct. Trevor looked right at her, and she read his desire for her stamp of approval. She appreciated that he checked in with her. It highlighted how much she absolutely loved being part of this team. Even Chris's outrageous ego couldn't rain on her parade.

"Hey, if you guys say this'll work, far be it from me to throw shade." She rolled her chair backward, conceding the spotlight.

"We just have the small task of getting the AUSA on board." Trevor winced. It was well known Briana's aggressive drive was equally matched by her commitment to safety. This was going to be a hard sell.

"It's Briana Logan." Chris waved Trevor off, all but assuring her approval was in the bag. "She loves me."

Gross. Dylan hated when people misinterpreted attention paid to them for doing their job as actual romantic interest. Good-looking men were the worst offenders, in her opinion. They simply couldn't get past their own vanity to see that interaction was required to accomplish work.

"She does?" Trevor asked, seeming keen to use any leverage to get the green light.

"Bro." He flexed his chest and biceps. "Ladies can't resist me."

"You wish." Thank God Shawn called his bluff. Dylan was afraid if she even opened her mouth, she'd tell him to back the fuck off.

"No, I'm serious." Chris crossed his arms and rocked back and forth on his heels. "We had, like, a thing. She was into me. One part of me in particular."

Dylan barely registered his smug laugh. She was too busy trying to make sense of what he was saying. There was no way this jerkoff could be telling the truth. Briana had rules. She didn't cross lines.

"Let me go talk to her," Chris said. "If I have to take one for the team, so be it." He puffed out his chest. "As good as Logan is in the courtroom, she's even better in the bedroom." His smile was full of grotesque pride at what he obviously considered a conquest. "She ain't bad on the couch either."

"Enough." Shawn threw both hands up, shutting Chris down. "That's our boss you're talking about. Have some respect."

It should have been her putting Chris in his place. Briana didn't need defending, but jerks like Chris needed to be told that slut-shaming was unacceptable in every circumstance. But Dylan could barely breathe, let alone talk.

The plant was so quiet that they all seemed to jump when the radio chirped. Ahmed's voice boomed through, saying that Benji was headed north on the FDR. Dylan couldn't even move to answer him. Thankfully Shawn grabbed the walkie and spat out a quick "10-4."

"I'm going to go talk to Briana," Trevor said. He turned to Chris. "Go catch up with the surveillance. Stay in the back, so you don't get burned before this even gets out of the gate."

Dylan wasn't sure if she detected frustration in Trevor's voice or if she was projecting her own feelings onto the entire situation. It didn't matter. She was angry and hurt, and all she wanted to do was talk to Briana.

It wasn't even an option, which was maybe for the best. As soon as Benji was on the move, the phones came to life, and she and Shawn kept busy monitoring the info and relaying it to the field team. It was a distraction, but not enough. Images of Chris and Briana popped into her mind with zero warning. An hour passed and then another, her emotions slipping from jealously to betrayal and back again on a kind of distorted, torturous loop. Countless times she picked up her phone to text Briana but hesitated every time.

She simply had no idea what to say.

Why hadn't Briana told her about Chris?

There'd been myriad opportunities, but she'd said nothing. As the day wore on, that distinct question ate away at her, and the second Trish arrived to cover the evening shift, she grabbed her gear in a hurry.

"Hey, Dylan." Shawn caught her as she was about to leave the plant. "You okay?"

"Yep," she lied.

"Karrakas will be here in five minutes. If you wait we could grab a drink."

"Not really feeling it. Thanks anyway."

"You sure?" He scratched his scruffy beard. "We don't have to talk about anything. You just look like you could use a friend."

"Another time. Okay?"

"Yeah, of course," he said. "Just don't drive yourself crazy. Chris is…" He shook his head. "He's a showoff. Don't let him get to you."

Dylan didn't have time to deconstruct whether Shawn was trying to talk her down over Chris's beefed-up role in the investigation or if he was advising her to chill out over the Briana bombshell he'd dropped.

"Thanks, Shawn," she said.

There was kindness in his eyes, and Dylan could see his offer of friendship was real. But her head was pounding and going in a thousand directions at once. She just wanted to be alone.

CHAPTER TWENTY-TWO

Dylan's phone vibrated in her pocket, and she had to put the laundry basket down to see who it was.

Dinner?

Briana. Normally she would jump on the invitation. But tonight she felt...uncertain. She closed her eyes and rolled her neck, hoping the right words would come to her. It was confusing. She wanted to see Briana, and she didn't. They needed to talk, but she wasn't ready.

Three hours of chores hadn't brought her any closer to peace over the situation.

I'm not really hungry, she typed back. It was the truth even if it was a cop-out.

I could pick something up and come over. I'm just leaving work now. It would still be a while before I get there...

Would you mind if we skipped a night? I'm pretty beat.

It wasn't entirely true, but since leaving work, Dylan churned through one emotion after the next.

There was the initial jealousy and anger over something that happened before they'd even met, and while she could talk herself out of those irrational feelings, it seemed nothing abated her sadness. Even when she told herself the past didn't matter—because it didn't—she kept coming back to the same thing. Briana had kept this from her, and she simply couldn't wrap her head around that fact.

Being kept in the dark undermined their entire connection. It made her feel disposable.

You need a night off from me? Briana asked, following it with a quick *LOL.*

Dylan swallowed hard, not knowing how to respond. It was kind of true, and it made her feel terrible. Her fingers hovered over the keypad as she tried for the right words. She was spared commenting when Briana sent another text.

It's fine, baby. I'll check in later. Briana dropped in the kiss emoji.

The relief Dylan felt triggered a kind of guilt. She found the big red heart and bounced it into the thread, hoping it was enough.

After another forty minutes of mindless household tasks, she slipped under the covers with some chamomile tea and killed the lights. She cued up an old episode of *ER*, hopeful that some scripted drama was just the remedy to snap her funk.

❖

Nine fifteen and the phones were already blowing up. Mornings at the plant were usually slow. Paul went to his day gig, being a lawyer to a mostly elderly clientele, likely stealing their prescriptions, definitely finagling their pensions. Benji hit the gym for two hours at a pop, and George never got out of bed before eleven.

Dylan typically used the time to catch up on admin tasks, but this morning was a whole different story. She'd planned to text Briana and try to convince her into a coffee date around the block just so they could see each other.

Those plans fell by the wayside when Paul started the day bright and early with a call to Benji. He ranted about a face-to-face he'd had with someone named Big Red. He repeated it over and over again, and even though he didn't give details he sounded stressed. Dylan looked at Shawn and said, "Big Red. It's gotta be Rojas."

"Bingo," Shawn said.

Dylan jotted details of the conversation, even though it didn't seem overly pertinent until Paul instructed Benji to wake up George and meet him at the Wine Bar at ten a.m. sharp.

"Nice," Dylan said, reaching for the portable radio to update Trevor in the field. Shawn turned on the plant monitor and cued up the Wine Bar surveillance equipment to make sure everything was working properly. It was only a few minutes before Paul showed up, followed by Benji and a truly bedraggled looking George.

"Is your fucking phone broken, man?" George's voice echoed through the quiet bar.

"Shut up, you lazy motherfucker." Paul stood in the center of the space, and it honestly couldn't have been a more perfect angle. He didn't even take his coat off. "Listen to me. While you losers were partying or whatever the fuck last night, I met with the big man. Big Red."

George looked confused, or maybe he just wasn't awake enough.

"Rojas." Paul spelled it out for him. "He's tired of losing business up in the Heights. He needs an in. George, who do you know up there?"

He ran his hands through his unkempt hair. "Fuck. No one, really."

"What about you, Goldenballs?" He nodded at Benji. "You got a piece of ass up that way?"

"Not really, cuz."

"Well." Paul shoved his hands in his coat pockets. "I suggest you find one. I don't know. Check out the schools, the clubs. We need to solidify this relationship. This is our retirement plan right here, boys. Make it happen."

"Seriously, Paul, we couldn't have had this conversation on the phone?"

"Grow up, George. Or get a fucking real job." Paul's smile was slick. "Until that happens, I'm your boss. Don't you fucking forget it." He opened the door, all but pushing them out. "Get to work, gentlemen."

Shawn whipped his chair around. "Did we just get all that on audio and video?"

"Fuck yeah, we did. Trevor's going to be pumped."

Dylan watched Paul leave the Wine Bar before shutting down the eavesdropping devices. "I'm only slightly annoyed that it proved Chris's intel was on the money." She coupled her admission with a laugh, so Shawn would know she was mostly kidding. "After hearing how eager Paul is to get in deep with Rojas, it sounds like his plan will really work."

"He's not a bad guy. Chris, I mean." Shawn was busy logging and documenting the footage. "I know he's arrogant as anything. And what he said yesterday about Logan was uncalled for—I'm not excusing that." He kept his head down as he wrote. "But he always had my back when we were assigned to Team 4. For whatever that's worth."

It was worth more than she wanted to admit. "I heard you had a rough time over there. I'm sorry about that."

"Some people suck." He shifted his eyebrows. "What can you do?"

"Are you happy here? With us on Team 2?"

"Definitely. Everyone is cool here. Anyway"—he swiveled in his chair and Dylan hoped she hadn't made it awkward—"you better call Trevor and give him the skinny. I'm sure he's dying for the details."

Dylan barely got a sentence out before Trevor hit her with a bevy of questions. She slowed him down and provided every last tidbit, not realizing he was driving to the office the whole time they were on the phone. It was only when he burst into the wire room and his voice echoed from two different directions that she put it together.

"Legal meeting at noon," Trevor said as he hung up his cell. "Trish and Ahmed are coming in early to cover the phones. I'll need you two upstairs with me since you both witnessed all of that." He pointed at the monitor with his radio. "Obviously I'm going to watch it. First, I need to get Conroy in here so he can join us." Trevor was always going a mile a minute, but this seemed a record even for him.

"How is all this in the works already?" Dylan asked.

"I had already called Hollander and Nieves before Paul's meeting with the two lackeys went off. And I texted Briana while I was talking to you."

"And you drove here." Dylan smiled and shook her head. "Trying to show everyone up with four burners going at once."

"Multitasking, buddy." He waved his phone and handheld radio for emphasis. "I just think with things being this hot, Briana is going to go for the UC op with you and Chris."

"She didn't bite yesterday?" It suddenly occurred to her that she'd never followed up on the aggressive proposal.

Trevor bobbled his head back and forth. "She wasn't sold on it. But with this new info, it's a lock. I can feel it." He checked his watch. "We have a few minutes. Shawn, pull together everything we have on Rojas. Pedigree, intel reports, financials. Same for Paul, if you can." He summoned Dylan with a finger. "You, me, and Chris need to iron out specifics for the new undercover plan. I want to present a well-oiled machine, so there's no doubt we can pull this off."

It was that simple. By the time they went up to see the legal staff on the tenth floor, they were a united front. Dylan could tell that Nieves and Hollander were proud of their team's ingenuity. Briana listened and asked a few questions, but she signed off on the operation without so much as a single protest.

During the twenty-minute meeting, Dylan avoided direct eye contact with her for as long as possible. Not because she didn't want to see Briana. The opposite was true. But she needed time with her girlfriend, not Briana Logan, AUSA. And if she was being honest, being in the same room as both Chris and Briana dredged up everything she hated about the whole situation. At least he'd brought his manners today. If not for his infantile comments the day before, no one would have a clue there was any history between him and Briana.

As the briefing wrapped, she caught Briana looking at her. There was a quick flash of pain and confusion behind her eyes, and it hit her right in the gut. Dylan needed to fix this, like now.

The second she was back in the plant, she pulled out her phone to send a text, but Briana had beaten her to it.

Are you ghosting me?

Dylan couldn't help but chuckle at the terminology. *Lol. No.*

Then are we fighting?

What would we even be fighting about? As far as Dylan knew, Briana had no idea she was even aware of her past with Chris. Not that the knowledge would be grounds for an argument anyway.

I don't know what's going on, Dylan. You blew me off last night. And you haven't contacted me since. You wouldn't even look at me in the meeting.

I didn't blow you off, she typed. *I was just tired.*

You didn't even say good night.

Dylan blinked long and slow, knowing it was a valid point. They'd idly slipped into the habit somewhere along the way. If she and Briana didn't spend the night together, they always texted before bed. Last night Dylan had drifted off mid-episode, and when she finally woke up, it was after one in the morning. She'd planned on explaining that fact this morning, but the day had taken on a life of its own.

I'm sorry. We do need to talk. Not here, obvi. Dylan still had no idea what to say, but not talking was making it worse. *My house after work?*

Ok. Briana's message appeared, but there were bubbles until a second text came through. *One thing.*

Yes?

Are we okay?

Dylan could sense the stress in Briana's words, and it killed her to know she had any anxiety about their status. Despite the inane jealousy she felt over Briana and Chris, and the slight sucker-punch she felt over Briana's omission, Dylan knew this would not break them. She didn't even have to think about her response.

I love you, Bri.

When her buzzer sounded at six fifteen, Dylan was totally thrown. It had to be Briana, but this was record time for someone who rarely left the office before six. In socked feet, Dylan padded down the hall and the stairs to the front door.

"You did not have to rush here," she said as she wrenched the door open. "Whoa, what's all this?" She reached across the threshold and took two huge bags from Briana. She bent forward to drop a kiss on her lips.

"That's dinner." Briana touched her back gently as she followed Dylan up the stairs to her apartment.

Dylan placed the food on the counter, and she couldn't help but feel warm everywhere when Briana's arms wound around her waist. The simple touch seemed to melt all her negative thoughts right away. Briana kissed her shoulder. "Whatever it is, we'll get through it," she said. "But I thought, Wilkie's takeout never made anything worse."

"I don't know." Dylan smiled even though Briana couldn't see her. "Depends on whether or not you remembered corn bread."

"Double order." Briana scooted between her and the counter and shrugged. "But since I really wasn't sure what I was walking into, I picked up this." She reached into one of the bags and pulled out a pint of ice cream. "Just in case."

"Haagen Dazs pistachio. Pulling out all the stops." Dylan laughed at her own joke as she took the ice cream and put it in the freezer.

On her way back she grabbed plates and utensils and reached for napkins. "Do you want wine, beer, seltzer? What are you feeling?"

Briana covered her hand as she set everything down on the counter. "Dylan. I'm trying to be chill." She let out a measured breath. "The truth is I'm freaking out." Her brow creased and her eyes were heavy with doubt. "I know it's only been twenty-four hours, but something's off with us. I can feel it. What's going on?"

Fuck. There had been part of her that believed she could just move past it. Never bring up Chris Conroy ever again. Work it out on her own and get over it by herself. Because for all her analyzing over the past day and a half, Dylan had no idea what to say. There seemed no way to admit she felt both insecure about Briana's past and betrayed by her lack of candor that didn't make her sound possessive and overbearing.

"I can see you thinking." Briana squeezed her hand. "Please just talk to me."

Dylan took a deep breath, done searching for magic words. "It's nothing," she lied.

"Obviously it's something." Briana's tone was soft. Pleading almost. "In the whole time I've known you, it's never been like this. You're quiet. You won't talk to me or look at me. You're shutting down. And it makes me feel like we're not okay."

"We're okay," Dylan said. It was possible her silence was making this worse. "Me and you are fine." One look at Briana, and Dylan saw the uncertainty in her eyes. It rattled her. She'd better just come clean. She licked her lips and rolled her neck, feeling like a petty jerk that this was her hang-up. "It's just…I heard about you and Chris Conroy." Dylan unpacked the food mostly to avoid eye contact. "That you used to date." She raised her eyebrows, qualifying her statement on the spot. "Or whatever."

"We didn't date."

"That doesn't really make it better, actually."

Briana was quiet, and she pursed her lips repeatedly. Even though Dylan had brought it up, she hated that Briana was in the hot seat.

"Look, you don't owe me an explanation," Dylan said, hoping to cut the tension. "I have a past too." She opened a container of Wilkie's signature mac and cheese. "The thing is…" She gripped the edge of the counter and focused on the tin of corn bread. Why did it sting so much to talk about it? "I wish you would have told me about Chris. It's stupid, but finding out from him kind of sucked."

"I'm sorry, Dylan."

The last thing she wanted was for Briana to think she needed justification for having a life before she was in the picture. "You don't have to apologize. That's not what I'm saying."

"I do." Briana reached across the small distance and touched her face. "Will you look at me?"

Dylan felt a twinge in her throat and tipped her head back to keep her eyes from watering. She clenched her jaw and willed her emotions to regulate. It was no use. Briana could see she was losing it.

"Baby, you're hurt." Briana got up from her seat and moved right into Dylan's space. She caressed her face and kissed her cheeks. "I am so, so sorry for hurting you." Dylan felt her full soft lips cover her neck as she whispered, "I love you. I never want to hurt you."

"Why didn't you tell me? That's what bothers me. Does that make sense?"

Briana took a long second, and Dylan wondered if she was trying to come up with an answer that wouldn't upset her. "When he got transferred to the case along with Shawn Fisher, I was going to tell you. I almost did."

"But?"

"I don't know. It's a combination of things, I suppose." Briana's touch was gentle as she smoothed over the pocket of her button up. She looked up, and Dylan saw nothing but honesty and love in her gorgeous hazel eyes. "I went out with Chris a few times. It was before he was in Major Case. We met through a mutual friend. God, years ago." She was so serious and beautiful that Dylan almost wanted to stop her with a kiss, but she'd asked for an answer, and Briana was honoring the request. She owed it to her to listen.

"The truth is…" Briana chewed her lower lip. She looked stressed as fuck. "At the risk of sounding completely cold, Chris didn't have that monumental an impact on my life. Telling you seemed not worth the door it might open."

"What does that mean?"

"It means…ugh." Briana dropped her head against her chest. "This is hard."

"What is?"

"This," Briana muffled into her shirt.

Dylan lifted her chin up and found her lips. She kissed her long and slow and soft. "I love you. Talk to me."

"Okay." Briana sighed, clearly giving in. "I didn't tell you about Chris because I was afraid if I brought it up, we'd start talking about the past. Yours and mine." Briana toyed with a tiny button near her collar, and Dylan felt the imprint of her fingertips through her shirt. "I don't like to think about you with anyone else. Which is a challenge, especially in this neighborhood. But I do my best to block things out in order to protect myself, my heart, my ego. Discussing Chris seemed to fly in the face of that strategy."

Dylan was blown away by this revelation. Her mind had gone in a thousand directions over why Briana had kept Chris a secret. A door to jealousy was not among them. "But you don't get jealous—you even told me so when we met."

"Funny thing," Briana pouted. "Turns out, I do."

"Bri—"

Briana stopped her with one finger to her lips. "This is all new to me. Love, jealousy. What if I'm not wired that way? What if I screw it all up?"

"Look, babe." Dylan kissed her forehead and hugged her tight before ducking down a little, so they were eye to eye. "This is new to me too. I've only ever been in love with one person, and I'm looking at her."

"You don't have to say that."

"I'm saying it because it's the truth." Dylan dotted a kiss on her nose. "You don't want to know about my past. That's fine." She shrugged. "It's kind of boring anyway. This. Us. That's what matters."

Briana leaned in for a kiss. "You're sweet."

"You are." Dylan kissed her again. "Do you think we could agree to an open line of communication? Maybe one where we adjust the parameters as we go along?" Dylan was shooting from the hip, but it felt right.

"So we talk about issues as they arise but only go full disclosure on a case-by-case basis?"

"Look at you with the fancy legalese." Dylan bit her lip and threw in an exaggerated nod to suggest she was down for the role-play. "It's hot."

Briana rolled her eyes and whacked her biceps. "Jerk."

"All kidding aside, do you think that could work?"

"I do." Briana placed a tender kiss on her arm in the spot she'd just playfully punched before scooting over to her seat. "I really do."

CHAPTER TWENTY-THREE

Briana reached for Dylan's shirt off the floor. It was barely nine thirty, but she knew the pattern by now. Dylan would be out cold for at least an hour. She headed to the kitchen and grabbed the ice cream and a spoon and slipped back into the bed next to Dylan, ready to shut off her mind and get lost in social media.

"Is that ice cream? In bed?" Dylan's voice was a mix of judgment and intrigue beneath the thin veil of slumber.

"I thought you were asleep." Briana scooched slightly lower. She loaded a spoon full of pistachio decadence. "Here, bae," she said, delivering Dylan the first bite.

"Mm. That's good." Dylan rolled onto her back, and Briana stole a glance at her perfect naked torso. She was all smooth skin and lean muscle. Briana leaned forward and kissed her chest before she indulged her own sweet tooth.

"You can sleep," she said as she ruffled Dylan's sex hair. "You do not have to entertain me."

"I feel bad. I don't want you to be bored."

"Baby, I have my phone. I have Haagen Dazs pistachio." Briana gave Dylan another taste. "Close your eyes. It's fine." She anchored the spoon in the center of the ice cream and combed Dylan's hair with her fingers.

"That feels nice."

In the moonlit room half under the covers, spent and satiated and sleepy, Dylan looked so opposite the strong brave detective she witnessed in action on the daily. Briana was always acutely aware of the hazards of police work. But in this moment the reality of potential danger hit her right in the heart.

"Do you ever worry about getting shot?"

"No." Dylan didn't even open her eyes.

"Never?" she asked.

Dylan's smile was soft and her eyes opened to half-mast. "Are you worried about me getting hurt at work?"

"Yes."

"It's not going to happen." Dylan reached for her hand and kissed her fingertips. "I promise."

"You don't know that," Briana argued. She didn't know why she was getting worked up, but Dylan's nonchalance didn't put her at ease.

"Do you want to hear about how I got stabbed?" Dylan wore a wicked grin, and Briana wasn't sure if she was kidding or not.

"Are you serious?" Briana paused, leaving a spoonful of pistachio midair as she waited to find out if this was some kind of sick joke.

Dylan laughed and nodded at the same time.

"Why are you laughing? Getting stabbed is not funny."

"See, that's where you're wrong. It was hilarious." Dylan seemed suddenly awake as she propped up on one elbow and hijacked a bite of ice cream.

"Go ahead. Make fun of how you almost died, and watch my heart break. That's nice."

"First of all…" Dylan leaned forward and kissed her. "I didn't almost die." Dylan scooped up more ice cream and offered it to her. "Second, it was really no big deal. Definitely not the hero moment you're picturing."

"We'll see." Briana reclaimed the spoon and leveled off the pint as she feigned indifference. "I'm listening," she said.

She watched Dylan lean back into the pillow, lacing her fingers behind her head as she channeled the memory. Her mouth curled into a half smile, and her eyes sparkled. Briana could get lost just looking at her, and when she spoke in her sleepy, husky voice…forget it.

"I was basically a rookie," Dylan started. "Maybe I had a year on." She shrugged as though that detail wasn't important. "My partner and I responded to a radio call for a domestic."

"Okay."

"Thing is, domestic violence calls can be hairy sometimes. Those and traffic stops are probably the two most dangerous situations you can get involved in as a police officer. Because you never know what you're stepping into."

"This." Briana waved her spoon in a circle. "The preamble of harrowing stats…" She put on a syrupy smile. "Not helping."

"It's fine. Just listen." Dylan reached into her open shirt and brushed a knuckle along her bare skin. It was such a subtle action, but it lowered her blood pressure immediately.

"So we show up at the residence. I'm all geared up, ready to race in and save the day. Got my vest on, extra cuffs, pepper spray, you name it."

"Prepared." Briana nodded in support. "That's what I like to hear."

"I was buffed out for sure." Briana felt Dylan's finger trace the outline of her panties as she spoke, and it made her instantly wet. She tried to ignore it and focus on the story. "I was not ready for what I was about to walk into."

Briana's mouth went dry, and her heart raced. Even Dylan's soft touch couldn't soothe her as she waited in anticipation to hear the outcome of an event that Dylan had clearly survived.

"This couple was fighting. Typical for a domestic violence call. They were just arguing, though. Screaming at each other, but nothing physical. And it was all about their pets. They had something like six cats, if I'm remembering correctly."

"If you are about to tell me that any cats got hurt, stop right there." She started to cover her ears, but Dylan stopped her and clasped her hands over her heart, clearly pretending to be affronted.

"And here I was thinking you were concerned for my well-being. I see how it is." Dylan laughed. "None of the animals got hurt. I promise."

"I'm sorry. I just can't handle any kind of animal cruelty."

"You and me both. The lady at this call too."

Briana wondered what that meant, but instead of interrupting she took a bite of ice cream and let Dylan finish.

"Anyway, we're standing there with all these cats climbing around us, the couple yelling at each other, and out of nowhere a swarm of birds flies into the living room."

"Wait? They had cats and birds?"

"Crazy, right?"

"Bizarre and brave."

"Exactly." Dylan licked her lips, and Briana could see her recalling the details. "These birds start flying all over the living room, and I'm freaking out and swatting at them because I'm, like, scared."

"Of what? The birds?"

"Yeah. I don't like birds. They creep me out."

"For real?" Briana was curious just how deep this fear went, but she was overwhelmed with finding out the facts. "Where did they come from? And are we talking pigeons or domesticated birds?"

"They were parrots. Or parakeets. I don't know the difference." Dylan rubbed her eyes and shook her head. "I guess they came from the kids' room. I don't know. But I'm there covering my head and trying to keep these creatures from using me as a perch. Of course the woman thinks I'm out to harm them, so she goes after me with the first thing she sees."

"Oh no."

"A tweezer. Gets me right in the arm." Dylan tapped her biceps as proof. "I have a scar and everything."

"No!" Briana said through a gasp. She tried to keep from laughing as she leaned in. "Show me."

"We'd probably need to turn the light on. It's miniscule." Dylan reached for her hand and guided it over a tiny bump near the top of her arm. "You feel it?"

"My poor baby."

"That's it. My big line of duty injury."

"Did you need stitches?"

"One." Dylan held up a single finger. "One stitch."

"No." She peered closer but still could barely make out the mark.

"I did have to get a tetanus shot. Which oddly hurt more than the tweezers." Dylan grabbed a bite of ice cream and swallowed it with a certain amount of finality. "I never really told anyone that," she said, returning the spoon.

"Why?"

"Um…it's embarrassing."

"No, it isn't. I'm glad you didn't really get too hurt, though." She placed a kiss in the vicinity of the old wound. "It's cute that you're afraid of birds." She took a bite of ice cream. "Are you still?"

"Yes."

"See, that's adorable."

"I think you're making fun of me." Dylan narrowed her eyes, but she didn't really seem upset.

"Maybe a smidge," she teased. "I like knowing stuff about you. Things that other people don't know. It makes me feel kind of special."

"You are special." Dylan pulled her in close for a kiss. "Your lips are cold."

"Ice cream."

"Right."

It clearly didn't put Dylan off because she went back for more and then some, kissing the way down her neck to her semi-exposed breast. Briana didn't dare stop her. On the contrary, she followed Dylan's momentum when Dylan lay back on the mattress and used the collar of her shirt to pull Briana on top. Miraculously, she held on to the pint of Haagen Dazs.

"I should put this away." She maneuvered into a straddle to get up, but Dylan held her in place.

"Not yet."

"You want more?"

"I just like where you are right now." Dylan's grin was more than suggestive, but Briana didn't need any encouragement. She was beyond ready to go again.

Dylan urged her hips lower, so their bodies aligned. "That's better," she said, holding on to her waist and grinding just the slightest little bit. "I love the way you feel," she said. Her voice was raspy as hell, and her hands wandered. "Tell me something no one knows about you."

Leave it to Dylan to ask a random question while she was trying to get her hormones under control. Briana was so turned-on she could barely think. Her underwear was saturated, and she was positive Dylan could tell. "For real?" she asked.

"It can be anything." Dylan's pout was cute and sexy at the same time. "Please?"

The request was simple, yet deep. Dylan was literally asking for an inside track. The crazy thing was she already had it. Briana had never let her guard down this much with anyone. Ever. But Dylan wanted details that could be hers alone. Briana understood the desire, and she racked her brain to come up with something good. "Things no one knows about me. Let's see."

"I'll just entertain myself while you think." Dylan drew lazy designs on her belly and her breasts, and Briana felt her body react.

"I have one." She twirled the spoon in her hand, almost disappointed something surfaced so quickly.

"Hit me."

"I can't catch anything with my left hand. No matter how hard I try. Just can't do it."

"Bri, you're left-handed. That makes no sense."

"I know." She offered Dylan a spoonful of ice cream. "That's what makes it crazy."

"Fair enough."

"Oh," she said, immediately coming up with something better. "I can play the harmonica."

"So random. I love it."

"What can I say—I went through a Bob Dylan phase."

"Do you play guitar too?"

"Yes."

"Wait, do you sing?"

"I can hold a tune." Briana knew her voice wasn't star quality, but she'd sung in the choir through high school.

"I did not know any of this." Dylan seemed gratified and impressed. "How come I haven't been serenaded yet? You're holding out on me, honey."

"Well, I don't own a guitar or a harmonica at present."

"We're going to have to fix that asap. Because I need to experience this. Like, soon."

She loved the way Dylan looked in this moment. Impish and entertained. Content, playful, sexy. She wanted it to always be like this.

"Dylan," Briana said, fully aware she was about to change the momentum of the night. It was probably the wrong time to bring this up, but there didn't seem to be a golden moment, and it had been weighing on her for weeks. "I have to leave." She read the look of confusion on Dylan's face. "Not tonight. I'm talking about the case. The US Attorney's Office."

Dylan's groan sounded full of denial and protest. Briana needed to be strong.

"It's the right thing to do."

"Why?"

"You know why."

"But we're making progress. And if a legit heroin buy happens, everything could blow wide open."

Even though what Dylan said made sense, this decision still seemed the only real option. "I know."

"I know I sound selfish," Dylan said. "Obviously I want you at the helm because you're the best. Everyone knows that. But I also know how invested you are in this case. Don't you want to see it to the end?"

"Of course I do."

Briana had never bailed midway through on anything. Not impossible professors in law school, not cases she thought unwinnable. Not even the weird bowling class she signed up for during undergrad before she realized PE was an elective. She always followed through. As much as she wanted to bury the Raffertys and George Rivas with evidence and hold them accountable for their crimes, she wanted Dylan more.

"It's just getting too hard."

"But it's only for a little while longer."

"You don't know that."

"But we can control it."

"Only part of it. These cases, they twist and turn. There'll always be other targets. Spinoff investigations. There's already Rojas. You know how it goes."

"Yes, but someone else could handle it when, or if, that lead pans out. Or if another surfaces. It would be a fresh start."

"It wouldn't be, though. My boss would expect me to prosecute. I would expect that if I was the boss. Because it makes the most sense."

Dylan turned her head to the side, and Briana knew she was frustrated. She stood up to put the ice cream away before it completely melted and to give Dylan a second alone to process. She used the small walk to the kitchen to really think about what she wanted to say. There was a litany of logical and ethical reasons she could list to illustrate the soundness of her decision, but when she got back to the bedroom and saw the look on Dylan's face, she went straight from the heart.

"I'm in love with you." Dylan was about to interrupt her, probably to echo the sentiment, but Briana stopped her. "Just listen to me." She tipped her head up and stared at the crown molding. "It complicates everything." She walked to the bed and smiled in appreciation when Dylan pulled back the covers and made room for her to sit close.

"I'm in love with you too. Just for the record."

"I know." Briana ran her hand down the side of Dylan's chiseled face. "But there are times when I have to make case decisions, and my feelings for you"—she lowered her gaze—"they get in the way."

"I don't understand."

"You do all the legwork. The truly dangerous stuff. But I call the shots." She could see that Dylan still wasn't following. "When I'm going to prosecute a case, I want things to unfold in a certain way. Some people would say I'm too stringent, but to me it's a necessity for trial. It's why I'm successful." She hoped it didn't sound like she was bragging. She just wanted Dylan to understand where she was coming from. "I always require a minimum number of undercover buys. Usually three, but often more depending on how things play out."

"That's fair."

"And now we're talking about heroin. Which is great for the case. But, oof, it raises the stakes. And the risk."

"I can handle it."

"I don't doubt it." She knew Dylan was capable, but the knowledge didn't make her role any less terrifying. "Dylan. I have watched you— literally watched you—in action. I know you're good at your job. Even when you were putting on a show with Trish, I toughed it out and sat through it. For the case, yes, but also because I needed to know firsthand that you'd come out unscathed."

"I still feel awful about that."

"It's…whatever." Truthfully the angst she felt over the Trish situation paled in comparison to the direction the case was going. "Now the ante is upped once more, and you'll raise the bar with Chris. I am sure you will be great, but it will destroy me." Her chest tightened at the mere thought of Dylan engaging Paul Rafferty again. "I simply cannot be responsible for asking you to put yourself in danger over and over again." Her voice caught in her throat. "It kills me. And I can't bear to watch it anymore."

"Your mind sounds made up."

"This isn't a whim. I've been wrestling with it for a while. Please tell me you understand."

"I do." Dylan held her hand and kissed her. "I hate it, but I get it. I know this is ridiculous, but do you think we could maybe not talk about it anymore tonight? I know it's not really fair of me to ask. But first there was the Chris drama and now this." Her forced laugh was loaded with stress. "It's a lot."

"Of course." It would never be easy to discuss this decision. But then, there really wasn't much to say anyway. And Dylan had taken the news about Chris in stride, even though it was clear her ego was bruised as much over the past hookup as Briana's decision to not disclose it. "Let's sleep," she said, lying down next to Dylan and pulling the sheet around them.

"Funny thing." She felt Dylan smile against her neck. "I'm not tired anymore." Dylan's hand caressed her belly and inched lower by degrees as she dotted a trail of kisses along her neck and shoulder.

Briana had never turned Dylan away and she wasn't about to start now. Even though the night had been a drain both mentally and emotionally, her brain and her body were in full accord. She wanted Dylan. Now and always.

"I think I have a solution for that."

CHAPTER TWENTY-FOUR

"Testing one, two, three." Trevor looked right into Chris's buttonhole camera and then keyed the mic on his radio. "Shawn, you copy?"

"10-4." Shawn's voice cracked through the portable, and Dylan straightened up as she waited for Trevor to check her equipment. They were way off the set of the Wine Bar, tacking up ten blocks south at a small car park under the FDR Drive.

Trevor stood in front of her and waved one hand in front of her belt where the recording device was camouflaged. "One-two-three-four-five. Five-four-three-two-one." He spoke into the radio. "You got that, Shawn?"

"Five by five," Shawn said over the air.

Trevor looked between her and Chris. "You heard him. Five by five. How are you guys feeling?"

Dylan shook out her arms and bounced on her toes. Her adrenaline was going. She was pumped and ready with just the right amount of nervous anticipation to keep her sharp. The field team was in place, strategically positioned around the location without being too close to tip anyone off. "Good," she said.

"What about you, Chris? Any jitters?" Trevor asked.

"Nah, man. I'm cool."

Chris stood ramrod straight, and Dylan picked up on his tension. She nudged him with her elbow.

"So, listen. I told Benji we'd be by around eight. It's on the early side of when I usually meet up with him, but I laid it on thick that Trish has been giving me a hard time about being out." They'd been over it dozens of times, but Dylan could tell he was anxious, and she thought rehashing the plan would ground him. "I told him I was bringing my cousin—that's you—and said that you were interested in product. I didn't get specific, so he's probably assuming pills. But that's where you'll work your magic."

"I'm going to follow your lead," Chris said, "but when I see a natural opening to talk about heroin, I'm going to go for it."

"That works." Her strategy was helping relax him, she could tell. "I know you've done this before," she continued, "but you're new to this crew. Let me introduce you to the guys. They love to talk." She rolled her eyes, making fun of them. "If we're lucky, the Trish comments will open up some conversation about girls in general."

"I can mention my girlfriend Jocelyn who lives in the Heights."

"And then, boom." Dylan used her hands to mimic a rocket launching. "We're off to the races."

"All right." He clapped his hands and rolled his shoulders, seeming way more chill than he'd been three minutes earlier.

"You got this." She continued her last-minute pep talk. "And hey, if it doesn't pan out tonight, we get some oxycodone and call it a night. It's not a loss either way."

"You're right. Thanks, Dylan." His smile seemed genuine, and she hated that he was being nice. It was so much easier to detest him before she saw his human side. "I really think, though, based on the connection you've already established, we're going to nail this."

The second she and Chris entered the Wine Bar, it was game on. Benji hopped off his barstool and greeted them both with handshakes and shoulder bumps. Paul hooked them up with a new Californian vintage he was sampling. George even sought out Dylan's take on the Yankees' recent trades. It was like they were all buddies.

Everything else unfolded exactly according to plan. Dylan purchased painkillers, and Chris asked for an in, offering cash as he expertly segued into his desire for good heroin to offset the jones he felt for the more expensive stuff. He whined about staying with his girlfriend and how her neighborhood was dry for good H. He was suave and smooth without being pushy, but like he'd predicted, once Paul Rafferty realized they were talking about Washington Heights, he was all over it.

"That was fucking amazing." Dylan waited until they were on the subway headed back downtown to discuss what had just occurred.

"Fuck, I know." Chris laughed heartily before high-fiving her. He rubbed his hands together and bounced his knees. She knew it was all part of the adrenaline dump. Completing a risky operation with that level of success had an impact on the nervous system. Dylan knew it well. Right now she was happy and giddy and horny as fuck. And super bummed she'd be expected to celebrate with her team before going home to Briana.

The train rolled through the stops, and Dylan kept her excitement at bay, fidgeting and making idle small talk about the weather, New York City, the transit system, really anything but the case. Chris followed suit, and it wasn't until they were both safely inside the plant that she finally let her guard down.

Trevor, Shawn, Trish, and Ahmed cheered for them and clapped their backs. Even the tech team praised them for a job well done. Dylan knew she was beaming with pride as she shook hands with Sgt. Hollander and Lt. Nieves as they congratulated her.

"Great job, Detective Prescott." Briana's voice came from behind her, and she whipped around to see her outstretched hand. Dylan was more than stunned, but she shook Briana's hand, resisting every urge she had to pull her close and kiss her senseless.

"Thank you." She was curious why Briana had hung around, not that she was complaining. "We usually don't see you here after the operation," she said. Of course she knew the reason Briana typically bolted, but there was an audience, and she was trying to act normal.

"Special circumstances." Dylan saw absolute love in her eyes, and it made her feel warm all over. "High stakes and all," Briana added calmly. "Plus, I hear there's celebratory drinks happening." She scrunched her nose in her adorable way. "Who am I to turn down cocktails with New York's Finest?"

"Awesome," Dylan said. "Any idea where we're headed?"

"Miri texted me the address of the bar—I'll forward it to you now."

Dylan watched her thumb out a text, and she reached for her phone to check the location.

Do you have any idea how wet I am right now?

Briana's text was not the address of a bar, but it was a thousand times better. Dylan was instantly hard and throbbing, and probably red as all get-out. She didn't have a clue how to appropriately respond, but there was no time anyway because Trevor was suddenly right next to her.

"Go see the tech unit and get all unplugged and downloaded. We have a quick debrief scheduled in ten minutes, and then Baxter's." He wagged his finger between her and Briana. "You're both going, no excuses."

"Yes, sir." Dylan fanned over her body as she looked at Briana. "Let me go deal with this stuff. See you at the brief?"

"And after," Briana said with a smile. "You heard Trevor. It's basically an order."

❖

"I still can't believe you stayed." The crowd was big enough for Dylan to lean close to Briana without drawing suspicion as they waited for their drinks. "Thank you." She looked around to make sure no one was paying attention. "I don't even think I said that. I know it's hard for you to watch."

"And I know how much it means to you when I'm there."

"It does, you know." It was odd but true. Just knowing Briana was in the plant when she went undercover at the Wine Bar had a strangely calming effect on Dylan. For whatever reason her presence translated as a kind of unconditional support. It made her feel confident.

Under the lip of the bar, Dylan felt Briana's fingers brush hers, and it gave her the best kind of chill. "I'm going to cut out after this drink."

"Tired of me already?" Dylan teased, even though she knew it wasn't the truth.

"On the contrary." Briana thanked the bartender with a nod as she took the first sip of her cosmo. "Stef and JJ are at a bar in the Village. Will you meet me there?"

"For real?"

"It's Friday night in New York City. Our case just caught a major break. Thanks mostly to you. I want to celebrate." Her shrug was just a little bit flirty. "I know JJ's not your favorite person, but it would be nice to be out together in public. In a way that we obviously can't be here."

"Yes." Dylan didn't even have to think about it. More than anything in the world, she wanted to be with Briana. Even having to share her with JJ couldn't diminish the excitement she was anticipating at acting like a real couple, even if it was for one night in a bar across town.

"I'll text you the name of the place. For real this time," Briana said with a wicked grin. "Maybe stall a little after I leave?"

"Stagger our departure?" Dylan smiled into her drink. "How devious."

"I'd like to avoid scandal, even if it's only for a little while longer. Does that bother you?"

"Not at all." She was, however, mildly curious about Briana's wording that their romance need only be a secret for a little while longer, but maybe she was just being optimistic. Either way, now wasn't the time to inquire, especially since Shawn and Trevor were upon them.

"How great is Dylan?" Trevor was clearly feeling his drink as he tossed an arm across her shoulders.

"She's pretty amazing," Briana said.

Shawn nodded into his beer. "You were really good. This whole team is great."

Selfishly Dylan was glad no one had brought up Chris's role in the operation. As nice as he'd been tonight and as well as they'd worked together, she didn't feel like singing his praises in front of Briana. But she also didn't want to hog the credit for what was most definitely a team effort.

"It was your records analysis that led us to Big Red," Dylan said, praising Shawn with a raise of her glass. "We're a solid crew."

"I'm glad to hear you say that," Trevor said. "I wasn't going to mention anything until it was official, but Nieves put in a request to have you guys permanently assigned to our team. I always forget that you're technically on loan from other squads."

Dylan had the tendency to block that detail out too, but suddenly it seemed it might not matter. "You think it'll get approved?" she asked. She hated the thought of getting amped up for something that might not come to pass.

"It's basically a done deal," he said, clapping her back. "Paper-work's with the inspector right now." He took a sip of his drink. "We're doing great stuff. And we were short people anyway. Two old-timers retired last summer, and we lost another guy to the Special Victims Unit. It's just a rubber stamp at this point."

"Nice." Shawn fully fist pumped, and Dylan was happy to know he'd never have to go back to work with the ignorant, nasty people at Team 4. Plus, he was a good detective, and with all the hours they'd logged together in the wire room, they were on their way to being real friends. There was only one caveat.

"Chris too?" she asked even though she really wasn't excited to hear the answer.

"He complements the unit really well." Trevor seemed on the defensive, and Dylan wondered just how much he was tuned into. "All of us together"—he made a circle with his beer bottle to reference the detectives scattered around the bar—"we have a really unique and varied skill set. We're a force to be reckoned with."

She knew he was right. And heck, more than anything, she was stoked to be included in a team that felt truly unstoppable. A permanent transfer was everything she'd hoped for since the initial overhear months ago. Now it was poised to happen. And they were on the verge of bringing down real bad guys. Plus she'd inexplicably fallen in love along the way. Even the prospect of a career alongside Chris Conroy couldn't ruin her night.

"Thanks so much, Trev," she said. Nieves might be responsible for filing the official request, but she knew Trevor was behind the reassignment. Dylan was almost speechless. Everything felt like a blur, but she registered Shawn thanking him as well and Trevor deflecting the credit back to their hard work. It was kind of a verbal group hug until Miri interrupted, stealing Briana away for a quick think tank with Lt. Nieves.

Dylan stayed with the gang as they celebrated the evening's success and toasted the future. She was idly aware when Briana slipped out but made sure not to move a muscle. Stay under the radar, that was the name of the game. When her phone buzzed in her pocket, she took care to read the message with caution.

I love you. Have fun with the gang. She dropped in a link for Greyson Blue, an upscale-looking pub on the corner of Hudson and Perry in the West Village.

Be there as soon as I can, she typed.

Briana responded with a kiss, and Dylan could do nothing to cover the sappy look she was sure was plastered all over her face. If anyone noticed, they kept it to themselves, and no one said a word to her when she raced through her drink and passed on a round of shots. Even the text she got from Trevor as she sat in the back of a yellow cab was nothing short of supportive to whatever good time she was chasing. She squinted at his words as she mused whether or not he was really on to her and Briana, but before she could really give it much attention, she was at the bar, and she realized it didn't matter one bit.

CHAPTER TWENTY-FIVE

H i."
Dylan was already swooning at Briana's lyrical greeting, but when she slid into the seat next to her girlfriend, the kiss that followed turned her into an absolute puddle. Briana touched her cheek, and her lips lingered an extra second, making the contact at once soft and sexy but also leading. And public. So very public.

"I'm glad you're finally here," Briana said, still holding her face delicately.

"Sorry it took me so long," Dylan said even though they'd only been apart for about an hour.

"Get a room." Stef laughed at her own joke and still managed to make her feel welcome when she added, "I'm just kidding. You guys are freaking adorbs."

"Hey, Stef. JJ," she added, making eye contact with her old friend. "How's everyone's night?"

"Glad you're here, buddy. It's been too long." JJ signaled their server. "Let's get you a drink already."

Two rounds later, it was like they were a regular foursome. JJ wasn't as unbearable as she remembered, but perhaps that was Stef's effect. Either way Dylan was downright flattered when JJ told a story from way back that painted her as the unsung hero. She'd forgotten how funny her old friend could be and how nice it was to be out with a buddy and a girlfriend. Rather than question the timing or challenge the choice of company, Dylan let her guard down and simply enjoyed it. There was genuine laughter and good conversation. With Briana by her side holding her hand as they talked and joked, the entire night was perfection.

"You about ready to leave?" Briana whispered.

They'd been gifted a moment of privacy when JJ stepped outside to handle a work call, and Stef had used the opportunity to run to the ladies' room.

"Whenever you are, babe."

"As soon as they get back, let's settle up and head to your place. Sound good?"

"Sounds perfect."

Maybe it was the alcohol hitting her, or maybe it was the tiny designs Briana was tracing on the inside of her thigh, but Dylan's restraint was officially waning. She wanted Briana, and she was about to show her just how much with a real kiss.

"I know that look." Briana's tone was full of playful desire as she pushed her away. "Nothing good comes of it."

"Disagree," Dylan said, dialing back to drop a peck on her cheek.

"Look at you lovebirds." Stef slid into her chair across from them.

JJ returned to the group at almost the same time. "Sorry about that." With dramatically wide eyes, she placed her phone on the table.

"Everything okay?" Stef asked as she rubbed her back.

"It's fine, hon." JJ took a hefty swallow of her cocktail. "Just one of my needier clients. Friday night and he wants to rehash his entire case."

Stef cuddled in and dropped a kiss on her shoulder. "Can't help being in high demand."

It was nice to see them being cutesy, and Dylan was happy for Stef—and JJ too, she supposed—but she was about ready to burst. She expected Briana was just waiting for a pause in the conversation to break the news that they were headed home.

"Not to worry, though,"—JJ would not shut up—"in precisely seventeen days he's your problem, kiddo." JJ smiled wickedly and winked at Briana. "It's already on your agenda. *Hyde v. The DiNapoli Contingent.* It's actually a great case. Breach of contract with a tinge of a pyramid scheme thrown in. You're gonna kill it."

Briana answered with a terse smile. "We're going to head back to Brooklyn," she said, not at all addressing JJ's bizarre comment.

"Cool." JJ looked at Stef, presumably to assess whether she was ready to hit the road.

"Hold on." Dylan was still trying to figure out the previous exchange. She turned to Briana. "What does that mean? That you're going to kill it. Kill what?"

"Shit." JJ winced and her blink was slow and measured. "I'm sorry, Bri," she said, making eye contact solely with Briana as she wobbled her tumbler between them. "I just assumed Dylan knew."

"Knew what?" Dylan directed her question to Briana. "What don't I know?"

"I was going to tell you." Briana looked more frustrated than apologetic, and that pissed her off even more. She hated being kept in the dark, and Briana knew it.

"You're going to work for JJ?"

"At her law firm, yes."

"Well, that's nice." How was she just hearing about this now? "And you have a start date and everything."

"Dylan..." Briana started.

"Can we go?" Dylan needed to be out of the bar right now. She stood and grabbed her jacket.

JJ got up and blocked the path, holding her hands up to further halt her exit. "I shouldn't have said anything, and I'm sorry about that. But I really think this is a good move for Briana." JJ's apology wasn't the one she wanted, and right now she couldn't give a crap about the rationale.

"Could you please move?" she said as calmly as she could.

"Come on, Junior. Sit down. Let's all relax."

"Fuck you, JJ. And don't fucking call me Junior." She turned to Briana as she pushed past JJ. "I'm out. Are you coming?"

Dylan asked the question but didn't wait to hear Briana's answer. She speed-walked down the dark empty street, trying to make sense of what just happened in the bar. Briana was going to work for JJ. There were details ironed out and everything. For fuck's sake, she already had a case lined up. And Dylan was clueless. What in the actual fuck?

"Dylan, wait."

Caught up in her sidewalk rage, Dylan hadn't even realized Briana followed her outside. At the sound of her voice, she stopped in her tracks and tipped her head up to the stars. She looked at the bright buildings against the night sky and tried to make sense of what she was feeling. There was anger, but also betrayal. And sadness. So much sadness. On top of it all she felt foolish and babied for being kept out of the loop. She opened her mouth but only a fog of breath came out with no words behind it. Above everything else she felt defeated. Completely and utterly defeated.

"Why are you being like this?" From behind her Briana's tone was a full accusation, and it put her right over the edge.

"Me." Dylan whipped around and faced her. "Me?" She could barely contain her outrage. "You're mad at me?"

"I'm not mad, but I do think you're acting selfish right now."

"After that stunt, you have some nerve coming at me like I'm in the wrong."

"It wasn't a stunt, Dylan." Briana crossed her arms, looking just the tiniest bit aggressive. "JJ obviously had no idea you didn't know."

"I hate that you're defending her right now." It was probably over the top, but Dylan was seething.

"There's nothing to defend. This wasn't some kind of coup."

"Oh no?" Dylan stuffed her hands in her pockets, her mind overcome with images of her girlfriend with JJ as they engineered the arrangement that would bring Briana away from the federal investigation into the private sector. "This all just happened by chance?"

"Of course not. But it's not like you're making it sound either."

"You mean underhanded and secretive?"

"That's not fair."

"Am I wrong, though?"

"How dare you act like I didn't try to talk to you about leaving the US Attorney's Office." Briana shook her head back and forth and her jaw was clenched tight. Dylan could see her eyes watering in anger or defiance. Perhaps both. "I tried so many times to talk to you. But you shut me down. Every time."

"You only ever mentioned it in passing."

"Maybe it seemed that way to you, but I did tell you this was something I had to do." She seemed anxious and distressed. "Dylan, this is my life." Her voice was softer now, almost pleading. "My reputation. My career on the line. And you never even want to discuss it. I'm sorry I couldn't wait for you to be ready. I honestly thought that day might never come."

Maybe Briana was right, but still none of it made sense to her.

The case was moving along fine. Better than fine, honestly. She didn't think it was necessary to change a thing. But even if she was wrong, that seemed secondary now. Stealing the spotlight was the exit strategy Briana had chosen, and she couldn't keep it in.

"JJ?" she said, trying to keep her voice from cracking. "Of all the places you could work in New York City. You picked JJ." Why did it hurt so much? "Do you know what that does to me?"

"This isn't personal, Dylan."

"Yes, it is." Dylan squeezed her eyes shut and covered her face with both hands, fighting to keep her composure. She didn't want to break down. Not now, not ever.

"Please, baby." Briana was gentle when she pulled her hands away from her face. "Do you think I want to leave this case?"

"I don't know, Briana." Everything about this decision felt wrong, and Dylan didn't know how to say that without sounding like a jerk. "It feels like you're leaving me."

"How can you say that?" Briana touched her face and brushed a thumb over each cheek. Dylan wondered if she was checking for evidence of her distress. "I stayed on this case, way longer than I should have, because of you. I broke all my rules. Because of you." With a hand covering her heart, she still seemed distressed but unwavering. "I'm changing the course of my career. Because of you. How are you so blind to all of that?"

"I don't want to lose you."

"You won't."

"You don't know that."

"I do, though." Briana rested her hands over Dylan's chest. "You love me, right?"

Dylan felt her shoulders slump at the ridiculousness of the question.

"Please say it." Briana's expression said she needed to hear it, and Dylan gave in on the spot.

"I love you. You know I love you."

"Then trust me."

It was just so much more complicated than that. But Dylan didn't want to fight, so she said nothing while she got them a car back to Brooklyn.

They rode in silence, graduating to small talk as they slipped under the covers, ultimately finding each other in much needed release. It was good. Fine. Definitely not earthshattering make-up sex, but then, their fight was sort of a dud too. Almost a blowout, but then not.

Afterward, Dylan lay awake staring up at the ceiling while her mind raced in a thousand directions.

What if JJ was trying to seduce Briana? What if Briana was into it? Logically she didn't think that was true, and Briana had never given her any reason to doubt her fidelity. But why hadn't Briana told her sooner? It was the one thing that kept needling at her. Shouldn't this have been a conversation, not a unilateral decision? The more she thought about it, the more she stewed. Not Briana, though, she slept blissfully sound next to her like their relationship wasn't on the verge of bottoming out.

She was even downright chipper in the morning. "Hey, Sleepy," Briana said from her seat at the kitchen island. "I made coffee."

Dylan honestly couldn't believe she'd slept so late. But then, it was almost three a.m. the last time she'd rolled over and checked the clock. "Hey," she mumbled as she reached for a coffee mug.

"There's a crazy story in the news this morning."

Without making eye contact, she poured herself coffee. "Oh yeah?" she said, but her tone was flat and she didn't even care.

"Over in Queens a bull escaped from...I don't know where exactly, but he made it all the way down Steinway Street before he ended up in some store that sells vintage housewares. It was literally a bull in a china shop."

"Funny." She reached for the cream from the fridge and stood by the sink as she stirred her coffee.

"Okay." Briana dragged out the word, and Dylan heard her put her phone on the countertop. "Not feeling the news. Noted."

"I guess I just don't really care much about a news piece that's gone viral because of a stupid pun." She fiddled with the water tap and wiped up a gooey bit of liquid soap that had dripped into the basin.

"Are you not even going to look at me today?"

Every muscle in her body was tight. She didn't want to turn around, and the worst part was that she wasn't even sure why. Briana nestled against her and hugged her from behind. Dylan was so in her own head that she hadn't heard Briana dismount the stool or cross the kitchen to her.

"Please talk to me."

"I just"—Dylan shifted to unwind from Briana's embrace—"I need a minute."

"Do you want me to go?"

Briana looked so hurt that even if the answer was yes, Dylan wouldn't be able to say it. The problem was she didn't know what she needed. Or wanted. Space might be helpful to process, to understand, to deal. But she also wanted to be around Briana. Pretty much always. It was a dilemma.

"In a way, yes. But really, no," she said, recognizing the distress in her own voice. "I honestly have no idea what I want right now." She forced out a laugh, but it was mostly an effort to defuse the tension.

"You want me to stay on the case." It wasn't an offer, just Briana verbalizing what they both knew was the truth.

"Yes."

"Dylan, I can't." In spite of her words, Briana's light brush along her forearm was apologetic. "I can answer any questions you have. Maybe put some of your anxiety to rest. Correct me if I'm wrong, but I think a lot of your stress over this is just insecurity."

Dylan ignored the emotion Briana had tapped into and took aim at practicality. "I want you to stay with the investigation because you're an amazing prosecutor. And together we're a great team. Unbeatable."

"We are a great team. And it's sweet of you to say nice things about my skills as a lawyer." Briana caressed her forearms. "I love hearing you compliment me. I doubt that will ever get old." She looked utterly sincere. "But, Dylan, I need you to understand that I'm doing this because I want to be with you. Fully and completely. Out and proud. I'm done with whatever this is. Hiding and sneaking around. I want to have a real life with you."

It was logic she couldn't fight. Except Dylan didn't think being a real couple had to negate their collaborative work effort. "I'm sorry for making it sound like I only care about the case," she said, knowing how one-dimensional her appeal sounded. She was avoiding the real issue like the plague. "Why JJ?" she finally asked.

"For real?"

"Yeah, I'm asking for real." For the life of her she could not keep the emotion out of her tone. "Why her?"

"Okay. Well then." Briana took a step back and leaned on the edge of the stove, crossing her arms, fully on the defensive. "Jill Jessup runs a superior law firm. They're aggressive, and they challenge the status quo. They're doing groundbreaking work. It will be good to get out of my comfort zone and grow my experience." Her shrug said that was reason enough. "And, if I'm being honest, the position comes with quite a substantial raise."

"Why didn't you tell me?" The whole situation sucked, but that detail stung the most. "That's what hurts."

"I was going to tell you this weekend. The offer wasn't official until yesterday morning, and I didn't want to tell you before last night's operation." Briana touched her forehead and she looked stressed. "I'm sorry if that was the wrong call, but I'm always so worried about you during these things to begin with. I didn't want you to be distracted with this too."

It made sense. Briana knew she would stew. In a way it was considerate, but she still felt slighted. "But JJ knew. And Stef too." Dylan sipped her coffee, annoyed that it was already tepid. "Why am I always the last to know?"

"You're not. It wasn't like that. I swear."

"I can't help feeling duped." It embarrassed her to admit it, but she swallowed the lump in her throat to get it out. "I was so stoked last night. The operation was such a win. You waited at the plant. It felt... special." Never had she ever allowed herself to be this vulnerable. She felt emotionally stripped. "I guess, I figured you felt it too. Because it was us. Our case. And I thought you were even willing to live on the edge, you know, risk being seen in public together, because it was our night." She rolled her head and closed her eyes. "Now I know it was only because you knew it was over."

"That's not true."

"It's not?" she asked. But it wasn't a question so much as a challenge for Briana to examine her own motives.

"When you put it like that, I can see how it might seem that way." In the moment she took to respond, Briana seemed to consider Dylan's words. "Dylan...last night...I just wanted to be with you. My amazing, smart, sexy girlfriend." She brought her steepled hands to her lips and closed her eyes. "That is the absolute truth," she said. "I suppose the knowledge that I'm leaving the US Attorney's Office may have subconsciously influenced my choices. I'm sorry for making you feel like it was some kind of calculated move. I would never do that to you."

"Promise?"

"Yes. I messed up. Maybe because it all happened so fast. Probably because I was scared about your reaction. But those excuses don't suffice. I should have told you before it got to this point. I'm sorry."

"Come here," she said, placing her coffee on the counter and pulling Briana close. She couldn't stay upset. She didn't want to.

"Baby." Briana rested her chin on her chest. "You do understand that this will be good for us, don't you?"

In theory Dylan understood. But reality had a way of taking good intentions and turning them upside down. She'd been around long enough to see enough good guys finish last to know so much of life was a gamble.

"What if JJ offered you a job to, like, get with you?"

"Get with me?" Briana mocked her outright. "Are we in tenth grade?"

She couldn't help but laugh even though Briana dodged the question. "You know what I mean."

"If that's the case, she's in for a rude awakening."

"She is JJ."

"Dylan."

"Briana." She mimicked Briana's gaping mouth but couldn't keep from laughing at her own dramatic effort. "I've seen her in action."

"Okay, well." Briana toyed with the crew neck of her T-shirt, and the pad of her finger brushed against her skin. "Aside from the fact that I believe JJ is interested in my litigation skills and my ability to craft a compelling legal argument, might I remind you that she is dating my roommate." Briana looked dead serious. "Stef is my best friend. So even though I don't share your sinister outlook, or your obsession with JJ's sex life, I want to put your mind at ease."

"I am not obsessed with her sex life," Dylan said through a smile.

"Shh." Briana shushed her with a finger as she baby-kissed her face. "You have nothing to worry about." Her kiss was sweet and seductive. "Even if JJ and Stef weren't together, it wouldn't matter. I'm in love with you. Case closed."

Hearing those words never hurt. Even if Dylan didn't have complete faith in JJ, she believed that Briana's heart was in the right place. She still hated that Briana was leaving the investigation, but she chose to find solace in knowing the decision was rooted in dedication to their future.

CHAPTER TWENTY-SIX

Briana straightened the framed photo of Dylan on her desk. It was such a nice change to be able to display her image and to see her gorgeous face anytime she wanted. Sure, it was no substitute for the real thing, but even daily coffee at the plant had stopped once they'd started covert dating officially. Over dinner the other night, she joked to Dylan that she saw her face more now—at least during work hours—than when they were working the case together. In response Dylan had forced out a chuckle, but Briana knew she was struggling with the separation.

"Conference room, ten minutes." JJ delivered the message with a double tap on her open door.

"Staff meeting?" she asked.

JJ didn't look up from her phone. "Nope. Just a development in the Hyde case I want to discuss."

"Okay. I'll be there."

Briana had hit the ground running. She'd devoured the firm's cases and researched hot-button civil law issues. She made herself available for every opportunity to assist her colleagues and even registered for CLE courses to broaden her professional development. First impressions were important, even if you were tight with the managing partner. All the prep work had her feeling confident and sharp, but her personal life was bearing the brunt.

Briana touched the picture of Dylan and reached for her phone. *I miss you,* she texted. Without stopping to overthink it, she followed with another message. *How about dinner later at Franny Lew?*

Dylan's response was quick. *What, no midnight oil to burn?*

She winced at the slight jab, even though it was true. The desire to succeed kept her at the office late most nights. *My treat,* she responded. *I know I've been an absentee girlfriend lately. Let me make it up to you.*

You did pick my favorite restaurant…

She could hear Dylan's defenses drop and it made her relax. *I'm no fool,* she typed. *How about 7?*

Can't wait.

Even though the invitation was spur of the moment, Briana was already counting down the minutes. *Me too.*

How's work today?

She could tell that Dylan was trying to be supportive, and it meant the world to her. *Fine. I have a meeting in five.* She dropped in the eye roll emoji just to keep it light.

Daydream about me?

Always, baby.

Dylan sent her a smiley face, and she smiled right back at the screen like a smitten teenager as she picked up the Hyde file and headed down the hall to the conference room where JJ was already lecturing an intern.

"Dennis Hyde called me earlier." JJ turned to her before she even sat down. "I don't know why he doesn't call you. He's your client now."

"He does call me. Pretty much nonstop," Briana said, as she nodded hello to the intern whose name she didn't remember.

"He is a needy little bugger." JJ swiveled in her chair. "Anyway, to cut straight to the point, Hyde says he has new witnesses who can substantiate his claims against DiNapoli."

"Great." Briana lifted her pen, ready to jot names.

"There's one catch."

Briana looked up.

"The witnesses are in Florida and will only talk to us in person."

She put her pen down, thinking that this sounded like Dennis Hyde was stringing them along. "What does that mean exactly?"

"Pack your bags, kid. We're going to Miami."

JJ continued to talk strategy and detailed a fairly comprehensive plan for where she believed there might be an opportunity for a settlement. Briana pitched in with detailed references to similar cases in other jurisdictions. It was a productive meeting as far as Hyde was concerned, but damn if she wasn't bummed over the Florida news. Not that she minded traveling for good witness depositions. And Miami… hello, fun. But deep down she knew, whether or not anything useful would come from it, a work trip with JJ was not going to sit well with Dylan.

❖

"Sorry I'm late." Briana sat kitty-corner next to Dylan at a table in the back of the restaurant. "It's not even my fault. There was a sick passenger on the F train."

"It's all good, babe." Dylan leaned over and kissed her, and Briana tasted the faint hint of gin and Campari on her lips. "I started without you," she said, eyeing her drink.

"I see that." Briana rubbed Dylan's thigh and inadvertently grazed her crotch, pleasantly surprised to learn she was packing. With an arched eyebrow she teased, "Someone has high hopes for tonight."

"What can I say." Dylan shrugged but her grin was impish. "I miss you. Like, a lot."

It was a sentiment both sweet and sexy, and it hit her right in the heart. And elsewhere, if she was being honest. Between the series of late nights and Dylan's constantly changing schedule, it had been over a week since they'd spent a night together.

"We could skip dinner." Briana was only half kidding. "Go back to your apartment. Order Wilkie's later…"

"We could." Dylan leaned in close and draped her arm over the back of her chair. Briana felt a soft touch on her shoulder. "But I kind of like the anticipation." She winked. "And it's nice to be out with you in a crowded restaurant." Dylan kissed her cheek, and Briana indulged in the singular perk of her career move. "Tell me how it's going at Jessup Finch other name, other name." Dylan grinned. "I want to hear everything."

"I will." From the high-end decor to the varied casework and the diverse staff, Briana was ready to spill the tea. She held a finger up, essentially hitting pause on the convo so she could order a glass of wine. "I promise to give you the whole scoop, but first tell me about the undercover op last night." She registered slight hesitation in Dylan's expression and edited on the spot. "Not details, obviously. I'm not trying to get info I'm not privy to. But tell me the sexy stuff." She threw in a shoulder shimmy. "You know…how you were sly and smooth while remaining safe the whole time."

"I was sly. And smooth." Dylan diverted her eyes and looked just shy enough to completely rock her smug air. "And safe."

"I know you're appeasing me, and I appreciate it."

"I really was safe, though. I always am."

"Thank you for that." She sampled her chardonnay. "I've been meaning to ask, how is O'Rourke doing?"

Dylan made a so-so gesture with her hand. "Meh."

"Give him time," she said in support of her former colleague. Davis O'Rourke was an acquired taste. "I know he's all over the place sometimes—"

"I don't mind his input, but he doesn't seem to fully grasp everything. It's like he's after the quick hit instead of playing the long game. I don't know." Dylan sounded dismayed, but there was really nothing she could do at this point.

"I pushed really hard for Kenisha Mubarek as my replacement. She's aggressive and smart."

"Eh, still not you." Dylan took a sip of her drink, and for a second Briana wasn't sure if the comment was a dig or a compliment. "Everybody misses you."

"Is that so?"

"Not like me." Dylan traced a finger over her wrist. "Trevor and Shawn and the gang have all been asking about you. Even Trish."

"Ugh, Trish." She made a face even though she was mostly kidding. "Is she still throwing herself at you at every turn?" Even making light of it, Briana felt her chest tighten at the thought.

"I think she might have a secret thing going on with Shawn."

"Really?" Briana nodded into her surprise. "I did not see that coming."

"And Trevor got engaged," Dylan said. "Did I tell you that?"

"Hold on a second." Briana waved her hands frantically. "I'm gone three weeks, and there's a hot new romance and a wedding?"

"Trevor popped the question last weekend. He just told me and Shawn yesterday."

"I love that you guys have this throuple bromance thing happening."

"Me, Trevor, and Shawn?" Dylan's laugh was hearty and sweet.

"Yes. You three seem to hang out a lot lately. It's nice."

"They're good guys. I miss you, though."

"I know." She reached for Dylan's hand. "It won't always be like this," she said, even though she was well aware the expectations of private practice were a far cry from punching the government time card. "Tell me about Trevor and Cate and their proposal," she said, guiding them back on track. "Wait. Fill me in on Trish and Shawn first. That's kind of blowing my mind right now."

"There's not much to tell. I'm purely speculating. But I'm picking up a vibe." Dylan smiled. "Trish is definitely seeing someone." She continued to voice her analysis out loud. "She has that new relationship energy. Plus she spends half the day making heart eyes at her phone." Dylan seemed to be assessing the possibilities on the fly. "I don't know for sure it's Shawn."

"How do you not know? You and Shawn are tight."

"He's quiet about stuff like that. Maybe they're still figuring it all out," she offered. "Or maybe I'm wrong."

"I bet you're not." Briana was genuinely happy for Trish and Shawn, and she offered a tiny toast to the would-be couple before taking a sip of her wine. "To them, if there is a them," she said with a smile.

"They'd be cute together, for sure," Dylan agreed. "I might be way off the mark, though. Still, I like to keep you in the know." Her wink was positively adorable.

"Love that about you." Briana leaned forward for a small kiss. "Speaking of…tell me about Trevor. That's big news."

"Cate's pregnant. I guess that makes the wedding stuff a little anticlimactic, so they're going to wait until after the baby's born to get hitched. But even though the baby wasn't planned, he's excited."

"That's great news. You'll have to congratulate him for me." Catching up on all the office gossip, Briana couldn't help but wonder if people had talked about her and Dylan like this. Or if they did still. "Does he, I mean do they…know about us?" she asked. She wasn't sure it mattered anymore, but she was curious.

Dylan shook her head. "I haven't said anything." She downed the last of her Negroni. "I don't know how to really bring it up. Plus I don't want the team to blame me for O'Rourke," she added with a small laugh. "But mostly I think I'm just holding on to hope that you'll change your mind and come back."

She looked so unbelievably sincere that Briana choked up. "I'm sorry, baby, I can't."

"I know." She tapped her empty tumbler on the table. "Sometimes I fantasize, though."

"I miss everything about the US Attorney's Office," she said honestly. "I'm in a good place, though. Even though this wasn't part of my original plan, I think it's going to be good for me." Sometimes she said the words just to put some positive energy out into the universe.

"I want to hear everything."

Briana walked Dylan through her first few weeks at Jessup Finch Silo Toussaint. Even though she'd given Dylan highlights every day, it felt nice to explain her transition like the narrative it was. Dylan asked a thousand questions, and over their entrees, she answered each one in detail. When she got to the Hyde case, she took her time with a thorough overview until she knew it was time to come clean.

"There is something you should know," she started.

"What's up?"

"I have to go to Florida with JJ."

Dylan looked up from her scallops. "Okay," she said, but her face dropped a little. "Just the two of you?"

"No. There'll be an intern or a law fellow with us," she said, even though she wasn't entirely certain of that detail.

"If I ask you something, will you be honest with me?"

She hated that Dylan had any doubts. "Of course I will."

"How is JJ with you?"

This wasn't about workload or cases, or professional experience. Or even friendship, for that matter. Dylan wanted to know if everything with JJ was on the level. But in the time it took her to respond, Dylan withdrew her question.

"You know what? I take it back." She placed her utensils neatly on the side of her plate. "Not gonna lie, I'm dealing with a fair amount of jealousy." She rested her forehead on the base of her hand. "And I hate it." She took a deep breath and added, "But I trust you. This is your job, and I completely support you."

"Baby, it is just work." Briana touched the tiny cleft in Dylan's chin, and Dylan kissed her hand.

"When's the trip?"

"Next week. Wednesday."

"Will you be back by Friday?"

"It's an overnighter. We are literally doing two interviews. Zip down. Take depositions. Fly back."

"Next Friday night is Kevin's promotion dinner out in Long Island. My mother's husband," Dylan clarified. "It's nothing fancy. Just my mom and Kevin and my little brothers." She fidgeted with the end of the tablecloth. "It would mean a lot to me if you were there. I'd like my family to meet you."

It was official. Vulnerable Dylan was just as hot as confident Dylan. Briana stroked the side of her face. "I wouldn't miss it." She caressed her thigh under the table. "I'm curious, though. Will I get the third degree?" She giggled at her need for advance warning. "I guess what I'm wondering is how your family acts with women you bring home."

"I honestly don't know." Dylan squeezed her hand, but her smile was filled with nervous anticipation. "Guess we'll find out next Friday."

CHAPTER TWENTY-SEVEN

C ome on, come on, come on."
Dylan checked her watch against the scheduled arrival time of Briana's flight from Miami. She'd been doing mental math all afternoon, trying to factor for the building weekend traffic as she calculated the travel time from John F. Kennedy airport to her mom's house in Suffolk County.

When Briana's overnight work trip expanded into two full days, Dylan willed herself not to hit the panic button. Briana loved her, and this was just work. She repeated it over and over in her head and even stayed calm when Briana called to say the final interview was pushed to Friday morning. Dylan went with the flow and offered to meet Briana's flight. JFK was en route to Long Island, and they could still make dinner with the fam.

The pit in her stomach started as she paced the terminal, but she ignored it. It wasn't foreboding. Maybe she was just hungry. Briana's flight would land soon, even though the arrival board was posting a delayed status. She just had to stay positive. It was probably just air traffic control trying to manage hundreds of flights coming and going. Nonetheless, she sought out airline staff to see if she could get any additional details. Human resources referred her to the airline app, which was frozen. All she knew was that the clock was ticking down, and Briana was still in transit.

Like a gift from the gods, her phone buzzed, and she felt her pulse regulate at Briana's name on the screen.

"Please tell me you're circling JFK, waiting for a runway to land," she said.

"Dylan, I am so sorry," Briana said. "I've been on the tarmac for two hours. We had no cell service, nothing. I couldn't even contact you until right now."

"Wait. Where are you?"

"At the airport in Miami. They just had us deplane after boarding hours ago."

"No." There was no way this was happening. "I don't understand. You're still in Florida?"

"I tried to text you. Nothing went through. My messages all failed to send." Dylan doubled over, like the wind had been knocked out of her. Briana was talking, but her explanation was muted by the sound of her head pounding like a pile driver. She closed her eyes and tried to control her instant nausea as she focused on Briana's voice. "After the storm passed, there was some issue with the plane itself. Allegedly we'll be boarding a new aircraft in twenty minutes."

Dylan stood up just to get some air in her lungs. "You'll never make it."

"I'm so, so sorry, baby."

"It's fine." She needed to get off the phone. "I gotta go."

"Are you okay?" Briana asked.

"Yep," she lied.

"Dylan?"

She'd almost hung up but caught it just in time. "What?"

"I am really sorry."

Maybe she was, maybe she wasn't. It hardly mattered right now. "Sure," she said, knowing her voice sounded as cold as she felt. "I guess, let me know when you make it home," she added.

"Dylan, wait." She heard Briana's plea in the distance as she ended the call and mentally prepared to head east and face her family solo.

❖

Dylan slipped the basketball between her legs as she dribbled up the street. She hated the amount of restless energy she had. It was only three o'clock, and she'd already caught up on all her laundry and completed a few handy projects at her brownstone. She was actually annoyed at how simple the install of her video doorbell turned out to be because she'd been counting on the task to occupy some serious time. Now she had to come up with other means of stimulation. She'd even reached out to Trevor to see if they needed any extra help at the plant. But everything was under control. Everything except her personal life.

It was colder than it should be for May, and the shorts and hoodie she'd opted for weren't really cutting it, so she broke into a light jog to warm up. Once she hit the outdoor court, she began with Mikan drills, using the exercise to shore up her post play and rebound game. Side to side she banked layups from under the hoop. Simple, straightforward, effective.

Why wasn't life this easy?

She'd posed the question to herself rhetorically, but the answer was clear as the blue sky above. Life had been this easy. Until she'd gone and complicated things. If there was a reason she didn't do serious relationships, the last twenty-four hours was an example highlighted in bright yellow marker.

Briana had sent several texts over the course of last night and this morning. But other than a thumbs-up to Briana's arrival home at ten thirty, Dylan couldn't bring herself to respond. Logically, she knew the flight fiasco wasn't Briana's fault. But she also knew her angst was about way more than a missed dinner. She was stressed about Briana being away with JJ for three days. What if she suddenly didn't measure up? And even if those fears were just insecurity besting her, what if she and Briana ran out of common ground now that they didn't have work to fall back on? If the last month was any indication, their competing schedules would always make it a challenge to find time for each other.

But maybe that was by design. Briana had left the US Attorney's Office. She accepted a case that had taken her out of New York for days in a row, and by her own admission, that lawsuit was just getting underway. Who knew how many more out of state trips were in her future?

Dylan took an ugly shot from the perimeter. How had she missed the signs?

Briana was pulling away. Of course, she was. And suddenly it all made perfect sense. New job, late nights, work trips. Dylan had been so caught up in her own emotions that she'd shut her eyes to it. Briana was letting her down easy. Pulling the bandage off slowly, giving the exposed wound time to scab and heal, so as not to leave her completely damaged and bleeding when she walked out of her life.

Fuck that.

This wasn't her first heartbreak, not by a long shot. Even if it was her first experience with falling in love, she'd been let down plenty of times before. A therapist might argue it was exactly why she'd avoided serious relationships at all costs. She'd taken Psych 101, she knew the drill, and she didn't need to be analyzed to know the remedy. Acknowledge, cope, recover. Most importantly, move on.

She needed to go back to basics. Do what she did best. Draw upon her training and experience and keep things simple. Channeling her anger into resolve, she fanned out to three-point range and sank a jumper, registering an odd sense of satisfaction at the crisp snap of the net.

"Nice shot."

Briana's voice was a surprise, but her internal pep talk gave her the strength she needed to deal.

"Thanks," she said, shuffling in for the rebound before dropping a fadeaway in the paint.

"Did you play in college?" Briana asked.

"I did." She dribbled to the top of the key. "I went to Kingsborough," she said idly, remembering her old uniform. "We were pretty good for our division. I liked it because I got to actually get in the game. If I'd gone to a real university, instead of community college, I doubt I would have had much success."

"Why do you say that?"

"I don't know," she said, taking another shot. "Because it's the truth, I guess."

Briana awkwardly grabbed the rebound. "You're avoiding me," she said as she passed the ball back.

Dylan shrugged. It was the truth. To pretend otherwise was pointless.

"I'm sorry about yesterday. Did I mess up things with your family?"

"Not really. Cynthia asked what happened. My brothers made fun of me for not being able to maintain a relationship. Typical teenage bullshit."

"Ouch."

"Whatever." She popped a shot from the baseline. "Not really sure I disagree."

"What?" Briana looked confused and offended, but Dylan wasn't ready to qualify her statement, so she changed the subject.

"How did you find me?" she asked.

"After you didn't answer my calls or texts, I went to your house. I was sitting on the stoop for twenty minutes. Your tenant finally came outside and said you left with your basketball. She was kind enough to point me in the direction of the court."

"Marie." Dylan clenched her jaw. "Remind me to raise her rent when I get back." She was obviously kidding, but it came out sharp, and Briana didn't miss it.

"Why are you being like this? I'm sorry I missed dinner. I really am. I get that it was a big deal. And I know you're hurt. But I had no control over what happened at the airport."

"You did have control over leaving, though." She raised her eyebrows in challenge as she directly referenced Briana's departure from the US Attorney's Office. "Let's not forget that."

"Dylan, we've been over this. I did that for us."

"Really?" She bounced the ball hard against the concrete and winced when it jammed her finger. "Right now"—she squared her shoulders at the hoop—"it feels a whole lot like you did it for you."

"Why would you say that?"

Dylan knew she was being harsh, but it was the only way she could stay firm. And while she didn't believe her statement was wholly true, she didn't think it was totally false either. "Look, Bri." She grabbed her own rebound and held the ball against her hip. "Maybe this, us," she said, waving between them as she caught her breath, "has just run its course. You know?"

"No, I don't know." Briana looked completely dumbfounded, and it broke Dylan a little. "Are you breaking up with me? Over a messed-up flight?" she asked.

Briana hugged herself, and Dylan could see she was cold. It took everything not to drop the ball and go to her. Fold her in her arms to warm her up, kiss her, and forgive her all transgressions, past and future. But this was about more than a delayed flight, and she needed to stay strong.

"It's not over the flight. Not really."

"But you are ending this?" Her tone was more anger than pain, at least in this moment, and Dylan didn't really know how to make her understand that it was the best to cut ties before it got any harder.

"Look, you're busy with work. I'm busy with the case," she said. "I just think it makes sense right now."

"Um. It doesn't. Not to me, anyway."

Dylan didn't have the heart or the patience to break it down for Briana. She was too busy using every ounce of her being to keep from falling apart in the middle of the basketball court. And where Briana might not consciously see the connections, Dylan knew this path all too well.

"Trust me, this is for the best."

"None of this makes any sense." Briana sniffled and squared her jaw, and Dylan could see the tears forming. "I'm honestly at a total loss right now."

Dylan didn't know what to say. She couldn't attribute her actions or her apprehension to any one thing in particular. She just knew that this was what she needed to do right now to protect herself. "I think in your heart you know I'm right."

"You're wrong." Briana swiped at a tear. "You're scared. I know it's different now than it was. Harder, in a way, because we're not working together. The opportunity to see each other just to check in and get that reassurance is gone. I get it. I'm struggling too. But I'm not running away."

"You already did."

Briana looked like she was going to sob, but she crossed her arms and pursed her lips and said nothing.

Dylan fought the sting in her throat. "I'm sorry," she said, hoping her apology covered both her mean-spiritedness and initiating their split. She pulled Briana close, so she wouldn't see that she was on the verge of losing it.

"Please." Briana begged through her tears. "Please don't do this."

Dylan hated every second of saying good-bye, but she blocked out her pain and channeled the part of her that knew the end was inevitable. Even if Briana was still partially invested in their relationship, it would wane. Nobody stuck around for her. That was a fact. Not her dad when she was a kid, not her mom when she was in high school. Even her grandfather had chosen to spend his final years in New Jersey with her uncle rather than stick it out with her in Brooklyn.

It was better to end things now before it was impossible to let go.

Dylan held her tight and closed her eyes even though she knew it would force her own tears to fall. Unable to speak any words at all, she kissed the top of Briana's soft, gorgeous hair before she found her lips one final time.

CHAPTER TWENTY-EIGHT

Where some people went through the stages of grief in order over time, Briana was busy experiencing a medley of the full cycle on a daily basis.

Anger and depression battled it out for the bulk of her attention, but there was no denying she was still in shock over the turn of events, even a month later. She simply could not come to grips with the fact that Dylan had dumped her. So much for acceptance, she thought with a laugh. Most days, moving on seemed a summit she might never reach. Much of the time she didn't even particularly aspire to it. Because she knew that milestone would mean Dylan was gone for good.

"Do you think she misses me?" Briana had been leaning on Stef for emotional support since minute one. This was probably the hundredth conversation they'd embarked on as she struggled to find meaning.

"Honey." Stef handed her a glass of white as she joined her on the couch. "I am one thousand percent sure of it."

It was nice to hear her bestie say it even though her opinion did nothing to change the circumstances. "If you're right, and Dylan misses me…" Briana held one finger up as she paused to sip her wine.

"I can't believe you're doubting me," Stef teased.

"I want to believe you," she said. "The thing is, if she misses me and I miss her, isn't this just a waste of time?"

"Yes." Stef leaned forward the way she did when she was crafting a summation. "Which is why we need to put our heads together and come up with a strategy to fix it."

"Well, she won't even talk to me. So good luck." Briana raised her glass, pretending to give up.

"What if you sent flowers?"

"Me?" Briana pointed at her own chest completely on the defensive. "You think *I* should send flowers to *her*?"

"Don't get all gender-stereotypy about it. Or in this case, bogged down by what might be expected from traditional butch-femme roles."

"Oh, I'm not." Briana couldn't believe Stef thought she was so shallow. "First of all, I don't think the binary breaks down like that."

"Why are you so horrified, then?"

"Flowers are so…I don't know." They just seemed wrong. Briana cozied into the sofa, trying to find the right words to explain why the suggestion irked her. She wasn't above a grand gesture that might get Dylan to reconsider their relationship, but flowers felt like an apology, and she didn't think she'd done anything wrong. "Flowers feel like an admission of guilt."

"I don't think that's necessarily true. At least I hope it isn't." Stef let out a nervous laugh. "JJ sent roses to my office last week."

"That's different. She loves you," Briana said.

"Here's hoping you're right," Stef countered with a raised glass and wide eyes. "I wonder sometimes."

"You wonder if she loves you?"

"Yeah." Stef looked out the window as she spoke. "I wonder if I'm enough for her. She can be so hard to read," she said. "It doesn't help that she's been a little distant lately. I know work is crazy. Believe me, I understand that. But I'd be less paranoid if some law fellow named Kara wasn't blowing up her phone all the time."

Kara Kennedy. Oofa.

Briana knew she was supposed to fill in the blanks. Ease Stef's nerves. Tell her she was crazy—everything was fine. The problem was she didn't have a clue if there was something going on between JJ and Kara. She was too busy trying to keep her head above water to notice anything else. All she knew was Kara had accompanied her and JJ to Miami weeks ago. At the time Briana had been too focused on the case during the day and too interested in talking to Dylan at night to even hang out beyond dinner.

"I'm sure it's fine, Stef," she said. "Kara's nice. But she doesn't hold a candle to you."

"Is she pretty?"

Briana winced. Kara was attractive and smart but young enough to be impressionable. She probably thought JJ was the shit. "She's not you. She's a kid."

"And my girlfriend is a silver fox with an insatiable sex drive and a massive ego." Stef waved her comment away, pretending it was no big deal. "You're right. I'm sure I have nothing to worry about," she said with a laugh.

"Insatiable sex drive. Hey-o." Briana tried to spin the convo into less thorny terrain. "Spill," she said, settling farther into the couch. "Spare no details. Remember I'm living vicariously through you these days."

"I'm sorry for making this whole conversation about me." Stef rubbed her knee. "We were talking about Dylan."

"It's okay. There's really nothing to say." It was the truth. In the month since their random ball court breakup, Briana had called and texted Dylan a fair amount, if she was being honest. But other than a few bland text responses, Dylan had iced her out.

"We were trying to come up with ways to win her back."

"But that's just it." The situation ate away at her, but she shrugged it off for the moment, knowing there was nothing more she could really do. "Why should I have to make another overture? I gave up my career for our relationship. And she flushed it down the toilet." Briana snapped her fingers. "Over. Just like that."

"Still makes zero sense to me."

Briana felt exactly the same way. Every night she told herself she was done trying to understand it, but then she lay awake in bed wondering what she could have done that might have made a difference. She hated that Dylan still took up so much space in her mind and heart. But at the same time, she wasn't ready to let her go. Not in any capacity. No matter how much she dissected it, the timing of their breakup seemed arbitrary. Dylan's reasoning, paper-thin. There was just no making sense of it.

"Let's talk about something else," she said.

"Come out with us tonight," Stef said with enthusiasm. "Me and JJ will be your wing-people. We're staying local. Just heading up to Connolly's for a few drinks."

Connolly's. Ugh.

The very location she'd shared her first solo drink with Dylan. Even all those months ago, there'd been a part of her that knew she was going to go for it. Despite the initial protest and the cat-and-mouse game that followed, Briana had always known what her heart wanted. Dylan had captivated her from the very start. The thought of going to Connolly's now, without her—there was no way she had the strength for that tonight.

"Nah." Briana swallowed her heartache. "I'm just going to stay here. This bottle of wine is my wingman."

"That's a healthy plan." Stef nodded in jest before her expression turned slightly serious. "Bri, maybe if you come out, you'll see Dylan. I honestly think if she sees you—"

"Nope." She knew she was being severe. But she didn't have the faith that Stef seemed to be holding on to. And she was barely staying afloat as it was. If she saw Dylan out, talking to someone, flirting, knowing she was going to take them home…no way. That was a reality she simply could not handle. "You guys go. Have fun. I'm going to order sushi and find something ridiculous on TV."

"No sappy romances," Stef ordered.

"No worries," she responded.

But despite her best intentions, she landed on a movie whose plot was part suspense, part love story, and by the end she was barely keeping tabs on the murder mystery as she sighed at every sweet thing the main characters did for each other, inadvertently reminiscing over the good times with Dylan.

Just after midnight, she was sleepily aware of Stef and JJ laughing and talking in the kitchen. Even though she was still sad for herself, it made her happy to hear them getting along. If she'd had any energy, she would have joined them for a late-night snack, but in her heart she knew it would only be to find out if there'd been a Dylan sighting. And honestly, whether the answer was yes or no didn't change the fact that she wasn't here.

Every minute of Monday was accounted for.

It was nearly eleven, and Briana had already ironed out the nuances of the Hyde settlement. Next on her agenda was reviewing the brief JJ asked her to look over before the noon interview she was sitting in on with Kara. Honestly, she loved being booked solid. It kept her from thinking about Dylan non-freaking-stop. As a bonus, today she'd get one-on-one time with Kara. Fingers crossed the personal connection would give her enough info to put Stef's fears to bed.

"Nose to the grindstone. As usual." JJ's voice echoed in her doorway. "It almost makes me feel bad that I make more money than you."

Briana smiled at the twisted compliment. "You are the boss," she said without looking up. "Shouldn't you be off golfing away your billable hours?"

"Eh, too rainy." JJ smirked at the good-natured jab and took a seat in the chair opposite her desk. "I was hoping you could spare a minute for me."

"Like I have a choice." Briana crinkled her nose, so JJ would know she was kidding. "Of course I have time for you. What's up?"

JJ's face was so serious that she almost wondered if she was in trouble. What if this was an informal performance review? Despite JJ's remarks to the contrary, she was dragging a little. Hopefully JJ knew her best work was still to come.

"I have it on fairly good authority that they're taking your case down soon."

"My case?" she asked, immediately thinking about Dennis Hyde. "I just finessed the settlement."

"No." JJ leaned forward and dropped her voice to a whisper. "Your drug case with the US Attorney's Office."

Her head started to spin. How did JJ know those details? Why was she sharing them with her? Did this mean Dylan would be in danger? So often drug takedowns involved a sting, and with Dylan's undercover role, she might be exposed. Her pulse raced, but she tried to stay cool.

"How did you come upon that information?"

"I think they're looking at the end of the week," JJ said, not bothering to address her question.

Briana was keenly aware of her heartbeat. "I'm serious. How do you know this?"

JJ kept her poker face as she selected a business card from Briana's desk and ran a finger over the embossed lettering. "Let's just say a little birdie told me."

"Well that sounds highly unethical."

"Before you go reporting me to the bar association, this hunch is based on being able to read between the lines, not leaked information." She returned the card and folded her hands precisely. "Anyway, I can be trusted."

"You're literally in here telling me."

"Sharing a hypothesis with you," she corrected. "With good reason."

"Which would be?"

"Briana." JJ looked her dead in the eye, her expression somber. "Call your girlfriend. Your ex. Dylan," she said. "Tell her to be safe. To come home in one piece. Let her know you're thinking about her. Because you are."

"Even if I was inclined to reach out, once I do that, she'd know you know."

"I can handle Junior," she said with a smug laugh.

Lord knew she wanted to tell Dylan to be careful, to wear every last piece of protective gear she owned, to come home unharmed and ready to give them another chance. But she'd played these cards already.

"Honestly, JJ"—Briana tossed her pen on the desk in surrender—"I did the heavy lifting here. I left my job." She shook her head still in awe over the way it had all unfolded. "The NYPD has hundreds of diversified units. Robbery, Homicide, Special Victims. Christ, if you want to ride a horse and be a cop, you can. She didn't put in for a transfer. She didn't ask to go back to Vice. No." With two fingers, she pounded her own chest. "I did the hard part. I gave up my dream."

"I'm pretty sure Dylan doesn't even want to ride a horse."

Briana rolled her eyes, annoyed that JJ was making a joke of her sacrifice.

"Look, Briana, we all know that you're going to run the US Attorney's Office someday. I don't think there's a single soul in the New York legal community who'd take that bet." She held her arms to the side and looked around at the upscale office decor. "Your stint here is going to help you reach that pinnacle. The varied experience and exposure you'll get, you haven't even scratched the surface. Plus, you'll make a healthy living. Win-win."

No doubt JJ was making good points, but her hard sell seemed to ignore the main hurdle. As if JJ could read her mind she said, "As far as Dylan is concerned, the kid's tough as nails. On the outside." She leaned forward and buffed out a scuff on her expensive shoes. "Thing is, Dylan's not actually bulletproof. The Kevlar vest"—she waved one hand over her torso—"does nothing to protect the heart, I'm afraid. Not from breaking, anyway. She's taken a fair amount of hits in that area, and I imagine the scar tissue built up from those wounds is impressive."

Briana let JJ's words sink in. Even though she put up a front, Briana knew Dylan felt a certain sense of abandonment where her parents were concerned. She'd even put up a wall in her friendship with JJ. Through this lens, she could see it now. Dylan's perspective on things. Was she so afraid of losing her that she ended things first?

"She's scared of looking weak," JJ said seriously. "She'll never ask for help. Or admit that she needs something. Or someone, in this case. She puts up all these defenses. Got that cock of the walk thing down pat."

"Hmm, where'd she learn that, I wonder?"

"I don't call her Junior for nothing." JJ's chuckle was filled with pride. "Deep down, though"—she shrugged—"she just wants to be loved."

"Ugh. Women." Fully frustrated, Briana closed her eyes. "So complicated."

"I prefer complex." JJ's smile was just a touch slick. "It's what keeps us interesting."

"I did love her. I still do."

"You have to tell her."

"And I should do that how? She barely answers my messages," she said remembering a cool *10-4* Dylan had shot back at her in a recent clipped exchange. "Am I to rent a skywriter? Take out a billboard?"

"That's very dramatic," JJ said, clearly pretending to take her seriously. "Involves a ton of logistics as well. I was thinking along the lines of something more conventional. Go to her apartment, perhaps. Wait for her after a Sunday basketball game. Something manageable but directed." She clapped both hands on her knees and stood up. "You'll figure it out."

"And what if she rejects me? Again, I should say."

"You give up this easy on cases?"

It wasn't a question at all. It was a wake-up call to fight for what she wanted. For what she needed. For Dylan. For love. God, she could fucking hug JJ right now.

"JJ," Briana called out just as her boss reached the door. She was planning on expressing her appreciation for the unexpected kick in the behind. It didn't matter that she had no clue how to proceed—JJ's roundabout pep talk fueled her drive. It felt like a vote of confidence for her, for Dylan, for their chance at reuniting. And for that she was thankful.

"Yeah?" JJ said.

"Are you screwing around on Stef?" she asked, surprising herself when the accusation trumped her moment of gratitude.

JJ hung her head, and a slow sly grin emerged. "I have to admit, I thought you were going to thank me."

"I was. I just…I don't know." Briana wasn't sure she even wanted to know the answer. "Thank you," she said shifting gears again. "Your weird mini-lecture has me feeling…hopeful. And thank you for hiring me. I'm not sure I ever properly expressed my gratitude for the opportunity."

"I know you don't see it yet, but it's going to be a good career move. Trust me."

For some reason she did. "When did you get so wise?" she teased.

"Remember, I have a decade on you. I might have collected a few nuggets of wisdom along the way."

"I don't doubt it." Briana straightened the file on her desk. "One more thing." She looked right at JJ.

"What is it?"

"Do right by Stef," she said, not willing to let her off the hook. "She deserves that much."

JJ's serious expression said she was taking the advice to heart. "I'll take your counsel under advisement," she said, knocking twice on the doorframe before she began to back away. "I suggest you do the same."

CHAPTER TWENTY-NINE

Dylan cracked the window to let the crisp morning air filter through her car as she stared at Benji Rafferty's house. This was it. The moment of truth and justice, the singular payoff for months of solid police work.

Good ol' Goldenballs was about to get arrested.

She should be brimming with anticipation. Even a little pride. After all, if not for her random overhear and initial gut instinct, the team might not be where they were right now—ready to hit the doors on their suspects and take them into custody. Reveal themselves as cops and watch the faces drop. But instead of being exhilarated, Dylan felt hollow.

It was crazy. This was literally what she'd been waiting for, in a way, since the day she took the oath to protect and serve.

But everything was wrong.

Her personal life was a mess. In the precisely six weeks and three days since she'd called it quits with Briana, nothing seemed right. Or normal. Or good. Dylan barely left the house unless it was to go to work, which these days didn't provide much solace. Even this takedown seemed all over the place. O'Rourke had moved it up in the eleventh hour just so he could include the arrest stats in some kind of quarterly assessment. It was complete nonsense and a stunt that Briana would never have pulled.

Briana. Dylan closed her eyes and swallowed hard. Everything she did, every last thought all came back to Briana. If time truly healed all wounds, why didn't she feel any better at all?

"Five minutes out." Trevor barked his ETA over the radio en route to apprehend Paul Rafferty at his residence in New Jersey. "Everyone else in place?"

"Copy," she said, keying the mic. "We're set up outside Benji's." She peered at the facade of the house, but it was dark inside. It seemed the whole neighborhood was still sleeping soundly.

"All quiet over here at Georgie-boy's." Ahmed and his crew were only a block away, and it was nice to know they were close enough to back each other up if needed.

"Great," Trevor said. "I'll give the signal when we're ready to roll. Stand by."

"10-4," Dylan said.

The coordinated takedown was designed to play out in unison. Executing all three warrants at the same time mitigated the opportunity for collusion by the perps. Benji would have no clue what, if anything, might be happening to George or Paul. And the reverse was true as well. It was a nice dose of uncertainty that played to the strengths of the good guys. And with any luck, one of the targets might panic enough to turn government witness.

In the light breeze, a leaf fell on her windshield, and she remembered the time Briana told her that Carroll Gardens ranked high on a list of New York City neighborhoods with the most trees per square mile. It was such a random tidbit, but God, it made her so happy. Back then and now. But fuck, even at this critical moment, her mind was on Briana.

"All right, folks." Trevor's voice pulled her back to reality again. Thank freaking God. She needed to be sharp. Get her head on straight. "Everybody check in when you're in the clear. Be safe. Let's roll."

Day was just beginning to break as Dylan exited her car and saw Shawn and the other members of her crew doing the same. They were an odd sight for sure—a pile of cops in ballistic vests and raid jackets descending upon the quiet suburban street. As wild as it was, the image was just enough to pump her up.

"You three go around back." Dylan directed three loaner detectives from Team 4 to the rear of the house, just in case Benji tried to bolt. "You guys are with me," she said, pointing a finger between Karrakas and Shawn as she approached the front door.

"You good, Dylan?" Shawn asked.

"Never better," she said.

"Okay, kids. Let's do this," Karrakas offered with a deep breath as Dylan knocked on the door.

There was no answer for a solid thirty seconds, so she pressed the doorbell and knocked again. Finally, they heard movement from inside.

"Here he comes," Shawn said.

Dylan kept her firearm holstered but gripped the handle of her Glock, ever ready if things went south.

But then Benji opened the door. He never asked who it was. She never even uttered the movie-famous *Police, open up*. The door swung open, and Benji Rafferty stood in front of them, a barely awake, rumpled mess in boxers and a T-shirt.

Dylan smiled and held her badge up so there was no mistake about what was happening. "Good morning, Benji."

Benji leaned back against the door and pressed his hands to his forehead. "Fuck," he said in a low defeated tone. He pounded his temples angrily before stepping to the side to grant access to his home. "You guys coming in or what?"

Dylan had always expected Benji would be the weak link—she just didn't think he'd fold so willingly. He almost seemed eager to be taken into custody as he dressed quickly and never shut up. He was so chatty, in fact, that Dylan felt compelled to repeatedly remind him of his rights.

Everything was going smoothly as she reread him the Miranda warning, going nice and slow to keep him at ease. But then a series of distinct pops sounded in the distance. It was gunshots, for sure, and Dylan had not one doubt they were coming from George Rivas's house. On autopilot she slapped cuffs on Benji just as the frantic cries came over the portable.

"*10-13. 10-13.*"

It was Ahmed screaming out the code that an officer needed help. Unmistakably she heard him yell repeatedly, "*Shots fired. We have an officer down.*"

Dylan's radio crackled to life as dispatch went over the air asking for details.

There was a ton of commotion and radio traffic, more cries for help, the sense of chaos unfolding nearby. In the distance sirens whirred and tires screeched. In a blur, Dylan let her instincts take charge. She ordered the supplemental cops from Team 4 to take control of Benji while she grabbed Shawn and Karrakas and sprinted to George Rivas's house.

They arrived ready to draw down and take action. But Rivas was already disarmed and cuffed up. Chris Conroy hovered over him panting and sweating.

Dylan touched his arm. "Hey, Chris. Chris," she repeated. "You okay?"

He had tunnel vision fixated on the perp beneath him.

"Where are you hurt?" she said, trying to snap him out of shock.

"It's not me," he said, still not making eye contact. "It's Trish. This motherfucker shot Trish."

Dylan spun around to see Shawn crouching next to Trish just as paramedics and uniformed cops flooded the scene and pushed him aside. In a flash, the medics had her up on a gurney and whisked her out of the house.

In a corner Ahmed was talking to Miri Hollander.

"What happened?" Dylan barged into the conversation.

Ahmed shook his head and seemed dazed. "He answered the door in a bathrobe. The lunatic blew off a few rounds before we could even pat him down."

"No one else was wounded," Miri said before she could ask. "Chris tackled him immediately."

"Wow." Dylan shook her head in disbelief. She surveyed the crime scene, which was already overloaded with emergency response. "You need us here?" she asked.

"I think it's under control," Hollander answered.

"Okay. I have the detectives from Team 4 transporting Benji to intake and processing," she said as she looked over at Shawn. "We're going to follow the ambulance to the hospital."

"Be careful," Miri said, granting permission in the kindest way. "We'll be there as soon as we can. Dylan, keep us posted, okay?"

"Of course, Boss," she said, backing away to grab Shawn.

Dylan went full lights and sirens to the hospital, but by the time they got there, Trish was already in surgery. That was good news, she supposed. And by all accounts, Trish's wounds were likely non-life-threatening. But since they'd been directed to a waiting area loaded with uniform cops who'd arrived in support and monitored by hospital staff who hadn't triaged Trish, it was difficult to get an accurate account of her injuries. Everything had happened so fast that Shawn couldn't even remember seeing where she'd been hit. Dylan set him up with fresh coffee and went in search of some real answers.

She tinned her way up to the charge nurse on the surgical floor who clearly took pity on her and used her position to confirm that Officer Patricia Suarez had sustained two gunshot wounds—one to her upper arm, one to her abdomen. The nurse made no promises but swore Trish was in excellent hands.

Dylan was hyperaware of the nurse's hand on her forearm, expressing her gratitude for the collective bravery of police officers everywhere. The mild flirtation was flattering, but only that. A year ago, she would have pursued the advances on the spot. But that was before Briana. Before love. Before her whole world changed. Before she lost everything.

Enough. She internally scolded herself for getting lost in her own drama.

But even as she walked back to the lounge, her mind drifted to Briana. Dylan couldn't help but wonder what she would think about the takedown, about Benji's eagerness to talk, George's unexpected violence. Rolling in right behind those queries were the questions she had about Briana personally. Was she content working for JJ? Was she dating anyone? Did she miss her?

Pacing through the sterile hospital, she let her mind sift through better times when she and Briana were together. Those memories made her feel safe and happy. It was a therapy she indulged in every night. Escapism as a reward for surviving each day. Right now she needed a dose, so she allowed her mind to slip into her secret comfort zone. It was a self-defense mechanism but one she needed desperately.

"Oh my God, Dylan." Out of nowhere, Briana's soft voice was in her ear. She'd been so deep in the rabbit hole that she didn't even see the love of her life standing in the waiting room. "Thank God you're okay."

For a second she thought she was dreaming. Like her fantasy life had taken over and morphed into the most unpredictable reality. But before she could make sense of what was happening, Briana's arms were around her, her face buried in her neck. If this was some kind of PTSD delusion, Dylan never wanted it to end. She let her whole being sink into Briana as she held her close, every part of their bodies pressed together.

"What are you doing here?" she whispered.

Briana pulled back, and Dylan could see her anguish. "I heard there was a shooting. The report came out that it was a female plainclothes police officer. My mind went crazy. I just…I feared the worst."

"It was Trish," she said, even though she was sure Briana knew the details by now.

"Is she okay?"

"She's in surgery. The nurse I spoke to said her injuries appear to be non-life-threatening." Dylan realized they had a small audience anxious for an update. She squeezed Briana's hand and looked into her gorgeous puffy eyes. "Will you give me a second?" she asked.

"Go." Briana wiped her cheeks, even though her tears had already dried. "I know this is a crazy day for you. I probably shouldn't have come. I just needed to know you were okay."

"Wait here?" Dylan's request came out like a plea, because it was. "I'll be right back," she said, hurrying over to pass along the few details she'd acquired. But damn if everyone didn't have four thousand questions. By the time she was in the clear, Briana was gone.

Dylan scanned the crowd to see if she was anywhere, but all she saw was mayhem.

A swarm of officers buzzed the hallway waiting for word on Trish, rank hovered in their own section, humblebragging about their own FUBAR experiences on the job, and news outlets brushed the fringes, fingers crossed some rookie might break the gag order.

But in all the hustle and bustle, the commotion over the case, the shooting, the media blitz, the drama, one fact stood out.

Briana had come to find her. To make sure she was okay. In person. Okay, so she didn't profess her love. Not in words anyway. She didn't need to. Dylan saw it in her eyes. At least she thought she did. Dylan tried not to overthink it, but she couldn't help it. Her mind was racing. She wanted to rush to Briana. To hold her. To kiss her. To admit she'd made a mistake. To beg for another chance.

"Hey, Dylan." Trevor's deep voice brought her back to the present. "How are you holding up?" he asked, thumping his hand on her shoulder.

"Yeah, I'm okay." She turned and hugged him good and tight, so grateful he was here. "How'd you guys make out with Paul?"

"Fine. Straightforward. He went willingly and said nothing." Trevor nodded toward the corridor beyond the waiting area. "Nothing like this craziness."

"Insane."

"I heard you guys raced over to the scene when it happened."

"Benji was in custody. Without incident," she added. "It was a no-brainer."

"You did the right thing," he said with an affirmative nod. She couldn't help but notice his affect held a mix of satisfaction and pride.

"Thanks, but things were basically over by the time we got there."

"Not the point."

She folded her arms and nodded in acknowledgment of his heartfelt sentiment.

"What's the word on Trish?" he asked. "Miri said you got some intel from a doctor."

"It was a nurse," she corrected. "She said Trish was in surgery, but her wounds were not life-threatening. She's gonna make it."

He breathed an audible sigh of relief. "Thank God." He hung his head, and Dylan wondered if he was praying.

"It's all good, buddy." She rubbed his shoulder for comfort.

"I know, I know." He rolled his neck and his shoulders to release the tension. "Hey," he said, switching gears, "I heard Benji was quite the motormouth already."

"The guy would literally not shut up. I think he was bummed when we left." She smiled, thinking about the bizarre turn of events and how ready Benji was to talk. "He's gonna sing like a canary."

Trevor laughed at the old-school expression. "The Team 4 guys said on the way to central booking he asked for two people. His lawyer and Dylan the cop."

"Stop it."

"I swear," he said with a smile. "Goldenballs is going to be the key to everything." Hot damn, if that didn't make her feel great. "That's all you, Dylan." His nod was downright proud. She thought he might cry.

"Well, you trusted me right from the start. You get credit too."

"We are going to have our hands full once the dust settles. I spoke to O'Rourke briefly. He's already angling for a spinoff investigation."

"That guy." Dylan sighed at O'Rourke's meddling, even though she was on board with the plan. "He's always seventeen steps ahead, and not necessarily in the good way. Not everything needs to be rushed."

"Yeah, yeah." Trevor threw his arm across her shoulder. "They can't all be Briana Logan, you know?" His smile was telling. "Let's grab coffee," he said, steering them toward the cafeteria. "I think it's time we had a real talk about you and the good prosecutor."

She laughed out loud at his direct approach. "My treat," she said, not bothering to put up the semblance of a fight. She was beyond ready for this conversation.

"No argument here." His shoes squeaked when he turned the corner into the caf. "So let me just cut right to the chase," he said, handing her a large coffee cup. "Are you going to win her back or what?"

Dylan wondered if he'd been onto them from day one. She filled her cup and considered both his question and how the heck she was going to convince Briana she'd panicked when she called it quits. "I am," she said, reaching for the half-and-half. "At least I'm going to try."

"Awesome," he said, stealing the cream from her. "Tell me what you need from me. Whether it's scheduling changes or just someone to talk to. You don't have to go through anything alone, you know." As he put a lid on his coffee, he ticked his head in the direction of the waiting area, and she knew he was paying homage to their entire crew. "We're family."

Dylan was more than choked up, and his words gave her an idea. It was so right in front of her that she was almost mad it hadn't come to her sooner. "That means so much to me—you don't even know."

"I mean it," Trevor said. "Whatever you need, say the word."

"There is something you might be able to help me with. Or at least I can pick your brain for options."

"Oh?" He looked genuinely intrigued.

"Let's see if there's any news on Trish," she said, leading the way back. "Then I'll fill you in on my master plan. You know, the one I just came up with right now."

"Better late than never," he said.

Better. Late. Than. Never.

CHAPTER THIRTY

Dylan found a parking spot across the street from her brownstone and paralleled in sloppily, too rushed to care about getting the alignment right. The day had taken on a life of its own, which was expected, but Jesus, she had stuff to do. Namely, track down the woman of her dreams and beg for another chance, convince her she wouldn't panic again. From the second she'd spotted Briana in the hospital hallway, her whole future came into focus with absolute clarity. Briana was who she wanted, who she needed, and she was willing to do just about anything to make it so.

She'd even concocted a silly shtick to make her pitch cute. Between the takedown and the shooting, the aftermath, the mandatory debriefing, and the brainstorming session that followed, the day had stretched on forever. Dylan made sure she stayed sharp, but in the background her brain worked on the plan to win Briana back. On her ride home she laughed out loud when she realized while it centered mostly on professing her feelings, it also featured Sour Patch Kids, Keurig crème brûlée, possibly even a harmonica just for good measure.

How the hell she was going to acquire all those items tonight was to be determined. It was a tiny problem, but one she could solve while she was in the shower washing off the day's grime.

At the front door, she fiddled with her keys and almost dropped them before getting it open. It was all excited energy as she bounded up the stairs to her apartment, ready to set the wheels in motion.

"Hi."

Briana's perfect voice hit her like a ton of bricks. For a second

Dylan thought she might be hallucinating, and she stopped mid-staircase to peek back at the front door just like people did in the movies.

"I'm sorry," Briana said from her seat on the top step. "I realize I'm ambushing you. Again." Her voice held a fair amount of nerves, and all Dylan wanted to do was hug them away. Hold her and kiss her, assure her everything was going to be okay. They could fix this.

"Do not be sorry. It's fine." What was she saying? It was so much better than fine. It was perfect. "I'm glad you're here."

"Marie let me in. I hope that's okay."

"Of course," she said. "Have you been here long?"

"I don't know." Briana checked her watch and seemed to laugh at herself. "A while."

"I am so sorry. Work was…crazy. As you obviously know." Dylan shook her head, still in disbelief over everything.

"How is Trish?" Briana asked.

"She's fine. The doctors say she'll make a full recovery."

"Thank God." Briana touched a hand to her forehead. "Dylan, I don't know what I would have done if it was you."

"I'm right here." Dylan leaned forward and rubbed Briana's knee delicately, their awkward staircase positioning getting in the way of real intimacy. "I'm okay." She brushed her finger over Briana's hand. "Hey, look at me." She leaned slightly back. "No cuts or bruises."

Briana reached forward and touched her stomach as though she needed proof. "Don't ever do that again."

"What? Not get shot?" Dylan chuckled and Briana laughed with her. She forgot how sweet it sounded even underneath the tears. "No problem."

"I just mean…I hate that your job is always so dangerous."

"It's not always. Today was a fluke. You know that."

"But, Dylan. Crazy stuff happens all the time. I hear stories. I know at least some of them are true."

"Cops exaggerate. Grossly," she said. "Anyway, I'm careful. I swear to you."

"I know I'm being dramatic." Briana pressed her temples. "I could have called instead of just showing up here. I suppose I'm using what happened today as an excuse, as messed up as that is." She licked her lips, seeming a little nervous still. "I wanted to see you. Yes, to know that you're okay. But also just to see you."

"You never have to call. You are always welcome here. Day or night." Dylan looked from Briana to the door of her apartment a few feet away. "Preferably both," she said in a whisper. "Should we go inside?"

"In a minute. Let me just talk before I lose my nerve." Briana looked so wrecked that Dylan thought she was going to cry. "Dylan, when I heard the news today, I lost it." She covered her mouth, and Dylan saw tears on the verge of spilling over. "I can't even imagine my life without you. I don't want to."

Briana had been the first person Dylan thought about when everything went down. Both during and after. Not because she envisioned her own death. Far from it. It was simply that in the face of mortality, the important things in life had a way of prioritizing on the spot. And Briana was at the very top of that list. Nothing else was even close. "Me either."

"Do you mean that?"

"Yes." She wished she had time to organize her thoughts. There was so much she wanted to say, and she wanted to get it right. She needed to make amends for her mistakes, own up to her denial of their conflict over the case and her reluctance to discuss options for dealing with it for so long. And she needed to accept her role in the sequence of events that unfolded as a result. But right now, she just needed to tell Briana how she felt. "I love you. So, so much."

"I love you too, Dylan."

Even though she knew it, hearing Briana say the words made her relax.

"I made a huge mistake. I panicked." It was the absolute truth, and she planned on showing Briana, but for now she hoped her words sufficed. "I was selfish and so scared of losing you that I eliminated us as an option. It was stupid."

"It was human." Briana rubbed her arm softly, and Dylan felt it all over. "But you weren't going to lose me. I'm not going to let that happen. I need you in my life. It's that simple."

"I feel the same way. You know, I actually had a plan," she said, hanging her head and laughing to herself as she thought about the ridiculous idea that she'd need props to show her level of commitment. "I was going to find you tonight. And beg you for another chance."

"Begging would not have been required. Like, at all." One look and she could see Briana was all in.

"But, Briana, there is something we need to talk about," she said, remembering her coffee chat with Trevor.

"What is it, baby?"

Briana touched her face, and oh my God, she almost melted. Whether it was her use of her favorite endearment or her gentle touch or the absolute love in her eyes, she wasn't sure. But in that moment Dylan knew that everything really was going to be okay. This wasn't the end. Not even close. It was the beginning. Without even thinking Dylan leaned forward and kissed Briana with every last ounce of love in her body.

She felt Briana's hands in her hair, and she heard the baby moans she'd missed as they fell into a deep, loving kiss that she never wanted to end.

"Not that I want to stop this," Briana said as she pulled back. "You said you wanted to talk about something. And you sounded kind of ominous. It's got me a little spooked."

"It's not anything to worry about." Dylan touched their foreheads together as she spoke. "You did everything for us. For the case. For our relationship." Briana's lips parted, and Dylan didn't know whether she was going to plead her case or brush it off. "Shh," she said, placing a finger on her full lips. "I never thanked you. For putting us first. Above everything else."

"You are the most important thing in my life. No contest."

"The thing is, I feel the same. And I hate to admit this, but it took me forever to realize I could make some compromises too. And mine aren't nearly as drastic."

"I don't understand what you're saying."

"It's not fair that you gave up your career for mine." Dylan was embarrassed to say the words out loud. How had she been so dense? Regardless, this was her chance to make it right. Better late than never, after all. "I talked to Trevor today at the hospital," she said. "I know it's a little late, but if you want your old job back, I can figure out a transfer. There might even be a way to stay within Major Case. Kind of bounce around between the teams who have cases with other AUSAs." She and Trevor had come up with the idea of Dylan acting in a kind of utility role for the entire Major Case Division. "But even if that doesn't work out, I'll land somewhere." It didn't even matter. She'd happily go back to patrol if it meant having Briana in her life. "I'm not pressuring you," Dylan added, just to be clear. "Please don't think that I am. Especially now that my offer comes as the case is ending and because I was such a baby about you working for JJ." Her reaction had been so juvenile, it was mortifying. "I can't change the past—I wish I could," she said, admitting the truth. "But I can do better going forward, and I will. You have my word."

"I appreciate that." Briana kissed her lightly. "The offer does get me right here." She covered her heart. "For the record, in a million years I would never have let you leave this investigation. You *are* the case."

"That's not true."

"Eh." She scrunched her nose. "Debatable." Briana traced an outline on her forearm, and Dylan felt her heart speed up at the innocent contact. "If I'm being truly honest, though, I'm happy where I am. The timing wasn't great. But I doubt I would've made the leap without the circumstances, and I think it's going to be a good career move."

"Wow. That's fantastic."

"It's a good firm. JJ is a fair boss. I'm learning a lot, and it's exciting. Invigorating, in a way." Her expression said she was beyond content there. "Are you okay with that?"

"Of course."

"Even the JJ part?"

"Look, it's possible she's not the ogre I make her out to be. I know that." Dylan shrugged and swallowed her pride. "I put up a wall with people." She hoped baring her soul wasn't a total turnoff, but there was no room for pretense. Not with Briana. "It's entirely possible I could benefit from some therapy," she said frankly.

"No walls with me." Briana's order was firm and sweet.

"No walls with you," Dylan repeated.

"Do you promise?"

"Yes, ma'am. So does this mean we're back?" Dylan asked just to make it official.

"I hope so." Briana held her hand as she stood up. "Otherwise I've been sitting here for hours for no reason."

"Hours?" Dylan felt instantly guilty even though the events of the day had been beyond her control.

"S'okay." Briana gave her hip a light squeeze. "You're worth the wait."

"I guess we need to get you some keys," Dylan said.

"Ooh, big step," Briana teased.

"Yeah, well"—Dylan dropped a peck on her cheek—"turns out I love you."

Briana's cheeks were beautiful and rosy when she responded, "I love you too."

"Mm." Dylan ticked her head from side to side like she was deep in thought. "I love you more."

"Not possible." Briana stuck her tongue out in jest.

"Totally possible," Dylan said as she unlocked the door to her apartment.

Briana arched one eyebrow in challenge. "But can you prove it?"

"You attorneys." Dylan sighed and shook her head. "Always hell-bent on having proof."

Briana laughed her giggle of a laugh, and Dylan heard genuine happiness filter through. It evoked a level of joy and comfort and strength and confidence greater than she'd ever imagined.

Despite her joking around, Dylan planned on proving the depth of her love and commitment every minute of every day. Because Briana was The One. Endgame. OTP. All the euphemisms put together. Plain and simple, they were meant to be. She knew it in her heart. She felt it in her bones. It was honestly all she could do to keep from proposing right on the spot. She smiled to herself, certain that day would inevitably come.

She pulled Briana close and kissed her with everything she had, with everything she was, so ready to start living the dream right here and now.

EPILOGUE

One Year Later

A reading from the book of Ruth.
A selection of Rilke poetry.
Vows.
The exchange of rings.
Cocktail hour, followed by dinner and dancing.

Briana flipped the program over only to find the reverse was blank, save the date and the names of the bride and groom printed in fancy script at the very bottom of the page. She placed the paper on the seat next to her to hold the spot for Dylan as she took in the amazing skyline.

Steel and glass and skyscrapers against a vibrant pink sky, the East River in the distance, love in the air, and the hum of the greatest city in the world below. Briana felt the spirit of the celebration wash over her even though she'd be more inclined to choose a beach venue when that day came. Nonetheless, Trevor and Cate were lucky. For each other, yes, but also because a mid-July rooftop wedding in New York City was a serious gamble. But the evening was warm and pleasant, and the romantic energy nothing short of contagious.

From her seat Briana spotted Dylan with Shawn chatting up Trevor as he shuffled from foot to foot under the wedding trellis. They were probably talking him down from any last-minute jitters, although she imagined with a year of parenting under his belt, he didn't scare too easily. Dylan clapped him on the back and looked over her shoulder doing a double-take at making eye contact. She smiled her unbelievably sexy smile, and Jesus Christ, even two years in it still made her giddy like a teenager. She felt her heart speed up when Dylan walked toward her.

"Is he having cold feet?" she asked.

"Nah." Dylan moved her program and slid onto the seat beside her. "He's mostly just nervous that the baby will be fussy during the ceremony. It's almost her bedtime."

"She's been good so far." Briana crossed her fingers on their behalf just as Lt. Nieves scooted past her to grab the empty chair next to Dylan.

"Briana, we miss you," Nieves said in greeting. He inched forward to look past Dylan. "Is there any chance you'll come back to us?" He whacked Dylan's knee with his wedding program. "Dylan is expendable." His smile was big and his laugh hearty, and she appreciated his good-natured plea for her return to her old government gig.

"It's funny, Patrick just asked me the same thing," Briana said, boiling the fifteen-minute conversation she'd had with her former supervisor down to one line.

"I did notice you two chatting," Nieves said, giving himself up. "I guess I'm hoping there's strength in numbers."

"From where I sit, O'Rourke is doing good things." The press had buzzed with news of the grand jury indictment just last month. "If Dylan's hours are anything to go by, things are busy." Briana wasn't complaining—she simply loved to be able to be open about their union.

"Oh, you're right. O'Rourke is fine. But he's not you. We miss your...your..." He seemed to be searching for the right word as he waved his rolled-up program in a semicircle. "I don't know what I'm trying to say, really," he said. "He's just not you."

Briana was touched. She knew Nieves didn't expect her to say yes, the same way she knew Dylan was most definitely not expendable. The amount of weekly overtime her girlfriend put in proved that point. But even though working with Nieves hadn't always been smooth, he was paying her a compliment. The look on his face said his sentiment was one hundred percent genuine. "That's very nice of you to say, Dan." She gave him her best professional smile. "I think I'm going to sit tight a bit longer."

The truth was in the last year she'd felt herself blossom in ways she hadn't ever imagined. Civil litigation pushed her just far enough outside her comfort zone to force innovation and ingenuity. Thinking outside the box sharpened her skills and honed her craft. She was happy, and her career was thriving. She still felt certain her path would lead back to the United States Attorney's Office, but she was in no rush. For now, she was loving her life. Working hard made playing hard that much more enjoyable. And she relished every minute with Dylan. Whether they were hand in hand strolling their neighborhood or cuddling in front of the gas-lit fireplace in the apartment that had officially been her home for over a year, Briana never tired of spending time with Dylan. In fact, she was counting down the hours until it was just the two of them.

"What time is our flight in the morning?" she whispered.

"Early," Dylan said with a laugh. "I know we'll be tired after partying tonight, but I was eager when I booked." Her wince was playfully apologetic. "But a week on the beach will give us plenty of time to recover," she offered in consolation.

"I love that Trevor's tying the knot, but we're taking the honeymoon vacation."

"Eh, we've earned it. And he's got a needy one-year-old. We, thankfully, do not."

Yet, she thought. It was crazy that such a thing even popped into her head. But then her thinking on everything had evolved exponentially in the last twenty-four months. For the moment, her career was still ranked above the desire to have a baby, but motherhood no longer seemed out of the realm of possibility. Being with Dylan had taught her that she didn't have to choose one life over the other. With the right person, everything was attainable. Love, career, family.

Dylan leaned in and kissed her cheek softly. "What about Antigua?"

"What about it?" she asked. "Is that where Trevor and Cate are headed?"

"No." Dylan shook her head. "They're honeymooning in Myrtle Beach. The whole family is going. Like a reunion kind of thing."

"Right. Fun." Briana remembered Dylan giving her the details a while back. "So what's with Antigua?" she asked.

"I don't know." She looked cute and impish, like she had something up her sleeve. "The pictures online look amazing. There's these beautiful beaches. We could stay in one of those cool tiki hut things right on the water."

"That sounds fancy. I like it," she said with an enthusiastic eyebrow raise and a silly giggle. "But why are we talking about Antigua when we're going to Aruba tomorrow?"

"I just think it's not a terrible idea to plan some things ahead of time. And to treat ourselves. For special occasions," Dylan said. "You know…vacations and stuff."

"We haven't even gone on this vacation yet, and you're planning the next one." Briana smiled even though she was a little lost at the direction the conversation had taken. "I love it."

"Maybe I want to lock you in." Dylan reached for her hand. "This way there's no chance of you skipping out on me."

"As if."

"I don't know, Bri." Dylan made a point of scanning over the guests. "You're far and away the most gorgeous person here. Also the smartest, the sweetest, the sexiest." She looked down at their linked hands. "Sometimes I still can't believe you're with me."

The look on Dylan's gorgeous face was vulnerable and adorable and charming as hell. "Hey," Briana said just as the band started the first chords of Pachelbel's Canon in D. The entire congregation turned to see the bride, but for a split second she and Dylan were face-to-face. Briana held the eye contact, and it was as though everyone and everything around them blurred into oblivion. "It's you and me, baby. Forever."

"Promise?"

"I do."

Her answer felt oddly like a vow, and Dylan didn't miss it. Briana saw her confident, magnetic smile emerge.

"I like that answer," Dylan said with a wink and a subtle squeeze of her hand. It was in that small moment when she pieced it together. A beach getaway, plans for another a year down the line. Dylan was gearing up to propose. Briana saw the love in Dylan's eyes, and she felt it deep in her own soul. It had been there since nearly day one, if she was honest. But now, on the brink of a pivotal milestone she never even knew she wanted, her heart beat loud and erratic with excitement and anticipation. She envisioned the twists and turns a lifetime of true love and commitment promised. It was daunting and alluring and scary and enticing. And so full of Dylan.

She couldn't wait to say yes.

About the Author

Maggie Cummings is the author of six novels including the Bay West Social series. She hails from Staten Island, NY, where she lives with her wife and their two children. She spends the bulk of her time shuttling kids and procrastinating writing. To pay the bills, she works as a police captain in Brooklyn commanding a squad of detectives, which sounds way more exciting than it is. She is a complete sucker for indulgent TV, kettle cooked potato chips, and pedestrian chocolate.

Books Available From Bold Strokes Books

Aurora by Emma L McGeown. After a traumatic accident, Elena Ricci is stricken with amnesia, leaving her with no recollection of the last eight years, including her wife and son. (978-1-63555-824-1)

Avenging Avery by Sheri Lewis Wohl. Revenge against a vengeful vampire unites Isa Meyer and Jeni Denton, but it's love that heals them. (978-1-63555-622-3)

Bulletproof by Maggie Cummings. For Dylan Prescott and Briana Logan, the complicated NYC criminal justice system doesn't leave room for love, but where the heart is concerned, no one is bulletproof. (978-1-63555-771-8)

Her Lady to Love by Jane Walsh. A shy wallflower joins forces with the most popular woman in Regency London on a quest to catch a husband, only to discover a wild passion for each other that far eclipses their interest for the Marriage Mart. (978-1-63555-809-8)

No Regrets by Joy Argento. For Jodi and Beth, the possibility of losing their future will force them to decide what is really important. (978-1-63555-751-0)

The Holiday Treatment by Elle Spencer. Who doesn't want a gay Christmas movie? Holly Hudson asks herself that question and discovers that happy endings aren't only for the movies. (978-1-63555-660-5)

Too Good to be True by Leigh Hays. Can the promise of love survive the realities of life for Madison and Jen, or is it too good to be true? (978-1-63555-715-2)

Treacherous Seas by Radclyffe. When the choice comes down to the lives of her officers against the promise she made to her wife, Reese Conlon puts everything she cares about on the line. (978-1-63555-778-7)

Two to Tangle by Melissa Brayden. Ryan Jacks has been a player all her life, but the new chef at Tangle Valley Vineyard changes everything. If only she wasn't off the menu. (978-1-63555-747-3)

When Sparks Fly by Annie McDonald. Will the devastating incident that first brought Dr. Daniella Waveny and hockey coach Luca McCaffrey together on frozen ice now force them apart, or will their secrets and fears thaw enough for them to create sparks? (978-1-63555-782-4)

Best Practice by Carsen Taite. When attorney Grace Maldonado agrees to mentor her best friend's little sister, she's prepared to confront Perry's rebellious nature, but she isn't prepared to fall in love. Legal Affairs: one law firm, three best friends, three chances to fall in love. (978-1-63555-361-1)

Home by Kris Bryant. Natalie and Sarah discover that anything is possible when love takes the long way home. (978-1-63555-853-1)

Keeper by Sydney Quinne. With a new charge under her reluctant wing—feisty, highly intelligent math wizard Isabelle Templeton—Keeper Andy Bouchard has to prevent a murder or die trying. (978-1-63555-852-4)

One More Chance by Ali Vali. Harry Basantes planned a future with Desi Thompson until the day Desi disappeared without a word, only to walk back into her life sixteen years later. (978-1-63555-536-3)

Renegade's War by Gun Brooke. Freedom fighter Aurelia DeCallum regrets saving the woman called Blue. She fears it will jeopardize her mission, and secretly, Blue might end up breaking Aurelia's heart. (978-1-63555-484-7)

The Other Women by Erin Zak. What happens in Vegas should stay in Vegas, but what do you do when the love you find in Vegas changes your life forever? (978-1-63555-741-1)

The Sea Within by Missouri Vaun. Time is running out for Dr. Elle Graham to convince Captain Jackson Drake that the only thing that can save future Earth resides in the past, and rescue her broken heart in the process. (978-1-63555-568-4)

To Sleep With Reindeer Justine Saracen. In Norway under Nazi occupation, Maarit, an Indigenous woman, and Kirsten, a Norwegian resister, join forces to stop the development of an atomic weapon. (978-1-63555-735-0)

Twice Shy by Aurora Rey. Having an ex with benefits isn't all it's cracked up to be. Will Amanda Russo learn that lesson in time to take a chance on love with Quinn Sullivan? (978-1-63555-737-4)

Z-Town by Eden Darry. Forced to work together to stay alive, Meg and Lane must find the centuries-old treasure before the zombies find them first. (978-1-63555-743-5)

Bet Against Me by Fiona Riley. In the high-stakes luxury real estate market, everything has a price, and as rival Realtors Trina Lee and Kendall Yates find out, that means their hearts and souls, too. (978-1-63555-729-9)

Broken Reign by Sam Ledel. Together on an epic journey in search of a mysterious cure, a princess and a village outcast must overcome life-threatening challenges and their own prejudice if they want to survive. (978-1-63555-739-8)

Just One Taste by CJ Birch. For Lauren, it only took one taste to start trusting in love again. (978-1-63555-772-5)

Lady of Stone by Barbara Ann Wright. Sparks fly as a magical emergency forces a noble embarrassed by her ability to submit to a low-born teacher who resents everything about her. (978-1-63555-607-0)

Last Resort by Angie Williams. Katie and Rhys are about to find out what happens when you meet the girl of your dreams but you aren't looking for a happily ever after. (978-1-63555-774-9)

Longing for You by Jenny Frame. When Debrek housekeeper Katie Brekman is attacked amid a burgeoning vampire-witch war, Alexis Villiers must go against everything her clan believes in to save her. (978-1-63555-658-2)

Money Creek by Anne Laughlin. Clare Lehane is a troubled lawyer from Chicago who tries to make her way in a rural town full of secrets and deceptions. (978-1-63555-795-4)

Passion's Sweet Surrender by Ronica Black. Cam and Blake are unable to deny their passion for each other, but surrendering to love is a whole different matter. (978-1-63555-703-9)

The Holiday Detour by Jane Kolven. It will take everything going wrong to make Dana and Charlie see how right they are for each other. (978-1-63555-720-6)

A Love that Leads to Home by Ronica Black. For Carla Sims and Janice Carpenter, home isn't about location, it's where your heart is. (978-1-63555-675-9)

Blades of Bluegrass by D. Jackson Leigh. A US Army occupational therapist must rehab a bitter veteran who is a ticking political time bomb the military is desperate to disarm. (978-1-63555-637-7)

Hopeless Romantic by Georgia Beers. Can a jaded wedding planner and an optimistic divorce attorney possibly find a future together? (978-1-63555-650-6)

Hopes and Dreams by PJ Trebelhorn. Movie theater manager Riley Warren is forced to face her high school crush and tormentor, wealthy socialite Victoria Thayer, at their twentieth reunion. (978-1-63555-670-4)

In the Cards by Kimberly Cooper Griffin. Daria and Phaedra are about to discover that love finds a way, especially when powers outside their control are at play. (978-1-63555-717-6)

Moon Fever by Ileandra Young. SPEAR agent Danika Karson must clear her werewolf friend of multiple false charges while teaching her vampire girlfriend to resist the blood mania brought on by a full moon. (978-1-63555-603-2)

Serenity by Jesse J. Thoma. For Kit Marsden, there are many things in life she cannot change. Serenity is in the acceptance. (978-1-63555-713-8)

Sylver and Gold by Michelle Larkin. Working feverishly to find a killer before he strikes again, Boston homicide detective Reid Sylver and rookie cop London Gold are blindsided by their chemistry and developing attraction. (978-1-63555-611-7)